One of the five outlaws stood guard on the front steps while the other four took the woman inside to rape her some more.

They had her naked across a mattress when Captain Gringo kicked open the door with his machine gun braced against his hips.

The man holding the woman's arms froze, thunderstruck, as the man who'd been about to mount her rolled away to grope for his gunbelt. The two who'd been waiting their turn still wore their guns, so Captain Gringo opened up and spread a deadly fan of hot lead, blowing them off their feet. His second burst blew the highjacker's bare ass to raspberry jam as the one who'd been holding the woman raised his hands, shouting, "Please, I beg of you, Senor!"

Captain Gringo looked at the woman.

"Ma'am?"

She said in a venemous voice, "Kill him, please."

Captain Gringo said, "You heard what the lady said," and blew his head off with a short savage burst.

Novels by Ramsay Thorne

Published by
WARNER BOOKS

Renegade #9

HELL RAIDER

by
Ramsay Thorne

WARNER BOOKS

A Warner Communications Company

WARNER BOOKS EDITION

Copyright © 1981 by Lou Cameron
All rights reserved.

Cover Art by George Gross

Warner Books, Inc., 75 Rockefeller Plaza, New York, N.Y. 10019

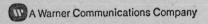 A Warner Communications Company

Printed in the United States of America

First Printing: June, 1981

10 9 8 7 6 5 4 3 2 1

Renegade #9

HELL RAIDER

Captain Gringo sat at a table on the hotel balcony with a glass of gin and tonic and a good cigar while he watched the town wake up as the sun went down. The Amazonian sunset was as Opera-Baroque as everything else in Manaus. It looked like God had set a flamingo's ass on fire. The sky was a big inverted magenta bowl with a black lace rim. For despite its spectacular architecture, Manaus was not a large town, and from any elevation one could see the soaring treetops of the surrounding Amazon Selva.

The electric street lamps were winking on the streets below and the natives were coming out to prowl the garish pavement, apparently left over from the streets of Rio de Janeiro, far to the south-east. By day the surrounding buildings looked like wedding cakes, blindingly white in the tropic sun. In the ruby light of the gloaming they looked like someone had covered them with strawberry icing. All the shadows were royal purple. The rich river port, dead center of the biggest jungle on Earth, looked like a Fairy Land designed by a drunken Maxfield Parrish. But Manaus had its disadvantages. Every street lamp below was blurred with a halo of flying insects. A roach as big as a mouse was waving its feelers at Captain Gringo from the balcony rail; a green something with wings was doing the back stroke in his drink, and a naked lady was creeping up on him along the line of balconies stuck on his hotel's side.

He took a drag on his cigar and blew an orange and

purple smoke ring as he pretended not to notice her. His side-kick, Gaston, had told him to stay put while he explored the possibilities of a safe passage down the Amazon. Manaus was a deep-water port despite its location. Ocean-going ships put in to load the riches of the selva and drop off the luxuries the brawling barons of the rubber boom demanded and could well afford. Finding an outward-bound ship was no big deal. Finding one that would be safe for two wanted men to board was another matter. Between them, Captain Gringo and his older comrade in arms, the former Sergeant Gaston Verrier of the French Foreign Legion, had accumulated a rather awesome number of wanted posters. They needed a skipper crooked enough to take them aboard without a lot of silly questions about passports, but honest enough not to turn them in for the reward when the ship cleared for the open sea at Para, almost a thousand miles downstream.

Now the naked lady was three balconies down. She rolled over the rails between balconies and flattened out to hide some more. The last time he'd had a better look at her out the corner of his eye. She looked as if old Maxfield Parrish had painted her, too. A slender blond nude in the sunset's soft glow. Highlighted dusky rose and shaded in lavender. Lots of shading. She had a nicely modeled body. He wondered what the hell she was up to.

Manaus had one of the highest homicide rates in the world, and it was famous for its whores. But the naked lady sneaking up on him obviously carried no concealed weapons and the whores of Manaus didn't sneak up on a man. They would walk right up to him on the street and offer to go three ways for three cruzeiros.

If she thought she as a cat burglar she was blind. She had to have noticed him sitting here as she played hide and seek along the front of the damned building. He wondered where she'd come from. The baroque plaster curls down the facade might be possible to climb from street level, but even in Manaus a stark naked blond strolling along the black and white sidewalks would attract *some* attention. They were in the center of town. The somewhat casual local police tried to keep things neat around the cathedral and opera house.

He knew he could go inside and lock the French doors, he thought as he reached for his glass, rescued the swimming bug, and sipped some gin and tonic. As he put his drink back on the metal table the naked lady slid over another rail and dropped to the deserted deck of the balcony next door. The sunset sure looked nice on her bare ass.

He shifted his weight in the chair and cleared his .38 for action just in case. She was smaller than he and didn't seem to be armed, but had to be some sort of lunatic; her next move was going to drop her almost in his lap. He could hear her breathing, the silly thing, and she sounded like she'd just run a mile and was scared skinny, too.

A couple of men came out on a balcony down the line wearing white suits, pink in the light. One was tall and thin, the other, short and fat. Looking around as if they'd lost something, the skinny one spotted Captain Gringo and waved, calling out in Portuguese. Captain Gringo understood it. Portuguese wasn't all that different, but he bought some time by calling back in Spanish, "No comprendo, Señor!"

The other guy switched to the polyglot creole used in these parts as the Lingua Franca. It was too close to Spanish to play dumb. He yelled, "Have you seen a woman out here, Friend?" and Captain Gringo yelled back, "Lots of them. The paseo is starting down there in the plaza."

"No, no, I meant up here on the balcony: A blond. She, uh, might not have had any clothes on."

Captain Gringo laughed incredulously and yelled back, "Hey, I'd had noticed something like that! What's going on?"

The two men muttered to each other. Then the tall one waved and called, "Nothing. Just a little joke. We're having a party and one of our, uh, guests is missing."

"Sounds like a swell party. Is it private or can anyone join in?"

"Ah, meaning no disrespect, Senhor, it is a private affair. Good evening."

They went back inside.

Captain Gringo rose and stretched casually, then moved closer to the rail that the blond was hiding behind, and said in

9

a conversational tone, "Just stay where you are for now. They may pop back out to surprise you."

There was an audible gasp from the invisible naked lady. Then she held her breath, trying to remain quiet as a mouse. Captain Gringo hooked a rump over the edge of the balcony and now he could see her bare bottom. Her head was pressed against the rail between them. He said, "Oh, for God's sake, breathe. They can't hear us from the rooms you whatevered from. What's this all about, Doll?"

The girl sort of whimpered and murmured, "Por favor, no hablo Español."

Captain Gringo realized he'd been speaking Spanish and that the girl's very bad Spanish had an English accent. He laughed and asked, in English, "For God's sake, you are an American?"

"I'm Welsh, look you! And are you not one of these terrible Dago Dons then?"

He said, "I'm a Yank. My name's Dick Walker. What the hell's a Welsh girl doing in Manaus and . . . never mind, I can see it would take all night, and we'd better get you inside."

"Oh, and will you save me from them terrible Dago Dons, kind Sir?"

"Somebody'd better. You were doing a lousy job of saving yourself. What happened to your clothes?"

"Oh, it's terrible. I was brought here to meet a famous Brazilian gentleman who could help me with my career, but while I waited for him they gave me a drink. It tasted too strongly of the creature, so I poured most of it in the pot of a fern I now feel sorry for. I must have been overcome by the little I did drink, for the next I knew I was naked on a bed."

"Alone?"

"Oh, yes, Praise the Lord. But when I got up to peek out I heard Carlos discussing the price of my poor body with that other old fat thing. The rest you know, for it all happened only moments ago."

Captain Gringo muttered, "Quiet," as he saw the tall one come back out on the distant balcony. When the Brazilian looked his way he raised the half-filled glass in his hand and motioned the pimp to crawl over and join him. Carlos looked disgusted, and went back inside. Captain Gringo spotted the shorter one stomping off downstairs, heading out across the plaza. He glanced at the sky and said, "Okay, I'll cover you. Roll over this rail and crawl inside, fast."

"I have no clothing on, look you."

"I noticed. Didn't you see me sitting out here while you were steeple-chasing naked across the front of the damned building?"

"I did. I hoped you were not looking, you see. I tried each French door as I came to each balcony. But they all seem to be locked. Back in The Valley people saw no need to lock their doors after them, look you."

"Yeah, well, Wales is probably a little more prim than Manaus. You want to duck inside, or wait 'til the folks next door come home and ask you what the hell you're doing on their balcony in your birthday suit?"

The blond gasped and slithered over the rail on her belly, exposing only her shapely back and derriere, which was enough to give Captain Gringo a desire to see more. She landed at his feet on her hands and knees and crawled for the open doorway as he watched, bemused. He let her get inside before he finished his drink, rose, and followed casually.

The only light inside the suite was the ruby glow from the doorway. It got a little darker and redder when he shut the French glass doors. They had lace curtains. But he could see she'd helped herself to the chenille counterpane of his rented four poster. She had it wrapped about her like a toga. She licked her lips and gave him a timid smile before she said, "I am Glynnis Radnor from Cardiff Town, Glamorganshire. Is this not a bedroom I find myself in, good Sir?"

"It ain't a Methodist chapel. We booked a two-room suite in case one of us got lucky. So there's a bed in the other room, too. But relax, sit down. You didn't jump from the frying pan into the fire. I only shoot people for a living. I've never sold one yet."

Glynnis sank to the edge of his mattress as he crossed to fix himself another drink at the sideboard against the far wall.

11

He asked her if she could use one, too. She said she could, but not too strong. So he made her a Collins sans ice and cherries. You could buy ice in Manaus. You could buy anything in Manaus at a price, but ice cost more by the pound than ass in this tropic port, and on their last adventure Captain Gringo and Gaston had made little more than enemies. He took the disgusting drink to her and said, "Here—the gin is real, and when you get right down to it, that's all that matters."

"Can I trust you?" she asked, eyeing her drink dubiously. He said, "Hey, pour it over your head if you want. Do I look like a sissy who has to knock his women out?"

Glynnis laughed and took a sip, smacking her lips. He'd made it sweet because she looked the type who would. She said, "I think you are a kind brave man. I heard the way you tricked those villains for me. Many a man might have given me away, look you."

"Yeah, many a man has more sense. I don't know why I keep getting into these things. But here we are. I guess the first thing we have to do is find you some clothes to wear. Where are you staying, Glynnis?"

She grimaced and said, "Oh, I can't go back there, now. I was staying with Carlos at the Mirador. But that was before I knew what sort of man he was. I am beginning to think he lied to me about an operatic career in Brazil, too!"

Captain Gringo frowned at her and said, "Let me get this straight: the pimp, Carlos, brought you all the way from Wales with a dumb story about making an opera singer out of you?"

"He did indeed. We met at the Cardiff Singing Championships. I was most beside myself to come in fourth, but Carlos said I had too good a voice for those ignorant taffs to understand and . . ."

"Gotcha," he cut in. "You ran away with the daring young man on the flying trapeze to become an opera star here in Brazil. Did he have to marry you or are you one of those sophisticated milkmaids?"

Glynnis looked up and said, "Well, he said we were married in the eyes of the Lord or something. In truth I'm a bit confused as well as disappointed in Carlos. He didn't speak very good English. But I'm sure he never said anything about selling me to fat old men."

"So you have been sleeping with Carlos but now you don't like him any more, huh? I can't say I blame you. But this leaves you in sort of a pickle, doesn't it? How are we to get you back to Wales?"

She looked up at him with a puzzled frown and asked, "Why on Earth would I wish to return to The Valley? Did I not come here to sing in the opera?"

"I wish you wouldn't frown like that when you're trying to think, Kid. You're awfully pretty when you're not thinking, and I can see it's a waste of effort."

"I don't understand, kind Sir. There is an opera house here in Manaus, for I've seen it, look you!"

"So have I. It looks like the Paris Opéra built to half scale out of marzipan and vanilla icing. Can't you see what Carlos is? He's a white slaver, Doll. These Brazilian rubber barons have money to burn and they buy nothing but the best. I heard about one who imported a Japanese girl, just for the hell of it, just for one night. He wanted to hear if it was true what they said about Oriental women."

"But what was Carlos doing in Cardiff if he sells girls to the awful Dago Dons here in Manaus?"

"Buying trip. The local talent tends to be a little darker and, what the hell, they send all the way to Russia for their caviar. Don't try to figure out how you got here, Honey. Let's figure out how we get you *out*."

"Don't you know anyone here connected with the opera? One can see you are a gentleman."

He smiled crookedly and said, "I used to be. I'm not in the music business, Glynnis. I'm a soldier of fortune. The instrument I'm best on is a Maxim machinegun. I doubt if they'd want me sitting in over there at the opera even if they were playing the 1812 Overture."

He checked the time and said, "I can't go outside until I know for sure the coast is clear. If my friend gets back before the shops close, we might be able to pick you up some kind of dress. Then we'll start figuring out where you can stay."

13

"Can't I stay here with you, kind Sir?"

He blinked in surprise, considered, and said, "If you do, you'll have to start calling me Dick. I'm not that kind a sir, Kid. I'm as willing as the next guy to help a maiden in distress, buy my nobility has it's limits."

She finished her drink, put the empty glass on the bed table, and said, "Oh, I see, you mean that if I am to stay with you I'll have to be your wife in the eyes of the Lord?"

"That's a pretty grotesque way of putting it, but you're getting warm, and so am I. Look, Glynnis, this isn't going to work. We're both on the run, albeit not running from the same kinds of people. I'm not the Sir Galahad you're looking for. I'm a roughneck with a lot of enemies. I play a rough and ready game for high stakes. Maybe if you went to the British Consulate and told them your story they'd work something out for you."

"Do you think they could get me an audition at the opera?"

"No, and neither can I, and I doubt like hell that any other bozo you meet up with in this rough little town is going to even try. Don't you know where you *are, Girl?* This is *Manaus,* the toughest town between Singapore and Port Said! They'll kill a man for his shoes in this town. You were just about to be sold like any other imported luxury, for cold cash on the barrel head."

She let the wrappings fall partly away as she dimpled prettily and said, "I know, Dick, but you saved me from that fate and now everything will be all right, you see."

He saw one tit. It was getting too dark to see her expression clearly but, Jesus H. Christ, could anything that pretty be that dumb?

There was a knock on the door. It didn't sound like Gaston's knock. But his French confederate had said he'd send word if he was tied up along the waterfront after dark. Captain Gringo moved over to the door and asked, "Quíen es?" a voice from the other side of the panels answered, brightly, "Mensaje por Señor Walker," So he opened the door.

14

The tall man in the white suit, he'd seen earlier, stepped in, smiling and holding a six-inch blade near Captain Gringo's middle. He was good-looking and obviously self-confident. He shut the door behind him and said, "I got your name from the hotel register, my most clever friend." Then he nodded at the blond cowering on the bed across the room and added, "I am perhaps more suspicious than most, but I see I was right. That *was* my little Glynnis I heard through the door panels just now, eh?"

Captain Gringo ballanced on the balls of his feet as he said, flatly, "She's not your little anything anymore, Pimp. The lady is with me."

Carlos kept smiling, but he didn't look at all friendly as he replied, "Listen, I am not an unreasonable man. I will let you have her for a price, if she means that much to you. But you must understand my position. I have a great investment here."

"Yeah, she told me you were interested in music. You'd better take a hike, Carlos. No offense, but I don't like guys like you."

The procurer's eyes narrowed and he waved the knife between them, back and forth for emphasis as he purred, "You are not my cup of tea, either. Since we can't do business, I'll just take my woman and go."

"With a *knife?* You can't be serious."

Carlos dropped into a street fighter's crouch with his back to the door as he stared hard at his target above Captain Gringo's belt buckle and hissed, "I warn you, I am a very serious person."

"Bullshit, you're a lousy two-bit pimp. If you had the balls to cut a grown man you wouldn't have to work so hard preying on green country girls."

The Brazilian's tone bordered on hysteria as he shrilled, "Glynnis, get up and follow me. If this maniac wants to die I see no reason to continue this discussion!"

The Welsh girl started to get up, meekly. Captain Gringo snapped, "Down, Girl. That's an order. Can't you see this punk's about to wet his pants?"

Carlos said, "Nobody calls me a punk and lives. This is your last chance, Yanqui. Are you going to be reasonable, or do I have to put this blade in you?"

Captain Gringo laughed and said, "You can try. If you so much as make me move a step you're in big trouble."

Carlos slashed the blade through the space between them as the tall American stepped back into his own boxing stance and said, "Like I said, now you're in big trouble."

He moved in on the balls of his feet as the pimp backed away, waving the blade like a magic wand that didn't seem to be working tonight for some reason. His eyes were glazed with fear as he reached for the knob behind him with his free hand. Then, as Captain Gringo feinted with his left, Carlos opened the door with a strangled gasp and ducked out to slam the door shut between them.

Captain Gringo chuckled and locked the door as the little blond sprang off the bed, running over to him, sobbing, "Oh, My God, I have never seen anything as brave as that!"

She'd left the cover behind in her eagerness to comfort her rescuer. He took her in his arms and kissed her without comment. He figured she was entitled to her illusions. So he didn't say he'd never seen anyone who waved a knife and talked about it really use it. He noticed her kiss was not as innocent as her childish words. Glynnis was a mature, instinctive woman with a little girl's brain. But, what the hell, that wasn't so bad when you considered how it would be the other way.

He picked her up and carried her over to the bed. As he lowered her to the mattress she sighed and said, "Oh, I do feel as if the Lord intended us to meet like this, for I see we are fated lovers."

He undressed without comment as she prattled on. As he dropped his clothes on the floor and turned around he saw she'd reclined across the bed in childlike acceptance of this latest relationship with a total stranger She was a sweet little slut, too dumb to be allowed out of the house without a leash. As he mounted her, she co-operated with the folk wisdom of her primitive body. As he entered her, she rose to meet his

16

thrust and clamped down expertly. Yet her eyes smiled up at him in innocent wonder as she said, bitter-sweetly, "Oh, my, you have ever so nice a thing down there, Dick. You're a much better lover than Carlos or those other boys."

The last thing he felt like at a time like this was a conversation with a dim-wit, but he had to ask. He moved in and out experimentaly as he got in time with her and asked, "What other boys?"

"Oh, you know, back in The Valley. I've always liked to do this almost as much as I enjoy singing."

He kissed her to shut her up as he started pumping faster. She responded eagerly and wrapped her legs around his waist with her nails gently running all over his back, and that felt great, too. He tried to hold back, but in truth it had been some time since he'd said farewell to that missionary gal they'd rescued in the jungle, and while *she'd* been grateful, too, she'd favored the missionary position more than most. He knew he was coming too fast, but what the hell, Glynnis was beautiful and tighter than she had any right to be. So he knew there'd be more where that was coming from as he ejaculated in her, hard, and felt her clamp even tighter in her own healthy uncomplicated orgasm.

As they came up for air, she said, "Oh, that was lovely. I never got there so fast before. Do you like the way I do it, Dick?"

"Honey, if you sing half as good as you screw you'll *have* to wind up an opera star!"

She laughed and started moving again. It was as good as if they'd just started. He could see how old Carlos had expected to make money off his "investment," although no real man would have been willing to share a thing this good for lousy money. If the son-of-a-bitch had been getting this regular, he figured to miss it later tonight. The son-of-a-bitch deserved to. Captain Gringo had lost most of the Victorian inhibitions he'd been raised to have. But thinking of another man in this saddle annoyed him a bit. Glynnis apparently had no inhibitions at all. So she only giggled when he suggested a change in position. She willingly rolled over and presented her pale white rump to him with her knees on the edge of the bed. He mounted her from behind, standing on the rug, and yes, he could go deeper and it was less effort. Their mingled sweat on his chest and belly felt cool as he held a hip bone in either hand and pounded her dog style. She started rolling her blond head from side to side as she moaned that she was coming and he was almost there himself when some silly bastard knocked on the door again.

Glynnis gasped and shot off his shaft to grope herself under the top sheet as Captain Gringo dropped to one knee and scooped up the .38 from it's holster near his mosquito boots. He was pretty sure he recognized the knock, this time, but now that he'd dulled the edge of his desire he was getting a little tired of tricky pimps. It it were that asshole, Carlos, again, it was time to scare him good.

He moved in the gloom to the door and growled, "Gaston?" and a familiar voice from the other side replied, "Mais non, My Old and Rare, it is your President Cleveland bearing a full pardon for your unfortunate misunderstanding with the U.S. Army."

Captain Gringo grinned and opened the door. Gaston came in and said, "Merde alors, why is it so dark in here?" Then he sniffed and added, "Never mind, is the lady still here?"

In Spanish, Captain Gringo said, "Watch the mouth. She speaks English."

As Gaston followed, he moved over to the bed table and switched on the small tiffany lamp. He put the gun on the table beside it and sat on the bed between Glynnis and the standing Frenchman, saying, "Glynnis Radnor. Meet Gaston Verrier. Don't trust him. Just meet him."

Glynnis dimpled demurely, holding the sheet over her breasts as Gaston said, "Enchanté, M'selle. All right, Dick, where have you been hiding it?"

"Hiding what?"

"Alladin's Lamp, of course. I leave you safely locked up in a town you've never visited before and when I return, I find you with a trés beautiful . . . ah?"

"She's not and she doesn't want to be," Captain Gringo cut in, adding, "Grab a chair. I'm more interested in what

18

you've been doing. Did you book us passage down the river or what?"

Gaston found a small chair near the dresser and hauled it over by the pool of light to sit it backward, resting his elbows on the back as he grinned knowingly at them. Gaston did that a lot. He was a small dapper man a generation older than Captain Gringo. Louis Napoleon had sent him with the French Foreign Legion to fight Juarez in Mexico over twenty years before. Gaston had survived the Siege of Camerone as a legionaire and then, as a natural survivor. he'd joined the other side. He and Captain Gringo had met on the wrong end of a Mexican firing squad, and things had been sort of noisy ever since. The years on the dodge were catching up with old Gaston, but he was still nice looking in a gray satanic way. Older experienced women went for Gaston, even before they heard he was French. His goat-like smile hinted at total depravity, and oral sex was hard to come by in a world presided over by the aging Queen Victoria. Gaston probably would have drawn the line at cannibalism, but he was game for just about anything else a lady might want to do in bed.

He said, "My story is obviously less interesting than yours, Dick. I have, as I promised, been scouting the waterfront for old comrades in The Life. Alas, we are much farther south than usual, and while this rubber boom would seem to be attracting common criminals from the four corners of the Earth, the thrice accursed Brazilian government is too stable for anyone to seriously consider toppling. Hence there seem to be no soldiers of fortune I know in Manaus at the moment."

"What about smugglers? I don't want to join a revolution. I want to get the hell out of here."

"I, too, find this jungle life fatiguing. Alas, the liberal import laws make it pointless to smuggle anything up the Amazon these days. I saw some three island freighters moored offshore just now. It is hard to believe it, even when you know the river this far inland is deep and wide as Lake Champlaign. Finding a ship is no problem. Finding cheap passage is no problem. Getting past Para or any other port at the mouth of the Amazon is the problem."

Captain Gringo frowned and asked, "How come? You just said the Brazilians didn't give a damn who sails or steams up here to Manaus."

Gaston nodded and said, "True. They allow anything to be *imported*. I just saw them unloading another street car, and a rubber baron just imported an Indian elephant for reasons best known to himself. But while Brazil welcomes anything coming *in* it casts a jaundiced eye on things going *out*. "They are still most upset by that Englishman who smuggled out a shipment of rubber tree seeds. Brazil felt it was rude for the British to start rival rubber plantations in their own colonies. A sailor I just spoke to says the Brazilian authorities board every outbound vessel to make a distressingly thorough search for rubber seeds, diamonds, and gold dust."

"Ouch, we're both bigger than any of the three."

"Exactly. They even search the bilge and lifeboats. Our only chance would be to mingle with the crew. Passengers are expected to have passports if they are going anywhere innocent. Signing on as crew members is trés simple, if one can trust the crew. But how one is to trust a band of wharf rats one has never seen before eludes me."

Glynnis had been trying to follow the conversation. She asked, "What about me?" and Gaston raised an eyebrow and asked, "Oui, what about her, Dick?"

Captain Gringo sighed and said, "Glynnis was lured down here by a white slaver. She's from Wales."

"I don't wish to go back to Cardiff, look you," the girl protested.

Gaston said, "No problem. I have no idea how to get as far as Surinam."

"What's in Surinam, M'Sieu Gaston?"

"Nothing. The Dutch are about the only people who have as yet failed to post a reward on either Dick or my weary self."

"Do they have an opera house in Surinam?"

Gaston looked at her as if she'd just started frothing at the mouth.

Captain Gringo explained, "She sings, too. They told her she was coming here to be a star."

"Ah, the story is familiar as well as trés banal. I feel certain M'selle would be a star at anything she put her mind to. But I cannot swear to an opera house in Surinam. I remember none from my last visit, years ago. But it is a trés pleasant little country. The trade winds sweep the heat and insects inland, the living is easy, and the women, ooh la la! But, of course, M'selle is less interested in that part."

Before Glynnis could protest she didn't want to go to Surinam, Captain Gringo said it for her. He said, "We've got to get back up to Central America, damn it. Our money will run out soon and the Dutch don't hire mercenaries, do they?"

"Mais non, a most fatiguing race, the Dutch. One suspects they prefer the quiet life. They don't even fight enough with the natives to matter. But on the other hand, we both could use a vacation. Surinam would make a good base to quietly plot our next move. I have been thinking about all the troubles we've had with our employers of late. The best way to make sure one is to be paid off at the end of a revolution is to start the revolution oneself. There must be some country a pair of enterprising adventurers could take over with a machinegun. That way, the new presidente could not double-cross us, see?"

Captain Gringo grimaced and said, "Look, let's just eat this apple a bite at a time. We've got to get out of Manaus before the local police find out about those fun and games we just had up in the montaña country. Some of the shooting was on this side of the border."

Gaston said, "Relax, my old and anxious. While you have been holed up here, in more ways than one, I have been out on le street. The local police have enough to worry about without checking hotel registers. This place is like your Dodge City in the '70s, without your more formidable marshals to attempt some minimal control. They have shoot-outs and stabbings on the hour in Manaus and the underpaid police see few reasons to get involved."

21

"I noticed the knives. It's dark out, now. Maybe if we went prowling we'd run into some of the wild bunch we know."

Gaston stood and said, "I shall do the prowling. You stay here and keep M'selle company. A big blond moose like you attracts attention in this part of the world even when one has not seen the reward posters, hein?"

Captain Gringo knew he was right, and it wasn't as if he'd be stuck with nothing to read. Gaston's English was thickly accented, because he'd spent most of his days since deserting the legion speaking Spanish. His Spanish was good enough for the latin-featured Gaston to pass as a native. His short stature and nondescript middle-aged features drew few curious glances in any crowd. Captain Gringo said, "Okay, see if you can find some guys you know."

Gaston spoke in Spanish as he replied, "Are you insane? I'm going out to find a woman. I know your views on sharing and I'll be damned if I'm going to spend the rest of the night next door playing with myself."

Gaston Verrier was as cynical as he talked, and ten times tougher than he looked. He'd been raised in the festering slums of Rive Gauche before Louis Napoleon cleaned up Paris for the tourists. He'd killed his first sewer rat about the time he learned to walk and kick. He'd killed his first man when he was eleven. Boys of the left bank learned early to protect their virtue from the degenerates prowling the narrow streets and alleyways of the poorer quarters. Another more publicized killing in the Red Mill had led to an early enlistment in the Legion. That in turn had led to further education in the casbahs of North Africa, the sweltering stews of Indo China, and in the end, the brutal occupation of Mexico.

So Gaston was shocked at being shocked when he took a seat in an alcove of the Porta d'Ouro and turned to catch the floor show. A large black man was playing a piano, stark naked. That seemed reasonable. A large white dog was

22

mating with a girl atop the piano. That seemed reasonable. The girl was about six years old. That didn't seem reasonable.

The naked child was an almost white mestiza and she looked embarrassed, as well she might, to be on her hands and knees in a crowded smoke filled cantina as the dog humped away at her with it's shaggy forelegs locked around her skinny little waist. The Negro playing the piano was keeping time with the dog's thrusts as he tinkled a mocking ragtime tune. He had a hard on, too. A big one.

A stark naked waitress came over to Gaston and asked if he wanted a drink or a blow job. He said he'd settle for a cerveza for now. So she brought him a beer. He put a coin on the table. The waitress moved it to the corner of the table with a bored expression, then thrust her pelvis forward to pick the coin up with her vaginal lips, asking, "You like?"

Gaston had seen the trick before, but he laughed anyway, and said he'd think about that, too. So the waitress wiggled off to look for more sporting customers.

Gaston lit a smoke and tried to fade into the stucco wall behind him as he studied the crowd for familiar faces. He didn't touch the beer. He wasn't crazy. He'd just ordered it because they didn't let you sit there for free. If the cerveza wasn't laced with sleeping powders or Spanish Fly it would probably give him the jungle trots. He could see it was half water and a man had to be careful about drinking water in the tropics.

The little mestiza didn't look like she was enjoying her performance much, but the dog sure was. Gaston grimaced. He knew better than to feel sorry for the kid. Feeling sorry was for boobs and idiots like his Quixotic friend back at the hotel. He was glad he hadn't brought Captain Gringo. By now they'd be trying to rescue the little love slave, and they had enough to worry about. He knew Dick wouldn't just desert that stranded Welsh girl. So if he made contact, he'd have to book three passages, and of course, the blond couldn't pass for an able-bodied seaman. She'd been trying to cover her rather heroic tits, but Gaston had twenty-twenty vision and a good imagination.

23

A stranger in a white suit slid in beside Gaston, uninvited. Gaston sized up the pomaded hair and violet perfume and said, dryly, "I hate to disappoint you, but I feel it's only fair to warn you that I am queer for women."

The foppish man said, "I know. A woman is what I wish to discuss with you, Senhor Gaston."

"You know me? In that case, you know I seldom need the services of a procurer, either."

"I have not joined you to sell you another woman. I wish to discuss the business losses your friend at the hotel has already cost me. I am willing to forget the customer I had lined up for the blond, although in God's truth he was willing to pay an enormous sum when I was able to assure him she was a virgin as well as blond. I am even willing to forgo my finder's fee for the fun he's been having with her since, but enough is enough. I will not stand being robbed of my very bread and butter. I must have her back. Do you understand?"

Gaston chuckled and said, "I do now. But why are you approaching *me* on the subject? As you can see, I have no woman here, belonging to you or any other slaver. You really should be having this conversation with my friend."

"I tried to. He was very rude. I was in hopes you would be more reasonable, Senhor Verrier."

Gaston didn't answer as he ran that through for rough edges. He'd signed the hotel register with his right name because it went with the tattered identification he carried in the first place and the police never expected one's right name in the second. So, hopefully, that was how the pimp knew his name, and with a little more luck, that was all he really knew.

Across the room, the dog was running out of steam after ejaculating in the little girl again. It withdrew to drop to the floor and lick it's long red penis as the crowd laughed. The child tried to climb down from the piano but the big Negro snapped at her and stood up, his own shaft turgid in the gas light. Gaston shrugged and said, "There's nothing I can do for you. The last I saw of your blond and my friend they seemed intent on her other career as an opera singer."

Carlos laughed cruelly, and said, "Bah. Glynnis could not carry a tune in a bucket. But she's a very good lay. I want her back. You are going to explain this to your friend, the notorious Captain Gringo."

Gaston's voice was cautious as he replied, "Oh, you *have* been doing your homework, hein? May one assume M'Sieu dabbles in blackmail as a sideline to his usual profession?"

The pimp shrugged and said, "Call it what you will. If I do not get Glynnis back, I am going to the police with what I just learned."

The big Negro had the little girl faceup on the piano now, and as she whimpered in discomfort he pulled her skinny hips to the edge to insert his awsome shaft in her hairless little slit while the crowd whistled and clapped. Gaston would have liked to pump the pimp for more loose ends, but he saw even the two naked waitresses had turned to stare at the obscene floor show, and Gaston was a born opportunist.

He turned to face the black-mailing pimp with a crooked smile. He glanced down in mock surprise and asked, "Merde alors. What is that on your shirt?" The fastidious Carlos, of course, glanced down as Gaston put a hand in back of himself to draw. Carlos asked, "What is it? I see nothing?"

Then he saw the blade, but as he stiffened in shock it was too late. Gaston stabbed him skillfully under the ribs, rising to clamp the other palm over the pimp's mouth as he twisted and severed the aorta. The struggle was brief and went unobserved in the dimly lit corner as Gaston finished off Carlos with his back to the crowd.

He sat back down and gently lowered the dead man's head to the table as he wiped the blade clean on the pimp's pants below. Gaston took his own glass and poured the contents on the floor to soak into the filthy sawdust there. The big black man was still screwing the child in the center of the room but people were beginning to lose interest as the novelty wore off. One of the nude waitresses turned to saunter away with a bored look on her painted face. Gaston caught her eye and held up two fingers.

When she brought the drinks she said, "Your friend looks like he's already had enough."

Gaston laughed and said, "In that case I may have to drink for two." He paid, generously, and the waitress asked, "Would you like to fuck me for another cruzeiro? It's a slow night."

Gaston winked and said, "I'm too drunk to get it up. But here's another cruzeiro anyway. Surprise another customer, and tell him it's on me."

The waitress laughed and walked away. Gaston poured some of the watered beer on the floor, but left the glasses two thirds full. He knew she'd ignore this table until at least one was empty or until she started wondering why it was taking so long to drink a lousy beer. He rose, patting the dead man's shoulder encouragingly as he groped for his fly and deliberately walked unsteadily from the table. The little girl was sucking the Negro as a sailor screwed her dog-style on the piano. Gaston asked the entertainer where he could take a leak and the Negro said, "Out back, in the alley. This ain't a fancy place."

So Gaston tottered out a back door, found himself alone in a dark alley, and started running like hell.

A while later he found himself seated at another table in front of a sidewalk cafe on the plaza, telling a lady with a gold tooth how lovely she was. The street walker was as faded as the organdy rose pinned to the hip of her sleazy red dress, but what the hell, she looked like she might have been pretty, once.

She said, "Cut the bullshit, handsome, and let's talk about the money."

Gaston looked wistful and said, "Money? You certainly had me fooled, my lovely child. I took you for one of the girls walking the paseo for romance and adventure."

The flattered whore laughed and said, "Hey, I've had all the romance and adventure I'm about to have for *free!* But, no shit, couldn't you see I'm a business woman?"

"No, how could it be possible? You're so young and fresh. A high-priced courtesan, perhaps. You are beautiful enough, and they say this is a wicked city, but a woman of the streets, never! You must be trying to discourage me. I am too old for you, hein?"

She laughed again, incredulously, and said, "You're crazy, you sweet old fart. What are you, a fugitive from a monastery? Why do you think I'm in this red dress alone on the street at this hour?"

"You have had a quarrel with your lover, perhaps?" He replied, innocently, holding up two fingers to the amused waiter.

They heard police whistled in the distance. The waiter brought two glasses of rum and after sniffing suspiciously, Gaston raised his to her and sighed, "To romance, hein?"

The whore took a sip, but said, "You're nice. Most customers don't offer a drink first. But no shit, my going rates are three ways for five cruzeiros. That's for a quick trick, of course. The whole night costs twenty, usually, but I might make you a price. You're kind of cute."

A young man strode by and the waiter called out, "Hey, what's going on down the street, Chico?"

The boy called back, "Another knifing in the Porta d' Ouro. It was that pimp, Carlos."

The waiter shrugged and said, "It's about time."

The whore turned to Gaston and said, "I know the man they're talking about. He was sort of nasty."

"Shocking," said Gaston, adding, "Listen, I have a nice room at the hotel across the plaza. We could take a bottle and get to know one another a lot better, hein?"

"Honey, I'm ready and willing, but we haven't agreed on a *price* yet."

"All right. How much do you want to pay me?"

"Pay *you*? Senhor, you are totally and obscenely loco en la caveza! The woman does not pay the man. The man pays the woman, see?"

"Why?"

The woman in the red dress gagged on her drink and sputtered, "Why? You ask why? María, José, and Jesus! Who ever heard of a woman paying the man?"

Gaston smiled at her innocently and said, "I've been paid. Not recently, it is true, but when I was a boy in Paris there

27

was this rich older woman who couldn't get her husband to kiss her between the thighs and . . ."

"Ah, I was right about that slight French accent, eh, you naughty thing. But seriously, even if you are willing to go sixty-nine I never give it away."

Before Gaston could answer two uniformed policemen came along the walk to eye the couple at the table. One of them looked at Gaston but asked the whore, "Dolores?" and she nodded and said, "He's with me. What's going on, muchachos?"

"The usual. Your friend, here, fits a description one of the girls at the Porta d'Oura gave us. What do *you* think?"

She laughed and said, "Forget it. We've been here a while. He's crazy, but he's all right."

One of the cops told Gaston, "Stand up and let's see if you can close your eyes and touch your nose, Senhor."

Gaston rose with a puzzled frown and passed the sobriety test with flying colors. The cop nodded and said, "Sorry to bother you, Senhor. The man who knifed that pimp staggered out drunk as a lord only half an hour ago."

They moved on and Gaston resumed his seat. Dolores asked, "Hey, did you really stab Carlos?"

"Surely you jest."

"I keep good track of time, too. I have to, in my business. But look, I don't care one way or the other. Let's get back to business. Don't you think I'm worth twenty? All right, fifteen cruzeiros?"

Gaston thought she was, just. But if she suspected the reason he'd run around the corner to drop smiling across the table from her, only a few minutes before the police whistles, he had to convince her he wasn't hiding anything worth paying for. Killing two blackmailers in one night would be pushing one's luck, even in Manaus, and too many people had seen him with the slut.

He said, "Merde alors, such a quandry," deliberately letting a heavier French accent creep into his creole as he remembered speaking more fluently at the cantina. The police weren't looking for a Frenchman, but some drunken native of the town. He took another sip of his drink and said, "I am willing to go with you for free, but if you insist on being crass about money I don't see how this romance is going to work out."

"Don't you like me?"

"But of course I like you. Why do you think I have been trying to pick you up? But you see, I, too, have my professional pride. I have been paid for *my* services on occasion, I have enjoyed the favors of other professionals at the Red Mill or along the boulevardes, but pay, *myself*, never! It is not that I am cheap. I would simply be *embarrassed!*"

Dolores laughed and said, "I can see how some old housewife might have been willing, once, but confess, it must have been a long time ago, eh?"

"Well, none of us are getting any younger, M'selle."

Dolores stiffened and asked, "Hey, was that a comment on my age? I'll have you know I'm only ... Uh, how old would you say I was, wise ass?"

Gaston regarded her judiciously and said, "Oh, let me see. Perhaps twenty-five? Certainly no older."

Dolores giggled with delight and answered, "You crazy old dear, I'll never see thirty again!"

"That is impossible," Gaston replied. He figured she was about forty at least, even before armies had marched over her. She nodded her head and insisted. "It's true. You haven't seen me in daylight. Everybody looks younger by gas light, and you're obviously drunk no matter what those cops thought."

He grinned and said, "What does it matter, hein? I, too, have been ravaged by time, and even though I am French, I prefer to make love in the dark. How about it, Dolores? My place is only across the plaza?"

She thought and asked, quietly, "Do you really treat a ... girl like me like a lover?"

"Oui, I was born to be a gymnast and I desire to eat you up."

"Look, it's tempting. I like you, and once in a while it's fun to let myself go. But, Jesus, for *free?* A girl's got to draw the line *somewhere!*"

He sighed and said, "I am amorous enough to admit

defeat if you will meet me half way. Suppose I give you, oh, ten cruzeiros as a token of my esteem. That way, I can feel I am breaking even, since I will be making ten myself on the transaction, hein."

She thought, staring across the plaza and noticing it was beginning to empty. She sighed and said, "Well, we can maybe start for ten. I won't promise to spend the whole night."

Then, as he rose to escort her to his hotel, she locked arms with him, giggled, and added, "Not unless you're damned good in bed, anyway."

So, the next morning, Captain Gringo was still stuck with Glynnis and Gaston couldn't get rid of Dolores even after they'd had breakfast in bed.

The blond couldn't even get out of bed until they got her some clothes. Dolores was amused by the situation and offered to go shopping for Glynnis if they'd give her some money. Gaston found this most amusing, too, and even the more idealistic Captain Gringo saw certain disadvantages in the idea, but, on the other hand, he was smarter than Gaston. So he gave Dolores the price of a new dress and she left. When Gaston said they'd never see her or the money again, Captain Gringo nodded and said that was the general idea. They were one down and one to go.

The conversation was in Spanish, of course, as the dumb but pretty Glynnis ate a canteloupe in bed. Gaston laughed and said, "I see the method in your madness, Dick, but that was still a rather expensive way to ditch a woman, non?"

Captain Gringo shrugged and said, "Not as expensive as trying to shove a screaming whore off the balcony. We're paying for two singles, here. The landlord probably knows better, but if we advertise he'll be within his rights to demand occupancy for four."

Gaston said, "I agreed it was trés practique. I just said it was expensive. In the meanwhile, if you give me the measurements of that blond I, Gaston, shall march out to the dress shop for you."

Captain Gringo shook his head and said, "I know her measurements by heart. I'll pick her up some clothes. You still haven't found us a way out of this damned place."

Gaston frowned and asked, "Do you think it wise to go out in broad daylight, my old and rare?"

"Oh, shit, you got back with a good lay after knifing a guy with the lights on in a room full of people! Who's going to get excited about a guy buying stuff for a lady?"

"Someone who's looking for him, of course. I told you the pimp said he'd found out who you were from someone. Someone we don't know. Carlos was at another hotel. The rooms he'd rented here for the orgy means he knows people at both hotels."

Captain Gringo shrugged and said, "Probably more. Pimps get around and he was a native of Manaus. So what? Sure, someone here or someone there might have told him who we really were. But can't you see they had to be knock-around guys, like us?"

Gaston frowned and asked, "Why? Why not a professional informant?"

"Oh, shit, Gaston, police informants don't finger wanted men to pimps. They tell the cops where they are and collect the reward! I think what that black-mailing twit picked up was the usual lobby rumor. Some bellhop or another guest Carlos had serviced might have shot off his mouth, just guessing. We do fit the description on those wanted flyers, but so do a lot of other guys. When I was fighting Apache back in the states, guys were always pointing to some old Indian and saying he looked a lot like Geronimo."

"Ah? And what did you do about it, my military expert?"

"Nothing. My troops were out there to keep order, not to scatter chickens and break up rain dances. If any of the local cops had taken the lobby gossip seriously they'd have knocked on our door by now."

So they left the Welsh soprano to her own devices and

nobody tried to stop them when they marched through the lobby and out on the plaza. Gaston headed for the waterfront while Captain Gringo went shopping for Glynnis. It was almost too late. They'd screwed away most of the morning and it would soon be Siesta Time. Latin Americans took a siesta between about eleven and three every day whether they needed one or not. In Manaus, they needed one. They were almost smack on the Equator and while the surrounding rain forest could be surprisingly pleasant in the eternal shade, Manaus had been layed out with total disregard for Mother Nature. The broad streets and elaborately paved plazas got hot enough to melt rubber heels after a few hours of Amazonian sunlight.

Captain Gringo was half-broiled by the time he found a decent dress shop and went in to discuss the latest fashions with an elderly lady who spoke only pure Portuguese. He tried speaking Spanish with a French accent and after they'd both waved their hands a lot she figured out that he wanted to buy something. So all he had to do was point.

Paying has never been a problem in any language on the planet Earth, provided the purchaser is willing to meet the price and has the money, wampum, or whatever. The shopkeeper got vague again about his change, but he wasn't up to arguing about the price in any language. Captain Gringo very seldom bought dresses and lingerie.

He moved down the arcade to a shoe shop and while he had better luck with a Spanish-speaking clerk, he was stuck for shoe sizes in Brazil. He guessed Glynnis wore a size four shoe. He guessed the pair he picked out were about that size. Then he decided to play it safe and buy a size larger. The girl could get into shoes too large, but it wouldn't work the other way.

By the time he had his purchases bought and wrapped it was even hotter outside. He knew the hotel bar would probably be closed for siesta by the time he made it back. So he stopped at a sidewalk cantina, sat at a table under the awning, and ordered a tall cool drink. The waiter said ice cost extra. Captain Gringo told him to put plenty in with the gin and tonic, and not to bother with the tonic.

The drink and a redhead arrived at his table almost together. The waiter put the glass down as the woman sat down in the wire chair across from Captain Gringo. He raised the glass to her and said, "Cheers," in English. Aside from having Celtic features, the redhead was dressed as only the British in the tropics could dress without laughing. She had on a pith helmet and a thin khaki shirt that matched the color of her split whipcord riding skirts. The shirt was open at the neck and he could see she had a very nice chest. Her face was flushed, either from the heat or embarrassment, but it was still a nice face. Wide-set green eyes, with a little more determination in the jaw than he'd have asked for if he'd anything to say about it when they were designing her.

She had her well-manicured hands on the whipcord khaki bag she placed between them on the table. She licked her lips and said, "I'm Maureen Mahoney, Captain Walker."

He stared at her unwinkingly. She said, "I know who you are. If you'd be good enough to come with me I've something to show you that you might be interested in."

He took a sip of his drink and said, "I don't know who you think I am, Miss, but I'll buy you a drink."

"We haven't time. My place is just a short way from here."

"Swell, why don't you just run along to it, then?"

"You won't come with me?"

"You must be joking."

She sighed, reached in her bag and drew out a nickel plated Virtue .32 as she asked, "Pretty please?"

He smiled wryly and said, "Well, since you put it that way."

They both rose. She pointed with her chin and said, "That way. You go first." So he did. He didn't see anyone else watching them as the streets cleared for La Siesta. He knew she'd timed it with that in mind. He figured he had a better than even chance of reversing the situation, since she couldn't see anything but his back and he was packing a bigger gun. But she was kind of pretty to shoot and he wasn't in the mood to explain the noise, so what the hell.

She couldn't be a cop. No bounty hunter, or huntress, would try to take him alive. The reward was dead or alive, so why take chances? Okay, what did that leave? There was only one way to find out.

He rounded the corner she'd indicated and she fell in at his side, with the muzzle of her .32 against his floating rib. He said, "Put that thing away, Honey. I'm not going to say it twice."

She poked him with the gun and said, "Keep walking. That pink stucco building with the brass-studded gate."

He took another step, whirled, and dropped his hand on the little whore pistol as she tried to snatch it back. He grabbed it by the cylinder so it couldn't fire as he twisted it out of her hand. She stood rooted in place as she stared down at her empty tingling palm and gasped, "How did you do that?"

"It's a knack," He replied, putting her Virtue in his jacket's side pocket. Then he took her by the elbow and added, "Brass-studded gate, right," and started moving her toward it.

She shook her head and said, "They said you were good. Nobody told me you were part cobra. I don't think I could have fired even if I'd had bullets in the gun."

"You were holding an empty gun on me, Doll? Didn't your mother ever tell you the facts of life? Never point a gun at a grown man unless you're very serious indeed. That was a pretty amateur stunt, Honey."

She sighed and said, "I am an amateur, Captain Walker. That's why I've turned to you. I need the services of a professional."

They got to the gate. He told her to open it and go first as he covered her from the rear. The rear view looked very nice, but he was more interested in what lay on the other side of the mysterious portal. Her ass would still be there when he made sure this wasn't a trap.

It wasn't. The gate led into a small patio shaded by a big fig tree. A terra cotta lion was spitting a tickle of water into a corner font and it seemed ten degrees cooler off the sun-blasted streets. Maureen Mahoney asked, "Can I have my

Virtue back?" and then as she saw the glint in his eye she blushed and said, "I meant my gun. It's called a Virtue."

He said, "I know," and took her little pistol out of his pocket. He broke it open and checked the empty chambers before he handed it to her. She put it away, saying, "I told you it was empty. Don't you trust me?"

He said, "Not hardly. You said you wanted to show me something. I've seen a fig tree and a fountain before."

She said, "Step this way," and headed for the arched doorway of the pink house. He wouldn't have stepped that way on a bet, but he followed her. She really did have a nice little derriere and he liked the way it moved her skirt.

They went inside. As his eyes adjusted to the gloom he noted it was even cooler indoors and that she or more likely her native servants knew enough to close the jalousied shutters against the sun to keep the cool of night in. There was no breeze at noon in the tropics. You ventilated at night and shut out the heat of the day by barring every possible entrance just before sunrise.

Marreen switched on a fringed lamp near a big cordovan leather sofa in front of a baronial baroque fireplace. There was a gold paper fan on the spanking new andirons, of course, for a fireplace in Manaus was to show how rich you were, not to build a fire in for God's sake!

She took off her pith helmet and shook down her long red ringlets. Without the heavy shade of the brim to contrast with glaring sunlight on her rather boyish jaw she looked a lot better. In fact, she was beautiful in a sort of fox hunting way. He could see her jumping a fence on a big thoroughbred, sitting side-saddle and wearing hunter's pinks and a little black derby. Leading the pack.

She put the helmet down and moved over to a sideboard to pour two Waterford goblets full of sangria from an already prepared pitcher. The ice in the punch was worth almost as much, in Manaus, as the cut glass itself. It was nice to know she was well provided for.

She handed him his drink and said, "Come with me." He said, "I'd love to," as he followed her into another room. She switched on an overhead Edison bulb. A Maxim machinegun sat on its tripod atop a packing case with Belgian markings. She pointed her chin at the weapon and asked, "What do you think of it?"

Holding the drink in his left hand, Captain Gringo stepped over and ran a finger over the deady oiled steel of the breechblock. He said, "It's new. Still has the factory kosmoline on it. Belgian-made under Maxim's license so it takes 9mm instead of 30–30. You got?"

"I got. A dozen belts of Royal Belgique Fabrique 9mm, as you guessed."

"Honey, I don't guess when it comes to machineguns. I know. So what's this all about? You didn't import a new machinegun to tap rubber trees."

She led him back to the other room and sat him on the sofa before she took a sip of her own drink and said, "I have a steam launch, too. Thirty footer with a canopy and Corliss engine. We'll be going up the Rio Negro, to the north."

"You mean *you* will. I just came out of that green hell, Doll. I can't think of a single reason I'd want to go back!"

Maureen said, "I'm not offering a single reason. I'm offering a hundred a day, plus a thousand dollar bonus when and if we get back here alive."

He took a sip, swallowed, and said, "You must want to steam up the Rio Negro pretty bad."

"I don't want to. *I have to.* My father, Professor Bernard Mahoney of the British Museum is missing somewhere near the headwaters of the Rio Negro. He vanished a year ago on a field trip, looking for a lost ruined city reputed to lie deep in the selva near the Venezuelan and Colombian borders. I can't seem to be able to get any help from Brazil. So I've made up my mind to go myself."

"Good hunting. If you've been asking questions about me you know I'm wanted in Colombia. I was on the losing side in their last revolution."

"Are you wanted by Venezuela?"

"Not yet. If I stay the hell away from their border I might just be able to keep it that way."

"Listen, the territory where we'll be going isn't patroled by the police of any country. It's unmapped, unexplored

36

wilderness. Nobody lives up there in that corner of the Amazon, but Indians and perhaps a few outlaws."

"I've met both. I think I like the Indians better. You know that you're crazy, don't you? Leaving out the poison arrows and wandering flagelados who'd kill us for our boots, there's no way in hell you're going to find a man who's been missing in that rain forest a whole year."

"I live in hopes my father is still alive."

"You just hope all you want to. If your old man was alive he'd have sent you a postcard by now. If he's dead, well, this may not be delicate, but even bones and guns just melt into the hungry soil under that tall timber. I recently helped search for some ambushed missionaries in another stretch of the selva. They'd only been missing a month or so and we knew where to look. We found some rusty crumbs that might have been a gun or something one time. That was it. Aside from being constantly wet, the red laterite soil is mineral poor. It sucks up calcium and carbon like blotting paper. Iron lasts only a little longer. We wouldn't find anything you could identify as your father even if we knew where to look, and we don't. You're talking about big country, Maureen. You could lose the British Isles in the upper Amazonian headwaters. Hell, you could throw in France and lose that, too, while you were at it. Forget the trees or the fact you can't see more than a hundred yards in any direction. You wouldn't be able to find a body in an area that big if it were all open desert!"

"He may not be dead. He may have been captured by Indians and . . ."

"Oh, cut it out, you've been reading Rider Haggard. I enjoyed that book about the white goddess living with the natives, too, but Haggard was writing about Africa in the first place, and I've spent some time with Indians in the second. The natives up that way are Jivaro. I've met some Jivaro. If they don't like you, they cut your head off and shrink it a lot. If they don't think you're their enemy you couldn't ask for nicer people. They'd never hold anyone a prisoner for a year. If your father ran into Jivaro a year ago they'd have killed him on the spot or loaned him a canoe by now."

"What about those others? What did you call them?"

"Flagelados—the flayed ones. Jungle running whites, mestizos, runaway slaves or any mixture you can think of. Same deal. Some flagelados are just looking for wild rubber, chicle, Brazil nuts, and such. Others are bad apples on the run from the law. Friendly rubber tappers or hide hunters would have helped your father if he needed it. The other kind would have killed him for his matches and salt as soon as they got the chance. Nobody is about to feed and care for a prisoner a whole year."

"I've heard some Latin American bandits kidnap for ransom."

"A lot of Latin American bandits and some Latin American governments kidnap for ransom. But have you gotten any ransom notes?"

She shook her red head and he said, "There you are, then. No small expedition stands a chance of finding out what happened to your father. Haven't you asked the Brazilian government to help you?"

She sighed and said, "Of course. They told me the same things you just did. They also said they don't want to send any military forces near the border this year for some reason."

"I can tell you the reason. I was just in on it. Columbia just had a short sweet revolution and the new strong man is a bit testy on just where his borders are at the moment. I missed the attempted coup they had down here in Brazil a year or so ago, but even though the central government won, it's in no shape to have a war with anyone right now. I understand they had to purge most of their navy and a lot of their army to show folks who was boss in Brazil. This rubber boom has the Indians on the prod. Some of the rubber tappers have poor manners when they meet a lady alone in the selva. The Brazilian government has enough on it's plate this year without looking for a needle in one very big haystack."

"So I've been told. That's why I want to hire you and your friend, Gaston Verrier. I don't mean to just muck about up the Rio Negro. If we locate the lost city and start from there . . ."

"Hold it," he cut in with a frown. "Are we talking about a lost Inca something all covered with vines and strangler figs like that ancient city they just found in the Cambodian jungles?"

"Yes, my father's theory was that the ruins, here, must have been built by some civilization older than the Incas."

"Yeah, I read about that idiot. Not your father, the French Count or something who wandered out of the trees a few years back with all those sketches he said he made of a lost Atlantis in the middle of the rain forest. He drew pictures of stone elephants and even had his Indian girl friend sitting naked on a fallen pillar. I think they were in the London *Illustrated News*."

Maureen nodded and said, "Other explorers have reported seeing ruins in the unexplored selvas to the north."

He shrugged and said, "Somebody once reported seven golden cities in the Arizona desert and the old Spaniards spent a lot of time looking for 'em, too. Guess what? They weren't there. Nobody ever found El Dorado or the elephants Thomas Jefferson asked Lewis and Clark to keep an eye out for, either. I think your father was on a wild goose chase, and, to put it frankly, somebody cooked his goose. Forget it, Honey. I know how you feel, but I've got better things to do and you ought to start thinking about your own future, too. Your father's gone. You'll never know for sure just what happened to him. But that's the way it is, sometime. Just think of him as someone lost at sea. You know he's on the bottom somewhere, but there's nothing you can do about it."

Maureen had been toying with the top button of her shirt, either absently or by design. It popped open, exposing another inch of cleavage, as she said, "I told you I was willing to pay well. If, as you say, it's a lost cause, I'm the only one who'll lose money on the expedition. There must be some way I can convince you."

She was doing pretty well with that slow teasing strip and Captain Gringo was a man, so he was tempted. But he was a reasonably decent man, so he knew that if he took her up on her unspoken offer he'd be stuck with living up to his

39

end of the bargain. He didn't think she was an easy lay. He didn't think she was interested in him that way. She was a nice girl getting a little desperate and the nicest female knew, instinctively, how to play that last ace in the hole, which *was* a hole, when you thought about it. But thinking about it made his groin tingle and he'd made up his mind to be smart for a change. So he said, "It's been nice talking to you. I'm sorry I can't help you. I've got to find my sidekick and see what boat we're leaving on."

He picked up the package for Glynnis that he'd placed on the floor by the sofa. She said, "You can't leave now. It's siesta time." "I know," he conceded. "They'll probably think I'm a protestant, but it's not actually against the law to walk across the plaza during La Siesta."

"I'm sure I could make you more comfortable, here," she said, blushing as she stared down at her hands in her lap. He noticed how she was twisting the whipcord with her fingers. He smiled wistfully and said, "You really must love your father, Kitten."

"I'd do anything to save him."

"That's what I just said. Leaving's going to be sort of painful to me, too, but I have to look at myself in the mirror when I shave and I don't take advantage of widows and orphans, so . . ."

"How did you know I was a widow?" she asked.

He wished she hadn't said that. It was hard enough to pass on a sweet looking virgin. He said, "I didn't. I meant you were an orphan. But since you seem to be both, my point was well taken."

He rose. She got up, too, and wrapped her arms around him, pleading, "Please stay. I've nobody else to turn to. I'll give you more money. I'll do anything you ask, Dick."

He said, "I know. Look, it's not the money. I'm not oblivious to the fact that you're one hell of a nice looking dame. It's not that I don't want you to find out what happened to your father."

"What is it, then?"

"I've sworn off lost causes. I had a nice career going as a U.S. Army officer, one time. I stuck my neck out to help some Mexican rebels. I wound up losing my commission and had to run for my life with a price on my head and my old comrades hunting me. I've been in one damned mess after another ever since. I keep trying to help people because I think they're in the right, not because they're about to win. I've been shot, stabbed, beat up, and robbed a lot. Mostly robbed. I'm trying to break the habit."

"Do you think I'm trying to rob you, Dick?"

"I don't know. I don't want to know. I'm trying to get *out* of this neck of the woods and you're not about to get me *deeper* into them!"

She hugged tighter and started moving her pelvis just enough to remind him it was there. She *was* a widow, he could tell, and she'd made her late husband very happy. He said, "Look, if you're trying to give me a hard on, you're succeeding. If you want me to go to bed with you, I'm willing as hell. If you think that means I'm going up the Rio Negro with you, forget it."

"Why don't we talk about it, later?" she asked. Her tone was husky and brazen, but her face was beet red. He said, "It won't work, Maureen. I'd roll you in the hay and screw you every way but flying, if I thought you wanted it and that you wouldn't expect anything else from me. But I know what you really want. I know you know you're pretty good in bed. So you'd be mad as hell when I got up and left, wouldn't you?"

She murmured, "How do you know you'd want to leave, Dick?"

He said, "Honey, if I can make sense with you rubbing that thing against what you surely know is not a pistol in my pocket it would be even easier after I'd fired it at you a couple of times."

She turned away and moved to stand against the fireplace with her back to him, head downcast and shoulders shaking. He asked, "I didn't mean to insult you. You know I want you so bad I can taste it."

"Why, then?" she sobbed.

He answered, "Because I like you. I like you too much to be a rat."

She didn't answer. He turned and walked out of her life. The heat out on the dusty street hit him like an open furnace door and as he trudged toward the hotel he was already regretting his nobility. He knew she'd just keep trying until she finally found some ass hole to go up the river with her. She'd probably give herself to the silly son-of-a-bitch, too. If she was very lucky, she wouldn't get robbed and fed to the fish by some fucking flagelado or down-on-his-luck soldier of fortune.

But, damn it, she'd been warned by the Brazilian authorities as well as him. If she were going to do it, she was going to do it. That stubborn jaw of hers indicated that she'd keep trying.

"Stupid," he told himself as he walked on. "You'd be in a cool bedroom with a hot redhead this very minute if you weren't such a Don Quixote!"

He still had a raging erection and the way his pants were rubbing didn't do a thing to ease it for him. Then, as he saw the facade of his own hotel he remembered the little blond who was waiting in bed for him, stark naked, and started walking faster. He still had that maiden in distress to deal with, but at least she didn't want him to go tear-assing up a jungle river with her and what the hell, what could the redhead have done back there that the blond ahead couldn't do as well?

He found the lobby deserted during La Siesta. He went upstairs and let himself in with the key. The jalousies were shut over the windows here, too, and the room was pretty dark. He put the package down and started to shuck his sun-baked duds as he told the woman in the bed, "I got you a complete outfit. If it fits we'll go out later and let you pick out some other things."

She didn't answer. He heard her soft breathing and nodded. It had been a rough night for her, he supposed. She was sort of little and he'd sort of let himself go after doing without for a while.

He stripped and showered in the bath between the two ajoining rooms. The tepid water cooled him nicely, but soaping his erection only made it harder. He dried off and came back out, saying, "Glynnis?"

She murmured something pleasant and snuggled deeper into the pillows, purring, with her back to him. He grinned and crossed to join her, sliding under the cool sheet. He ran a palm along the angle of her hip and when he moved on his side to place his engorged shaft between the cheeks of her round derriere she arched her back to receive his piece offering without waking up. It was a game every couple played once in a while. He guided himself into her gently to see how far he could get before she woke up. She murmured dreamily but went on sleeping as he got it in and started gently moving. She started moving, too. And as they started really going at it she sighed and murmured, "Oh, that's nice. Let me turn over and do it right."

So he withdrew and as she rolled on her back, dreamily, he remounted her and flattened out atop her to really let her have it. She wrapped her arms and legs around him and started moving rather astoundingly as she gasped in Spanish, "Oh, my, there certainly is more of you than meets the eye."

In Spanish? He braced himself up on his elbows for a better look. Then he gasped and said, "Hey, you're not Glynnis!"

She said, "Of course not, my name's Dolores, but for God's sake don't stop now!"

He didn't. He couldn't have if he'd wanted to, and he didn't want to. He was coming. As he did so, the whore's flesh contracted tightly and she gasped, "Oh, shit, I don't believe this. It's going to take me days to get back in the proper frame of mind."

He stayed in, getting his second wind as he asked her, "Didn't you like it?"

She said, "That's the trouble. Between the two of you, I've been ruined for the day. I haven't come with a man's prick in me for years. The two of you have sensitized my poor business machine and now all it wants to do is come. This is really most annoying."

"You want me to stop?"

"Of course not. That's what's so annoying. But what the hell, since I'm no good for the street right now, I may as well enjoy it. Let me get on top."

He rolled off and over. As Dolores mounted him with a roguish grin, he asked her what had happened to Glynnis. She said, "I got back with the clothes you sent me out to buy, remember?"

"Oh, yeah, I'd forgotten about that. You're just full of surprises, Doll."

"Oooh, that is surprisingly deep, eh? Back to your blond, she put on the clothes and went out to see somebody about a job at the opera. Can she really sing?"

"Beats me. I never heard her."

"I thought this was all the two of you were doing in here last night. Is she any good at that?"

"Not as good as you," he replied, gallantly. Old Dolores wasn't as pretty as Glynnis and Glynnis wasn't as pretty as Maureen but it was hard to think how it could have been any better over at the redhead's. Nobody screwed like a whore on her day off. The experienced dark Dolores was finding the situation piquant, too, and obviously liked to show off her skills to her few friends. She hooked a bare heel in each of his armpits and began to move amazingly with her weight back on her braced arms. He asked, "For God's sake, are you trying to twist it off?" and she laughed and replied, "Yes, and I defy you to go soft in that position."

He tried. He ejaculated harder than he'd expected as she literally jerked him off with her bouncing bronze body. She giggled when she felt it inside her. She kept moving and he saw she was right as her rippling internal muscles kept wringing him out like a dish rag and held it erect and still throbbing. He laughed and said, "Jesus, have you no mercy, Dolores?" and she shook her head wildly from side to side, replied, "No, you are my prisoner and I shall never let you out of my dungeon cell."

But then she started to get there and suddenly rolled off to pant, "Oh, you do it to me, now. We seem to have awakened a sleeping dragon!"

He rolled into the saddle and pounded her unselfishly with what was left until she climaxed with a long shuddering moan and went limp, saying, "I surrender. It's not possible, but I just came again."

"I noticed. I didn't," he replied, as he went on, now aroused again. He was getting a little jaded and it was taking longer this time. He was a bit limp and Dolores had dilated until the results, while very nice, were a little loose. She locked her ankles around the small of his back and reached down to fondle his scrotum with her left hand as he attempted to get over the hill. She laughed and said, "Poor baby's tired," as he braced himself on locked elbows and tried to picture her as a redhead to keep his interest up. He slipped out, swore, and started to fumble his way back in.

Dolores gasped his moist shaft, steered it, and as he re-entered her he said, "Oh, that is tight and . . . hey, is that where I think it is?"

She laughed and said, "Yes, I want to try something very wicked. I never do this with a customer."

He moved more gently in her tight rectal opening, afraid of hurting her despite how good it felt. He asked, "Are you really getting out of it, this way?" and Dolores said, "Just do it," as she started to toy with her own clit while he sodomized her. He didn't know why it should excite him, but it did. He knew she was getting a perverse thrill out of openly masturbating in front of another as she gave her free Greek lesson. He didn't have to worry about pleasing her with his own sex organ, so he could just enjoy her, and he did. He had her selfishly and sinfully as she rolled her head from side to side, moaning with forbidden pleasure as she jerked herself off with her fingernails raking through his pubic hairs until they both climaxed and collapsed in a mingled mound of quivering flesh. As he relaxed atop her she slowly excreted him. He sniffed and said, "I think I need another shower."

She said she wanted one, too, so they went hand in hand into the bath. She sat on the commode and relieved herself as he adjusted the water taps. She got up and stepped under the shower with him, saying, "You naughty boy," as they began to soap one another. Naturally, they started getting interested in each other's bodies as they lathered each other's crotch. He leaned her against the tiled wall and started to enter her standing up, but she was too short or he was too tall so they wound up on the bath mat with her sucking his fresh scrubbed member and offering him the same opportunity. He knew she was cleaner than many a lady he'd met like this in less sanitary surroundings, but, damn it, she was a streetwalker and the idea made him remember Gaston for the first time. He said, "Hey, speaking of going French, where the hell is Gaston? I expected to meet him here during La Siesta."

She saw he was losing interest and sat up to say, "I don't know what happened to him. I thought you were he, until I woke up a bit more. Do you think he'll be jealous if he comes home to find us like this?"

Captain Gringo didn't know but he didn't want to go sixty-nine with Dolores, so he said, "I don't know. The point is that he's not here. There's nothing going on outside. There won't be anyone along the waterfront until after three or so. What in the hell could he have gotten into?"

"Another woman?" Dolores suggested, adding, "Both of you are sex maniacs. Maybe he ran into that Welsh girl on the street. Maybe some other woman. God knows it's not hard to find a woman on the streets of Manaus. The competition in this town is killing me."

Captain Gringo helped her to her feet and they dried each other off as he mused, "Gaston would have brought any other playmates here, he's too practique to pay for another room. The cantinas are closed. Everything is closed. I don't like this."

She led him back to the bed, holding him by the leash as she soothed, "He'll turn up, my Toro. He may have found a girl who has her own room."

She sat on the edge of the bed and began to kiss him all over his lap as he stood bemused and a little worried. He knew she was probably right and she was great at the wrong she was doing to him down there. On the other hand, Gaston could be in trouble. He said so. She kissed the head

46

of his half aroused organ and asked, "Where would you ever begin looking for him, then? He could be anywhere in Manaus and it's hot out there."

He said, "It's hot down there, too, and I just had this same dumb conversation with another lady looking for a dirty old man."

He rolled her back and mounted her with his feet on the rug for purchase. But as he started to enjoy himself again he decided he'd give Gaston another ten minutes and then he'd just have to go out and look for him.

The timing worked out just right. Ten minutes later Gaston was still missing and he couldn't have gotten it up again with a block and tackle. So he decided he'd better get dressed and go find the little bastard.

Manaus lay at the junction of the Amazon and Rio Negro. Despite its location in the center of a continent, the waterfront of Manaus looked like any other tropic seaport. The big bronze Amazon could technically be called a river, but it was just as much an inland sea. Some of its tributaries were bigger than the Mississippi or Nile while they'd barely mapped piddling side streams the size of the Rhine or Hudson. On the lower reaches of the Amazon you couldn't see the shores from mid stream and had to navigate as on any other open water. Up here near the head of ocean going navigation the main channel was still thirty feet deep and all the fleets of the world could have anchored off Manaus without being too crowded.

Most of the deep draft vessels anchored offshore, hanging on their anchor lines with all sterns downstream. Like most tropic ports, Manaus was a rummage shop or nautical museum. For many a vessel whose day had passed still plied it's trade in the backwaters of the world. Sleek new steam freighters anchored among tramp schooners and a few square riggers still earning their keep as carriers of imperishable cheap cargos that didn't have to be anywhere in a hurry. Captain

Gringo noticed a low gray gunboat flying the green Brazilian ensign. He recognized it as one of the ubiquitous Clyde-built jobs the Brits sold cheap to the less-advanced navies of the world. It looked like a cross between a tugboat and a battleship. The hull and main superstructure were, in fact, the same as those of a harbor tug. They'd simply made the whole thing out of armor plate and added a conning tower and gun turret. He figured it was there to show the flag. They were a long way from the Capitol at Rio de Janeiro and the dust was still settling from that attempted military coup a while back.

He noticed some luxury yachts closer in but they were no mystery. With the world demanding rubber for the new pneumatic tires and even carriage wheels, a lot of people in Brazil were getting rich. Guys who'd never owned a pair of socks were suddenly millionaires and everybody knew J.P. Morgan had a yacht, so what the hell.

Most of the riverside was occupied by cheek-to-jowl small craft, bows on the muddy bank. There were lighters, houseboats and dugout canoes. A whole community of mixed breeds lived on or near the water as fishermen, cargo handlers, or, when nobody was looking, thieves. He saw a gang of kids swimming off the stern of a cargo raft. Some were sunning on the rough deck or using it as a diving platform. Not one had a stitch on which seemed reasonable. Some were boys and some were girls, which seemed a little naughty. A few of the girls were starting to blossom, which seemed naughty indeed. They sported innocently, like south sea island natives, and he supposed clothes were sometimes a needless convention. The nubile maidens were probably in more danger of being eaten than they were of being ravaged on a raft. There were some very spooky things swimming under the tea brown surface of the Amazon. Caymans as big as Nile crocodiles and giant catfish that ate them. Everyone but those kids seemed to know about the deadly shoals of piranha. Oddly, he'd never met a native who seemed at all afraid of piranha, electric eels, or man-eating catfish. On the other hand, few of them seemed very bright. Superstition took the place of literacy in most places south of Laredo and he noticed most of the kids wore religious medals if nothing else.

Gaston wasn't swimming with the kids, and everyone else along the waterfront seemed to have taken off for La Siesta. He moved on to where quays on driven piles poked out into the sluggish current. Nobody was guarding the goodies piled helter-skelter here and there. Maybe the local thieves took La Siesta, too?

He moved around a small mountain of rubber bales. They looked like big licorice lollipops with their sticks broken off short. He knew the locals made them by repeatedly dipping the end of a stick in liquid latex and smoking each layer over a smudge fire of green leaves. The labor involved in the rubber trade was awesome, but human labor and lives were cheap on the upper Amazon. The barons who controlled the trade were too rich to believe. Their armies of flagelados and enslaved Indians were expected to be grateful for their lives and the scant rations they received.

He grimaced and moved on. It was like that in a lot of places. Brazil was no worse than any other tropic land he'd visited. It was easy enough to see why they had revolutions down here every few minutes if one studied the economy as an outsider. The insiders never bothered to try. Anyone who couldn't see the advantages of civilization was a wild Indian or a bandit born to hang, right?

He passed some mahogany logs and a huge pile of quinine bark slabs. It looked like the luxury imports were quickly cleared from the docks while the bulky export stuff could wait. It was true no smart crook would steal a slab of quinine or a mahogany log at the risk of his life when all he had to do was paddle up some side stream and cut his own. So there wasn't one watchman or cop in sight and where the hell was Gaston?

Captain Gringo knew his sidekick had been negotiating with the skipper of at least one of those vessels moored out there. Swell. Which one? He saw no sign of movement out on the river. He came to a closed chandler's shop with a closed cantina next door. There wasn't anyone he could even ask about a small dapper stranger passing by.

49

He turned and started back. He was just going to attract attention to himself by wandering about in the heat during La Siesta. He'd go back to the hotel and wait until three like the rest of the grown ups in town. With any luck, he might find Gaston there. Probably in bed with old Dolores if he knew Gaston, and Dolores.

As he retraced his steps he heard a shrill scream. He glanced over at the kids on the raft. One of them had swum out a ways and was trying like hell to get back in as his or her friends shouted encouragement but offered no help. It was easy to see why. That floating log following the frantically swimming kid was no log. It was a cayman. A big one.

Captain Gringo ran down the muddy bank, leaped aboard the raft, and ran to the stern before he'd really had time to consider what the hell he was doing. Naked boys and girls around him were shouting and pointing. He didn't understand their river Creole. He didn't have to. The long-haired tawny swimmer was damned good, but the cayman was gaining with almost lazy ripples of it's long armored tail. The cold-blooded meat-eater was awesome in its total lack of eagerness. It was probably dimly aware that the meat it pursued would never beat it to the bank and so it was simply reaching for a snack with no more emotion than a well-fed monkey reaching for a dangling fruit. It lay awash in the water, with only the tip of it's snout and twin periscope eye bumps breaking the surface. Captain Gringo saw its intended victim was a teen-aged Indian girl. She didn't have a chance, but he had to admire her spunk. She didn't scream or thrash in mindless fear. She kept swimming, gracefully, grimly determined to do the impossible. The best human swimmer in the world couldn't move faster in the water than the aquatic reptile after her. Even as he watched the cayman was closing the distance. The girl was the length of a swimming pool away from the raft. The cayman was ten, no, nine, no eight feet behind her! Captain Gringo drew his .38 and held it in both hands as the cayman raised it's upper jaw to make the final lunge. He aimed at the reptile's tonsils and pulled the trigger. Nothing happened, so he pulled it again. He couldn't be missing because he saw no splashes on either side of the monster's scaly head. He emptied the revolver into the gaping maw and as his hammer clicked on an empty chamber it did seem as if the girl was a length ahead. The cayman closed its jaws and vanished under the surface with a swirl of brown water, either to take its victim from below or to die. It probably had to think a while before it made up it's tiny mind.

There was no time to reload. Captain Gringo dropped to one knee on the edge of the raft and held out an encouraging hand, shouting, "Come on, Kid, you can do it!"

She could. She shot a small brown hand up to wetly clasp his, and as he literally yanked her out of the river she plastered her naked wet brown flesh against him and sobbed, "Ay, salvador mio!" as the others crowded around, grinning and slapping both of them on the backs.

Everybody was talking at once and Captain Gringo was suddenly aware that he was, one: soaking wet, two: an obvious child molester to any adult passing by, and three: he'd fired five gunshots in broad daylight, and it wasn't the Fourth of July.

He disengaged himself from the wet Indian girl, who was acting as if she wanted to screw him standing up. It was a good thing he'd sated himself with Dolores only an hour or so back. She was too young for him, but too mature to be swimming naked with the smaller kids. His wet pants would have betrayed him if he'd shown the erection her trim brown figure deserved.

Her face wasn't bad, either. He'd noticed she kissed pretty grown up and she had enough white Portuguese blood to make her pretty by European standards. From the little he could understand of her creole dialect she wanted to take him home to her own houseboat, either to taste some of her mother's chicken soup or to go to bed with her. He said he was late for another appointment and made his way ashore with her clinging to one arm and another naked girl, almost as pretty but really way too young. He wondered if they intended to walk all the way back to his hotel with him, stark naked.

Apparently there were some limits to what downtown

Manaus would tolerate, however. The naked swimming party only escorted him to the first paved street running in line with the waterfront shanty town. She insisted on kissing him goodbye, putting a lot of tongue into it, and told him she'd wait for him later that evening near the chandler's shop. It figured. She wasn't old enough to be served inside the cantina. He assumed she'd have some clothes on. He didn't think he wanted to find out. She was a sweet little thing, but he had to find Gaston and get the hell *out* of here!

As he headed along a narrow lane he hoped led toward his hotel, he spied two men in white uniforms coming down the block to meet him. It was still siesta time, so he knew that they thought it was important to be out on the streets. He saw they were looking at him but kept walking toward them until he came to a side alley and casually turned up it. He started running as soon as the uniforms were out of sight. The fucking alley dog-legged once and ended in a blank wall. The top of the stucco wall was guarded by shards of broken glass set in the cement. He knew how to get over the glass. He'd done it before. He could take off his jacket, throw it over the top of the wall, and roll himself over the stout linen.

But then what? He'd be landing smack in someone's patio during siesta when everyone was home and probably lounging by the damned tinkling fountain he could hear on the other side.

He looked around. He spotted a deep door niche on the shady side of his blind alley and stepped into it, taking out his .38 to reload. Those guys had probably heard his shots down by the river and were strolling over to investigate them. With luck they'd walk right past this alley.

They didn't. He heard the crunch of a boot heel on a gritty spot and flattened himself against the oaken door behind him, sucking in his gut. He couldn't see them, but apparently, from the sounds, they'd moved in as far as the dog leg. He heard one ask, "Well?" and the other replied, "He either went over that wall or he's in one of these houses. He may have had some innocent reason to be out in the siesta after all."

"Let's go around to the far side and see if he came out that way, eh?"

Captain Gringo allowed himself to start breathing again as he put the gun under his jacket. That had been close, but for once he'd made it without having to act surly.

But he knew his luck was running out in Manaus. That pimp had learned who they were. That Irish girl had known, too. Those kids over by the river would describe him when the cops asked them about the gunshots they'd just heard. He had to find Gaston and make some serious plans about getting the hell out of here.

He eased out of the door niche and resumed his interrupted walk back to the dubious safety of the hotel. If Gaston had been picked up, the police would have the hotel staked out even if Gaston refused to talk. Like himself, Gaston carried a key to their rooms with the hotel's name on it. It had seemed a good idea at the time. Knockaround guys didn't like to attract attention in a lobby by asking over and over for their room keys. On the other hand, the key tags made backtracking you simpler for the cops.

He reached in his pocket for his own key. Then he smiled thinly and saw it made no sense to get rid of it. He had to use it if he ever went back, so the question was, should he go back?

Where else? he asked himself. He didn't know where the hell Glynnis was, right now. Maureen would think he wanted to go looking for Dear Old Dad with her if he went back to her place. He might be able to stall her for a time, but she'd be sore as hell and maybe tell the cops on him if he double-crossed her. For all he knew, she'd already done it. Hell hath no fury and all that shit.

He took out his watch: it was almost two-thirty. In half an hour or so the shops and cantinas would be opening again. Maybe his best bet was to just kill time wandering around. He'd know the hotel was still safe if and when he stumbled over Gaston. If Gaston had made it back okay, he'd get tired of screwing Dolores by nightfall and come looking himself. There was that sidewalk cantina across from the hotel. That

53

was his best bet. Sooner or later old Dolores would wander by, even if she hadn't seen Gaston and . . .

Captain Gringo froze as something hard poked him in the floating rib from behind and a voice said, pleasantly, "Please raise your hands, Senhor."

There was nothing else he could do. He'd been suckered. Some son-of-a-bitch had been in another door niche and he'd walked past without noticing, like a fucking tourist!

As one man held the gun against Captain Gringo another pair of hands patted him down and relieved him of his own weapon. With any luck, they were hold-up artists.

They weren't. The man with the gun removed the muzzle from his rib and said, "Thank you. You can lower your hands now, Senhor Walker."

Captain Gringo turned around. They were the same two uniformed guys he'd thought he'd outfoxed. He smiled sheepishly and said, "Congratulations, you boys are good."

The one with the gun smiled back and said, "Thank you, Senhor. Coming from a professional like the Great Captain Gringo, that is a most pleasant compliment. Would you be kind enough to accompany us, Senhor?"

"Do I have any choice?"

"No, but there is no need for rudeness between officers and gentlemen. I am going to put my own pistol back in it's holster to save you the embarrassment of appearing to be under arrest in public. You, of course, are unarmed and one assumes intelligent. We have not far to walk. Shall we go?"

Captain Gringo noticed the silent one who'd taken his .38 trailed behind as he walked beside the one who'd arrested him. They wore white tunics like the local police, but now that he'd gotten a better look at them he'd noticed the anchors on their caps. He asked, "Are you guys Navy Shore Patrol?" and the friendly one said, "Brazilian Naval Intelligence, Senhor. Our superior, Commodore Barboza, will explain the details to you in a few moments."

So he let them lead him to wherever, his mind in a whirl. About the only people he couldn't remember tangling with in the past was the Brazilian Navy. He asked the one beside him, "Have you guys picked up any friends of mine, lately?"

and the amiable Brazilian said, "Yes, your comrade, Gaston Verrier, was trying to book passage on a rather rusty old tramp when we caught up with him. It's as well for you both that we did. It's a most slow freighter and I understand the cook is terrible."

Captain Gringo fell into a quiet funk. He didn't want to remind them of any charges they might not already have on paper by asking questions. They might want to talk to him about that Colombian gunboat he and Gaston had pirated that time. He wasn't about to remind them of it! Brazil had no extradition treaty with the States. But an underpaid officer or two might well turn them over to Columbia, Mexico, or Nicaragua for the various cash rewards posted on their heads.

The two Brazilians took him down another narrow alleyway and into a courtyard guarded by sailors with Krag rifles with fixed bayonets. They led him to a door and knocked. Another guard opened it from within.

They went in. The room was brightly lit by overhead Edison bulbs. A large scale map of Amazonia covered one wall. A man in uniform pants and shirt sleeves had been studying the pins in the map. As they entered he took a seat at the big desk near the wall map and indicated a big leather chair across from him, saying, "Please make yourself comfortable, Senhor Walker. It was so good of you to come."

Captain Gringo sat down and accepted the cigar the other handed him as he said, "These guys you sent after me are pretty good. Are you Commodore Barboza?"

The officer lit his guest's cigar with an expensive desk lighter before he took his own seat across the desk and said, "I am. But names are not important among those who follow our trade. I, ah, have some very distressing wanted fliers on one former U.S. Army officer known now as Captain Gringo. You are, of course, simply Senhor Walker, an American interested in exploration, is that not so?"

Captain Gringo took a drag of smoke and asked flatly, "Where's Gaston?"

Barboza said, "He's quite safe, aboard the gunboat you may have seen out on the river. By the way, those children

55

told us about your saving the girl from the cayman. It was most kind, and I admire a man who thinks on his feet."

"Okay, you're holding Gaston and you've got me, so what's all this pussyfooting about, Commodore?"

"We want you to do a job for us," Barboza answered. "You get your friend, new passports, and ten thousand American dollars when you've completed it to my satisfaction."

Captain Gringo whistled silently and said, "That's a lot of money. But how come the Brazilian Navy has to hire bums like us? Those are four-inch guns you have out there on that gunboat. You guys are supposed to be better than average down here. We're usually hired by bush league outfits who lack their own professional officers."

The commodore smiled thinly. "You have also done a few odd jobs for certain intelligence services on occasion, my innocent young friend. Greystoke of British Intelligence says you are a bit noisy for his taste, but that you certainly manage to wreck things nicely."

He rose and stepped over to the map to point at a spot with his cigar as he added, "I want you to go up the Rio Negro, to this area, and make hash out of everything you find there. I'm putting three steam lunches and a crew of, well, let us call them domesticated cuthroats, at your disposal. You will have a machinegun and some dynamite along with your other arms and supplies. The last launch will of course tow the usual line of dugouts to be cast adrift as you use up the extra fuel and so forth that you'll require on your way upstream. A couple of the men I'm sending with you know the country. One is a Christian Indian and the other tapped rubber on the upper Negro until a domestic tragedy forced him to flee the country a year or so ago."

"What kind of a domestic tragedy are we talking about?"

"He killed his wife and her Indian lover. She was the daughter of a Jivaro chief. The Jivaro do not understand our sense of honor."

"I'm sorry I asked. What about the other guide, the tame Indian?"

"He's a Colorado."

"Great. Aren't the Colorados enemies of the Jivaro?"

Barboza shrugged and asked, "Who can say? Both tribes are most truculent. Sometimes they act like *everyone* is their enemy. The one I'm sending as your guide no longer paints himself red and only acts savage when drunk. You may find both him and the half-breed Flagelado useful and, in any case, you'll have a map."

"Okay, what's the target?"

"A Fazenda. I want it destroyed."

"What about the people?"

"I want them destroyed, too, of course. You may spare women and children if you feel sentimental on the subject. I doubt if you'll take many male prisoners. They are desperate and should put up a good fight."

Captain Gringo took another drag and asked, "How many on the other side and how many on mine?"

"You will have about thirty followers, well-picked condemned criminals who understand they are to receive full pardons if they live through your punitive expedition up the Negro. They are all good shots and experienced jungle runners. Every man in your crew has killed at least one man in the past and should no doubt be willing to do it again. The people you are going up against number about a hundred fighting men and their dependents."

"Hey, that's better than three to one odds, Commodore!"

Barboza shrugged and added, "Not really. As a professional you know that less than half the men in an ordinary military unit fight at all, even on the front line. I read a very interesting report on the Battle of Gettysburg in your own Civil War. After the Union Iron Brigade stopped Pickett's charge dead in its tracks and fell back to regroup and resupply, one of your inspecting officers discovered something he could not believe."

Captain Gringo nodded and said, "I was taught that tale at West Point. After three days of heavy fighting, the Iron Brigade had half its ammunition left. Fifty percent of the soldiers had never fired their musket once in the whole battle."

"Exactly, and your Iron Brigade was the best in the Union Army. We can assume the picked killers I'm sending with you will do better. The people you'll be fighting will be average. So, you see, the odds are not as great as they may seem."

"Okay, let's say I'm crazy enough to take on a hundred guys with thirty. Why me? Doesn't that gunboat I just saw run anymore?" Barboza sat down again and steepled his fingers as he said, "We don't want that gang wiped out by the armed forces of Brazil. We want to be able to report it was hit by border bandits. It is close to the border of Venezuela. No Venezuelans live anywhere near, as it's almost trackless jungle up there, but border bandits are at least possible."

Captain Gringo nodded and said, "Okay, you want a massacre you can palm off to the papers as just one of those disadvantages of frontier life. So who are these guys you want wiped out, and what are they doing up there near the border that makes you so mad?"

"Oh, dear, they told me you were rather idealistic. Do you really have to know who and why? We're paying you a lot of money for this job, Senhor."

"Yeah, and it smells fishy already. I like to know who I'm shooting at, and why, Commodore."

"It's rather complicated. Let's say they're enemies of the state."

"Let's spell it out and I'll try to follow you. I can read without moving my lips and, yes, I do have to know who and why before I shoot folks."

Barboza conceded. "Very well. It's a delicate political matter. You know Brazil is a constitutional republic?"

"I'll accept that with reservations."

"Don't be picky. We did get rid of our Emperor a while back and we have been trying. But it's rather difficult to hold sensible elections in a county where most of the people don't read and the losers want to shoot the winners. As you know, we've just changed presidents again, after much excitement and the shooting of a few sore losers. A block of Army and Navy staged a most distressing mutiny in an attempt to put their own man in as a military dictator. Our side won, barely, and hopefully our new President Barros will be able to enjoy a peaceful administration."

"Prudente de Moraes Barros is not a dictator?"

"Ah, you do read. Listen, old Barros is trying. He's funded the national debt and made peace with most of the political blocs, which is not as easy as it may sound. For the first time in years the Paulists and Liberals have stopped assassinating one another. This rubber boom is helping. We're starting to ship a lot of coffee from the south-east coast lands, too. Give us a little time and we'll show you North Americans that we know how to run a democracy, too."

Captain Gringo grimaced and said, "That's why you want me to massacre some folks for you, huh, to buy you some time?"

"Exactly. Survivors of the attempted military coup have fled up the Rio Negro to join some local Paulists. We suspect they are smuggling in new arms from Venezuela. We know they are plotting a comeback. The Fazenda up the Negro is their headquarters. Do you understand, now?"

"No. I thought your new President Barros *was* a Paulist. How come other Paulists are plotting against him?"

The commodore rolled his eyes heavenward and said, "You Anglo-Saxons are so literal minded! The Paulist party represents the back country rubber barons, miners, lumber lords, and so forth, true?"

"Yeah, so?"

"So it is true Barros is, or was, a Paulist from the interior. It is also true he is now working with the east coast aristocracy and shipping interests to restore Brazil's economy. His wild and woolly former comrades are not happy about this. A stable government requires laws, and laws annoy the frontier mind. Some Paulists now consider Barros a traitor to his class. Others are proud to have one of their own in power in last and are waiting to see what happens."

"Gotcha. What happens, if Navy men fighting for Barros openly attack a Paulist stronghold, is another revolution! It's starting to make sense. You want the mutinous officers and frontiersmen wiped out quietly by person or persons unknown."

59

Barboza sighed with relief and said, "You do have a way of putting things in a nutshell. How soon will you be ready to leave for the Rio Negro?"

Captain Gringo studied the end of his cigar and said, "I've got a few loose ends to tie up here in Manaus. There was this Welsh girl who wanted an operatic career . . ."

"Done. We know about your little blond friend and my agents know where she is at the moment. The gentleman, ah, auditioning her for the part of Carmen has no connection at all with the opera, but I know someone who does. We'll make sure she gets a part, if not in Carmen, in something as noisy."

"Okay, I left another lady at the hotel."

"She's gone. She left soon after you did, taking a few easily carried things like the electric lamp with her."

"You've been tailing me for some time, eh?"

"Oh, of course. You have this reputation for violence and I told my boys to make sure they had the, how you say, drop on you before they moved in."

"Okay, that leaves Gaston."

"I told you where he was and, I am sorry, but you will have to leave Gaston indeed. I assure you we shall make every effort to keep him in comfort."

"Shit, are you afraid I'd double-cross you?"

Barboza smiled. "The thought had crossed my mind. But I don't think you'd leave your old friend behind if you decided to, how you say, skip out with our supplies and machinegun."

Captain Gringo took a drag of smoke, blew a thoughtful smoke ring, and said, "I don't like this deal much, Commodore."

"Nobody asked you to like it. We just want you to do it."

"The guys you want me to fight for you have never done a thing to me and mine. You're holding my pal a prisoner aboard that gunboat. That's not how you get on the good side of me, Commodore."

"Ah, but I'm not trying to get on your good side. I'm

60

trying to force you to strike a blow for Brazil, on my own terms."

"Suppose I tell you to go to hell?"

Barboza shrugged. "In that case, I would have to find someone else, of course. Both you and your French comrade would, in that case, make most convenient scapegoats for the terrible massacre up the Rio Negro, no?"

"You'd hang us for it, without a trial?"

"No, we'd *shoot* you both without a trial. But why are we discussing all these fantasies, Senhor? You know very well that you have every intention of leading that expedition up the Rio Negro to wipe out that rebel stronghold, don't you?"

Captain Gringo deliberately flicked ashes on the commodore's desk as he growled, "I sure am, Motherfucker."

Siesta Time was over, so the shadows were long on the courtyard's dusty red clay near the municipal jail as Captain Gringo stood morosely between the commodore and the younger officer who'd arrested him, facing the long motley line of rough-looking characters he was supposed to lead into battle. They ranged in ages from teen-ager to grizzled old-timer. A few were white and some were black, but most were that raceless blend of white, red, and black that Brazilians considered average. Some looked like they'd kill you for a plugged nickel; others wore the expression of choir boys who wondered what they were doing there.

"All right, Captain Gringo started, "the first thing we have to get straight is that I'm the boss and mean as hell. Does anybody here think he can lick me in a man to man fight?"

No answer.

He nodded and continued, "Okay, you had your chance. If any of you give me any lip on the way up the river I won't argue about it. I'll kill him on the spot. We're facing lousy odds. Some of the guys we're going up against are likely to be trained military men and, frankly, you look like a bunch of useless pobrecitos. I'll be in the middle launch and I know how to run a steam engine. That means we need two more. So how about it? Any of you assholes ever run a steam launch?"

Again there was no answer. As the men shuffled their feet and looked at one another Captain Gringo turned to the Brazilian officers. "Swell. I need two lousy mechanics and you offer me these illiterate thugs. You sure know how to pick 'em, Commodore."

The younger officer, who'd long since given back Captain Gringo's gun, said, "I can take charge of one launch, My Commodore."

Barboza frowned and said, "You are a commissioned officer, Lieutenant Sousa."

"True, but one can always change his shirt. I see a further advantage in going along, My Commodore. Not only will I be useful as commander of a second launch, but I will be able to keep an eye on the, ah, situation."

Barboza still looked dubious. Captain Gringo broke in, "Look, I don't give a shit who you pick, but pick somebody. Pick *two* somebodies. I can't run three fucking boats by myself."

Sousa said, "What about that engine room man we have in the brig aboard Sao Vincente, my Commodore? He is experienced enough with steam."

"He is also a fighting drunk who assaulted his superior and now faces a general court-martial, Lieutenant," Barboza added.

"True, but there will be nothing for him to drink on the Rio Negro but water. I am sure he would volunteer for this mission, my Commodore."

"So am I. He'd *talk* about it, too. I have to think about this problem. I was under the impression some of these flagelados had served aboard river boats in the past."

Captain Gringo spoke up: "While you guys are thinking, it's getting late. Where are these damned boats of yours?"

"Hidden, of course," Barboza said. "You and these men

62

should not be seen leaving Manaus. It was my intention you should shove off after dark."

Captain Gringo grimaced. "Jesus, you sure plan great secret missions. There's a full moon tonight and the whole town comes to life at sundown. I'm not about to shove off from a well-lit shore to cruise up the river in the dark with untried men. Our best bet will be mañana, during La Siesta."

"In broad daylight?"

"In broad daylight with everybody *home in bed*, damn it! That'll give us a quiet departure and a few hours of daylight for our shakedown cruise. If we're still afloat on the Negro by nightfall, we'll be well on our way. If we're not I'll never speak to you again."

Barboza looked dubious. Captain Gringo turned to the men and called out, "Okay, company dismissed. We'll be shoving off at eleven tomorrow morning, are there any questions?"

A shy-looking youth Sousa had pointed out as a mass murderer raised a hand and asked, "May one ask where we are going, Captain Gringo?"

The tall American was surprised they didn't know. But he shook his head and said, "You'll know when you get there. Some guys will be shooting at you."

Barboza hesitated, then nodded and called out, "Very well, you shall all be escorted back to your cells for the night."

That was a surprise to Captain Gringo who asked, "Are you saying these guys are still under arrest?" and Barboza replied, "Of course. Most of them would run away if we gave them the chance."

"Great. How the hell am I supposed to keep them under control once they're armed and in my boats with me?"

Barboza said, "We understand you have a way with roughnecks. You've led many a wild bunch before, eh?"

"Maybe. There's wild, and there's wild. I'm going to insist on a condition. If you want me to lead that crew, it's got to be my way. I want them turned loose."

"In the morning, certainly. If we let them go this side

of sunset I doubt if many would still be around by sunrise."

"You're probably right. I'd rather have the desertions here and now than later, up the river, when the sons-of-bitches have guns in their hands."

Again the commodore hesitated, then turned to Sousa and spoke, "I'm leaving this in your hands, Lieutenant. I have to be at a ball this evening and I'm sure you two can work the details out."

He walked off, muttering to himself. Captain Gringo turned to Lieutenant Sousa. "It's wonderful what having the right relatives in politics can do for a man. How long have you had to cover for that asshole?"

Sousa let that go by but he said, "I'll be commanding the second boat and I think I can get us another engineer. I am at your service, Senhor."

Captain Gringo turned and whistled shrilly with his fingers between his teeth to freeze everyone in place. Guards and prisoners alike.

The formation had of course broken up, but as they saw he wanted something they drifted back to fall in line with the guards watching from a distance.

Captain Gringo pointed at the gate across the courtyard and shouted, "All right, muchachos, we're starting with some new rules. As of now you guys are no longer prisoners. You're Captain Gringo's Guerrillas."

They stared at him with the wary blank look of the lifetime con who's heard it all. Gringo continued, "You know we plan to shove off tomorrow morning. We'll assemble here. You'll receive further orders then. Meanwhile, I'm giving you the night off. Try to keep out of trouble. If the first lady you ask says no, for God's sake ask another. I don't care if you get screwed or tattooed, but I won't bail you out if you're charged with rape, murder, or anything else as impolite."

The mass murderer raised his hand to ask, "Are you saying these guards will not stop us, now, if we just take off for town, Captain?"

The tall American turned to Lieutenant Sousa, who called out, "Guard detail, dismissed. These men have all been pardoned."

There was a collective gasp from the prisoners and somebody shouted "Viva Captain Gringo!"

Before anyone could break for the gate, he held up a hand and shouted, "You're still at ease, damn it! I've got something else to say."

They settled down, warily. He nodded and said, "Look, I know some of you assholes are already planning on your escape down river. The commodore just told me I was crazy to trust you. I probably am. You look pretty stupid to me, too. Nobody's going to be watching you tonight. It'll be easy to get away. But I want you all to think about where the fuck you're going before you take off. You've been told that you'll all be paid off and receive full pardons at the end of our mission. What the lieutenant, here, just said is conditional. Any man who's not here when I call the morning roll is going on the wanted list again. *I* sure don't want him, but I imagine Brazil will. The next time he's caught, and he will be, he gets no break. I'm banking on most of you being smarter than that. Not because I'm a good-hearted asshole, but because I want to lead men with brains, and I want them to trust *me*, too. Any questions? Okay, keep it down to a roar and meet me here again at ten-thirty in the morning. Leave in small groups and act grown up, for Christ's sake. Anybody in jail when we're ready to leave will stay here in Manaus to face the music. Company or whatever dismissed."

Nobody moved for a moment as they discussed the astounding orders of their new C. O. Captain Gringo took Sousa's elbow and whispered, "Let's get out of here. I'll buy you a drink and we'll discuss some details before we break up."

Sousa said, "I could use a drink. You know, of course, that we'll be lucky if half of them ever turn up here again?"

"So what? Would you rather go into the selva with fifteen men you could trust or twice that many you couldn't? How many guys do you have in the brig aboard that gunboat?"

"About five. The engineroom man is the only one worth anything. The others are just brawlers."

65

"Any of 'em killers?"

"No, just nasty drunks."

"Okay, leave 'em where they are. We might be able to recruit some more knockaround guys, if you could get Gaston out. He knows a lot of knockaround guys."

"Sorry, I couldn't do that," Sousa said. "Commodore Barboza's orders."

"Hey, we've agreed he's an asshole. If you still don't trust me, why did you volunteer to come along, Sousa?"

"Two reasons. I want to keep an eye on you. I want to fight the Paulists."

"Oh, personal hard on?"

"Yes. A Paulist guerrilla hit my family's coffee fazenda near Sao Paulo during the Revolution of '89."

"Ouch. Anybody hurt?"

Sousa's face was bleak as he answered flatly, "All of them. My father, my mother, sisters, and brothers. They raped the women before they murdered them, of course. I was away at the academy when it happened, but our few surviving workers told me what had happened."

"I'm sorry, Sousa. It sounds like you guys have a rough country down here."

Sousa shrugged. "The country is settled around Sao Paulo. Wait until you see the kind of country we'll be going into."

Captain Gringo lounged at a table just outside the doorway of the waterfront cantina, nursing a cerveza as he stared morosely across the water at the Brazilian gunboat. The sun was setting on the other side of the cantina so the eastern sky was purple with the vessels on the river gilded a rosy gold, while the river resembled a tray of brass that needed polishing. The planet Venus hung above the far shore like a rhinestone pinned to a purple velvet curtain. The moon would soon be rising like a pumpkin, magnified as always by the thicker atmosphere of the tropics. Somewhere a guitar was strumming a sad soft love song and nothing was in view but the sluggish river. If he'd been sitting there with a dame she wouldn't have had a chance.

But he wasn't there to pick up a dame. He was trying to figure his next move. Out there on the gunboat Gaston was probably planning, too, and if there was a way to escape, the slippery little Frenchman would find it. Captain Gringo couldn't communicate with his friend and nobody was signaling him from the dark mass of armor plate moored three hundred yards off shore.

If Gaston busted loose, he wouldn't come looking for anybody. He'd take off like a big ass bird. Captain Gringo knew the same would be a good idea for himself, too. He didn't owe the Brazilian Navy a nickel and since they didn't expect him to do anything until tomorrow morning he'd have a whole night's head start if he just swiped a canoe and started paddling.

Paddling was the problem. Those fucking gunboats moved faster than anyone could paddle a canoe and he doubted he could get anywhere important by the time they started looking for him. They'd take it out on Gaston if they still had him, too.

His next best move would be to go back to his hotel and get a good night's rest. Now that Barboza had cleared things with the local law he could relax a bit more in bed, knowing nobody was about to start pounding on the door, But it was still early and he was too keyed up to consider going to bed, alone.

He knew he could find Dolores against a lamp post somewhere in town. But even free she wasn't very appetizing, once the novelty wore off. He had no idea where Glynnis Radnor was tonight and wasn't sure he wanted to know. He'd managed to come out of that quixotic adventure without any bruises, but little Glynnis was a troublesome dame and as helpless as a cute little boa constrictor. The only other dame he knew in town was Maureen Mahoney and he'd already decided to stay the hell away from her. Maybe there was a mazagine stand near the hotel?

Two men came along the quay and when they saw him, came over. They both looked vaguely familiar and when one

67

of them saluted him as Captain Gringo he knew they were a couple of the condemned men he'd agreed to lead up the Negro. One of them started to sit down as Captain Gringo said, "Watch it, Muchacho, I'll let you know when I want to drink with the crew."

The man took a step back, with a frown. He had sullen Indian features. His more civilized-looking companion smiled and spoke: "We are most willing to drink elsewhere, Captain Gringo, but we have no money. When you turned us loose for the night we were given no money to spend."

"Tough tits," Captain Gringo said. "You'll get paid when you've *done* something for me. If you don't have any friends in Manaus you can sleep at the jail tonight. Tell the guards I said not to lock you in."

"Hey, we are not sleepy, Captain Gringo. We are thirsty, and a little ass never hurts a growing boy, either. Couldn't you lend us a few cruzeiros?"

"I could. But then I wouldn't have them, would I? What do you guys expect, egg in your cervezas? I got you out of jail. Bum your drinking money off someone else."

The two cons exchanged glances. The tall American was alone. Nobody else was in sight. He took a sip of his beer and said, "Don't even consider it, Muchachos. I could take you both, and your mothers, too."

The lighter mestizo laughed nervously, and said, "Hey, Captain Gringo, you sure are friendly. I thought we were your comrades-in-arms."

"We'll see about that at roll call, mañana. If you ever show up, you'll be armed and given a few coins, then. If you're the bums you look, I'll never see you again. Frankly, I don't give a shit either way."

They stood there, confused. He took another sip of beer and asked, "What are you hanging around here for. Do I look like a piece of ass?"

So they walked away, muttering unpleasant things about Yanquis. Captain Gringo chuckled. He knew how they felt. He'd been tempted to buy them a round of drinks. But he'd learned, the hard way, what happened to guerrilla leaders who allowed their semi-bandit followers to suck up to them.

One of the things that made his business so interesting was that everybody in the game wanted to be a chief and nobody wanted to be an Indian. Pride and ignorance walked hand-in-hand in the banana lands and a leader was expected to be more arrogant than his followers, which could take some effort.

His stein of cerveza was almost dead. He considered whether to go in and order another but decided against it. There had to be more action somewhere else. He stared out across the water at the gunboat Gaston was being held aboard. He took out a Havana Claro and lit up, leaving a quarter of his beer for later. Even if Gaston had some way to signal, he couldn't know anybody worth signaling was sitting here in the shadows of the cantina. So, how could he signal Gaston? He could strike another match and use his shielding hand to send morse. But the bridge watch on the gunboat would see it, and in any case, what was there to say that Gaston didn't already know?

He thought. Then he struck a match and held it in his left hand to wig-wag his right in front of it as he sent, "Are you there, G?" before the match burned down to his fingers and had to be shaken out. He took another drag on his cigar and then a shutter-light on the gunboat's bridge sent, "We are all here, Captain Gringo."

He thought about sending, "Fuck you" in morse, but decided it might seem impolite. He didn't know whether Gaston had read his signal or not. The damned watch officer had, and he seemed on his toes.

Captain Gringo finished his cerveza and put a tip on the table. But before he could rise to stroll back to the main drag a girl in a thin white shift sat down across from him. He stared soberly at her. She had a rose in her hair and as far as he could see in this light, she wasn't bad.

She said, "I was hoping you would return, my hero," and the penny dropped. It was the girl he'd saved from the cayman. She looked a lot more grown up wearing clothes.

But he knew she was just a kid. He smiled at her and asked, "Does your mother know you're out?"

"I live alone," she replied, adding, "My mother died a

year ago from El Vomito Negro. My father was drafted for to tap rubber up the river. My houseboat is not far. Would you like to see it?"

"Maybe. Who pays the rent on your floating digs?"

"Rent? I pay no rent. We have always owned the houseboat. We made it ourselves. I do not understand you, Senhor."

"Call me Dick. I was being subtle. It's a habit I've been trying to break. I meant how do you get the money to live on? You do eat, don't you?"

"Oh, certainly. I have a job. I am the chica of a rich Blanca widow. She pays me for to clean her casa and run a few errands. It is a very good job. There is little work and she never beats me."

"So how come you were playing tag with crocodilians this afternoon if you have a job in town?"

"Because it was La Siesta, of course. Nobody has to work during La Siesta. Besides, my Patrona gave me the day off. She does her own cooking and gives me much time off. Most chicas have to live at the casa where they work, but La Senhora says this is not necessary. She says she can get to her bathroom without help."

She giggled and added, "I think she desires privacy at night. You know what they say about rich widows."

"She sounds interesting. Is she good-looking?"

She shrugged and said, "She is too old for you. I am called Borita, and I saw you first."

He laughed and said, "I admire a subtle approach, kid. But while we're on the subject of women's ages, you can't be more than what, fourteen?"

Borita raised a hand to adjust the rose in her hair, pulling the thin cotton tighter on her cupcake breasts as she replied, "I don't know, exactly. My parents were Mission Indios, but I have never been baptized. I think I am somewhere between twelve and twenty."

"You haven't been twelve for a while, but you're a long way from twenty. Do you know what year this is, Borita?"

"No, do you? I started to learn for to read, one time, but

70

we moved up the river from the mission before I learned all my ABCs. I may be ignorant about some things, but one does not need to know how to read and write in any case when one is Indio."

He detected a little bitterness in her voice. His own voice was gentle as he asked, "What tribe were your people from, Borita?"

"My mother was a Bororo. That is why I am called Borita. The Bororo are very machismo but the others you saw me with are only teasing when they say I am a cannibal. My father is Flagelado, almost a Blanco. He even knows the place in Portugal where his white ancestors came from, but I have forgotten it's name. I don't think it was fair for the rubber barons to draft him, but they said he looked Indio enough for them, and everyone knows Indios have no rights on the Amazon."

He caught himself about to call her a poor kid. He warned himself to butt out. The world could be tough enough on a Connecticut Yankee, as he'd learned the hard way. He hadn't made the rules down here, and he sure as hell couldn't hope to change them.

He said, "I guess I'll have another cerveza after all. Would you like one, Borita?"

She shook her head and said, "Not here. The man who owns this cantina is most rude. One day when I was swimming he exposed himself to me and said bad things about my complexion, considering what he wanted to do to me.

"I have rum and some English gin at my place. Why don't we go there and drink. It will not cost you anything."

"Oh? What are you charging for, Honey?"

She looked puzzled and replied, "Charging? What would I be charging for? I own nothing but the houseboat, and me." Then her eyes widened and she asked, "Oh, do you take me for a wicked woman?"

"Of course not. I take you for a nice kid. It's the kid part I have to think about it. I, uh, don't play with toys anymore, Borita."

She stood up, saying, "I never had any toys. Come, let us go to my place and drink lots of rum and gin, eh?"

He rose, too, and as she took his hand, trustingly, he muttered in English, "You ought to be ashamed, Dick Walker" but he went with her anyway. He hadn't really been in the mood to read himself to sleep.

Borita's houseboat was really a thatched hut on a balsa raft, with its fore ashore on the red mud along the river's bank. The furnishings consisted of packing cases, a carpet of rush matting, and a hammock slung across the rear quarter of the small single room. Borita told him to make himself at home in the hammock while she fix them some drinks. So he tried to. It wasn't easy to sit up in a hammock but he managed, just, bracing his boot heels on the deck as he sat crossways. It was pretty dark in here. The moon was rising and a few shafts of golden light found their way through the side thatch. They added more to the confusion than they illuminated. The little Indian girl was painted with tiger stripes of moonlight and shadow as she knelt on the matting, tinkling glass. Her cotton shift was tight and she looked nude in the tricky light. He wondered why that should bother him. He'd seen her stark naked in broad daylight, yet for some reason she seemed more seductive now that he could only make out her general form, filling in the blank spaces with his glands. That was probably why dance hall girls wore tights. The male mind drew better pictures than Mother Nature. A guy could go crazy trying to peek under a strange skirt and then go home to ignore his wife taking a bath in the kitchen.

Borita rose to join him with two glasses. She handed one to him and climbed on the hammock with him. Naturally, their hips slid together as the webbing sagged under their combined weight. The rose in her hair smelled sweet and the rest of her was the musky odor of sunlight and river water. She snuggled closer and said, "There, isn't this nicer than sitting by that nasty old man's cantina?"

He took a sip from the cool glass she'd handed him and gasped, "Sweet Jesus, gin and rum, straight?"

"Don't you like it? I find it most refreshing."

"It takes a little getting used to. Do you drink alone, much?"

72

She sighed and said, "Yes, it helps me for to go to sleep."

"I imagine it would. You, uh, sleep alone a lot, too, eh?"

"Yes, alas. I used to have a caballero, but the rubber tappers took him away, too. I don't think I will make friends with any more Indios. They never make you Blancos tap rubber. Would you like to be my caballero, Dick, or am I too dark for you?"

He swallowed another sip of lava and said, gently, "You're very pretty and I'd love to be your hombre, but I'm leaving Manaus in the morning, kid."

"Oh, damn. Just as I was starting to get interested in you, too."

"Yeah, it's a tough old world. But you're young and beautiful, Borita. If you can just stay away from caymans until you meet the right young guy, you'll be all right."

She sipped her own drink, gagged, and added, "My, I did make it a little strong, didn't I? Where are you going tomorrow, Dick?"

"Up the Negro. That's all I can tell you."

"Can I go with you, Dick?"

"Hardly. What about your job?"

"Pooh, I can always find a job. I'm a good worker. Finding a man who pleases me is much harder, and you please me very much. If you take me with you I will cook and sew for you. I know the selva. I can find food where no silly Blanca girl can, eh?"

"I'll have an Indian guide, a male one, damn it. I'd like to take you along, honey. But I can't. It's not a butterfly hunt I'll be leading. It's an all-male expedition into rough country."

He knew he was bullshitting her. He wouldn't have offered to take her had he been going as far as the hotel, for there were limits to what a guy could walk through the lobby with, but she was a sweet little thing and it didn't hurt to let her think he took her seriously.

Borita took another gulp of firewater. "Well, if we only have this one night, we'd better make the most of it."

Then she stood up and pulled the shift off over her head. The tiger stripes of moonlight were enough to show she'd worn nothing under it. She dropped the cotton on the deck and climbed in beside him again, stark naked, and breathing faster. She husked, "Don't you want to take your clothes off, too?"

He did, but he hesitated. A passing boat's wake rocked the raft under them as he shook his head to clear it and said, "Jesus, this stuff is strong. You're, ah, not too drunk to know what you're offering, are you?"

"I have nothing to offer but my body, Dick. Don't you want it?"

"Well, I don't want to be rude to a lady. But you understand this is it? A one night stand? No promises? No more talk about going anywhere with me in the cold gray light?"

She said, "Oh, hurry and take off your clothes, my hero."

He chuckled and said, "That's right, I did slay a dragon for you, didn't I? I don't know what you put in that stuff besides the gin and rum, but I'm starting to believe in fairy tales, too."

So he stood up, drained the glass, then started to undress before he could pass out. Another wake swayed the deck under him and he almost lost his balance. He held on to his gun rig as he let the rest land anywhere it felt like. As he climbed back in the hammock the little brown girl was waiting with her dark slender thighs apart and a knee hooked over either side rope. He knelt on the webbing between them as he fumbled overhead for some handy place to hang his .38. She asked, "What on earth are you doing?" and he said, "Looking for a hook. I like to keep my hardware handy when there's no lock on the door."

She said, "Let me," and reached for him. She didn't grab his gun. She gripped his erection to their mutual surprise and said, "Oh, I knew you were a big man, but this may not work."

He found a peg and hooked the strap over it as he lowered himself on her, saying, "If it falls it falls." Then, as

74

he guided himself into the warmth between her trembling young thighs he added, "Damn, you may be right. I am in the right place, aren't I?"

"Yes, but it's too big. I don't think . . . Oh . . . !" and then she tilted her pelvis up to meet him as he slowly eased in, trying not to hurt her. He touched bottom as their pubic bones kissed. He lay still in the saddle, allowing her throbbing internal muscles to adjust to the idea. He said, "You told me you'd had a guy, Borita. For Chrissake, you're not a virgin, are you?"

She moved experimentally and said, "I didn't think I was, but Madre de Dios, I didn't know they came this big."

"Am I hurting you?"

"No. You are *frightening* me, a little, but I think I like it."

She wrapped her arms around him, flattening her small firm breasts against his chest, but she left her knees hooked over the hammock ropes as he gingerly started moving. She was right not to raise her knees. It was almost too deep this way. Almost, but not enough to hurt, apparently, for she started to move with him, thrusting down on the side ropes to make the hammock bob in a very interesting way. Her muscular young body was wildly exciting to him, but he deliberately held back. He been getting enough, lately, to maintain control and he felt a little shitty to be abusing little girls this way. Borita suddenly gasped and said, "Oh, this is impossible. We've barely started," and then she started moving up and down from side to side as she climaxed, twisting his shaft inside her like a dish rag. As she clamped down tightly in a shuddering orgasm he joined her. It was so good it almost hurt. They collapsed together and as he lay cradled in her arms and the curve of the hammock she was still pulsating wetly. She felt his discharge running down between her buttocks and his scrotum and sighed, "That was wonderful. But it was over so soon."

He said, "Honey, we're just getting started."

"Oh, you are not going to turn over and go to sleep like . . . like other men?"

"Hardly. That was just an appetiser. Now I feel like screwing."

He rolled off and stood with his bare feet on the matting as he swiveled her around to lay across the hammock broadside. It was a trick he'd learned in an Indian village a while back with another Indian girl who hadn't been this nice. He hooked an arm under each of Borita's knees and pulled her toward him until her tail bone was on the hammock rope. Then he moved in and his erection found its own way home in her more relaxed but still tight entryway to paradise. Borita gasped in surprise and delight as he started swinging her in the hammock. Legs braced stiffly and not having to move his own hips enough to matter as he hauled her on and off like a sock. She giggled and said, "Naughty boy. I'll bet you've done *this* before!"

He said, "It's kind of complicated to be old fashioned in a hammock. Do you want me to stop?"

"Never. Never! I could do this all night!"

That wasn't true. They only came once that way. Then he showed her dog style, kneeling on the matting with the wake from passing tugs adding odd pleasant surprises from time to time. He was too polite to say he could see she'd done *that* before. She wiggled her upthrust derriere at him like a saloon door on payday as he humped her from behind, enjoying the view. He'd always wondered what it would be like to make love to a tigress, and now he knew. She was striped pale brown and purple-black by the tricky light, and no real tigress could have acted more passionate or primitive.

They collapsed on their sides on the matting, gasping for breath as they recovered from the earthy love-making. He was still in her, caressing her hot brown flesh. She pressed his hand to her breast and sighed, "Oh, I wish you did not have to leave me, ever."

"Me, too," he gently lied. He knew he really was going to miss this, but what the hell, one night of Borita was almost too much. The tiny nymphomaniac was all woman in the body of a child. It was impossible to go soft in anything that tight. On the other hand, who wanted to?

76

She purred, "We are all sticky. Why don't we go for a swim, Darling?"

"At night, in a river full of man-eaters?"

"Caymans seldom attack in the dark. They are sluggish when the sun is not shining. I swim almost every day and night and until this afternoon I have never been attacked in the water."

"Well, you're pretty young. Give 'em time. I know man-eating caymans are considered rare, but one is all it takes, Doll."

She sat up and insisted, "Come, let us cool off and get back in the hammock clean and refreshed, eh?"

He saw she was determined, so he got up, too, muttering to himself about damned idiots. But when she led him to the rear of the raft and dove naked into the moonlit river he decided it was a swell way to die and dove in after her. The water was only a little cooler than the night air and when he opened his eyes under the suface he could see Borita's flashing long limbs as she sported above the moonlit bottom. There didn't seem to be anything else swimming near enough to matter, so he swam after her, enjoying the change as he used new muscles to slide his naked flesh through the silky cool water. Borita stood up, the water rippling around her nipples as he put his own bare feet on the sensuous mud of the shallows to join her. She threw her arms around him and kissed him, her wet nipples turgid against his cooled chest. He ran a hand down her spine, through her long wet strands of black hair. It didn't reach below her waist. Her firm little bottom felt marvelous. He put a finger between her buttocks to tease her rectum. She laughed and forked a thigh over each of his hip bones as he braced against the slight current. He hadn't planned it, but he didn't argue when she slid her own hand down, gasped him underwater, and guided his shaft into her again. It made for a slithery and somewhat tricky way to do it . . . and they'd have drowned if they'd let themselves go completely, but they managed to come again. It felt wild as he moved in and out to feel cold and warm wetness alternately.

They swam some more and then they climbed back on

the stern of the raft to lay side by side on the smooth balsa logs in the moonlight.

He stretched out on his back, staring lazily at the stars in the now black velvey sky. The stars looked close enough to touch. The moon had turned silver as it rose higher and Borita had changed to a nymph cast in pewter. She'd changed in other ways, too, having lost her first shyness. She still looked like a barely budded teen-ager, but he was feeling less guilty, too. He'd learned in a Jivaro village that the Indians started early down here. From the way she moved he knew she'd been at it some time despite her innocent looks.

She propped herself on one elbow to caress his sated shaft. He really wasn't up to any more sex at the moment, but he didn't stop her. It felt nice. He reached out lazily to put a hand in her lap, toying with the light wet thatch he found there. Borita giggled and lowered her head over him, trailing her long wet hair down his belly as she moved into a most improper position. He blinked in surprise but hardly felt like complaining as her lips kissed his limp virile member. It didn't stay limp long, as she began to tongue and commit what the laws of some states called a crime against nature. He didn't feel like pressing charges as she moved her pursed lips up and down, expertly. He made a mental note to tell Gaston the next time they met, that France was not the only civilized country after all.

He smiled crookedly as he thought about the ideas people had about the degeneracy of soft civilized races. He'd met some very primitive people, indeed, since he'd left the States one jump ahead of a hangman's noose. He knew, now, that so-called primitive natives practiced all the so called vices of Degenerate Paree. Borita was used to the smaller men of her people, but she could teach any French can-can girl a few things.

She'd known the cleansing swim would make her latest notion more appetizing, too. So he wasn't surprised when she rose on her knees and swiveled around to get a thigh on either side of his chest. The view was very interesting as he played with her spread groin in the moonlight. She said something with her mouth full and lowered herself on his face. He hesitated, then he decided one good turn deserved another and what the hell she was squeaky clean all over.

It drove her wild to have him kiss her clit as he drove two stiff fingers in and out of her. She clamped down on his knuckles as he massaged her cervix, deep inside, with his fingertips while she tried to swallow him alive. He could tell she was coming. He came himself, but, as always, it was less fully satisfying going sixty-nine, so he rolled her off and over to pound her hard with her buttocks against the logs and this time she was able to wrap her legs around his waist and take it all as she gasped, "Oh, yes, this is the only way to do it!"

He thought so, too, but all things must end and they were only human. So they went inside and snuggled together in the hammock. The next thing he knew it was morning. He lay quietly in the hammock with Borita's sleeping head nestled against his chest as he held her, wondering what had woke him up. The houseboat was bobbing gently in some passing steamboat's wake. But that wouldn't have done it. He had a vague recollection of a distant booming sound. Thunder? The sunlight peeping through the slits in the side thatch made a thunderstorm unlikely. Maybe they'd fired a sunrise gun somewhere. Whatever it had been, he was wide awake, now.

He tried to slide out of the hammock without waking Borita. It didn't work. She rubbed her eyes and said, "Oh, it is morning. What time is it?"

He climbed out and got his watch from the piled clothing on the deck. He checked the time and said, "Almost eight."

She said, "Damn, I have to go to work." And he said, "Me, too. I'm going to miss you, Borita."

"And I you, my hero. But listen, La Senhora is a late sleeper. We have time to make love one last time. No?"

He said, "I have a lot to do, honey."

"One last time, Dick? We have never done it in the daylight."

So they did, and it was very nice no matter what time you did it with Borita. But then it was going on nine and even she was worried about getting to work so late. She beat him getting dressed, since she had so much less to put on. She stood in the doorway, eyes downcast, and murmured, "Well?"

He said, "Do me a favor, kitten? Just turn around and start walking."

She started to object. Then she ran her eyes over him, wistfully, as if trying to engrave him on her memory. She suddenly sobbed, turned, and ran outside. He finished dressing and when he left the houseboat she was nowhere in sight.

He didn't have to be anywhere for another hour, so he decided to go back to his hotel. It seemed impossible that Gaston could have escaped during the night, but if he had, he might have left a message at the hotel. Captain Gringo knew Gaston would hardly stay there long. It would be the first place anyone would look for him.

The whole town would be considered small, back home, despite it's opera house and ornate architecture. So it him only a few minutes to make it back to the main plaza. As he crossed it toward the hotel he saw a crowd out front. Most were just passersby, but a few were wearing police uniforms. He hesitated. Then he kept going. If he were working for the Brazilian government, he didn't have to worry about a few cops.

He moved to the edge of the crowd and asked a Negro in a straw hat what was going on. The civilian shrugged and said, "A bomb. They say a chambermaid opened a door upstairs for to change the linens and the bomb blew her to chili con carne."

Captain Gringo whistled softly and, spotting a policeman writing on a pad, moved over to him and said, "Good morning officer. I'm a guest at the hotel. Could you tell me what room they placed the bomb in? I have friends on several floors."

The cop said, "Don't worry. No guests were hurt. The room clerk tells us neither of the foreigners staying in the suite came home last night."

Captain Gringo swallowed the green fuzz in his mouth and asked, "Uh, was it by any chance suite fifteen?"

"Yes, now that you mention it. Do you know the men who were staying there, Senhor?"

"No, I'm on the floor above. But I know the men you mean. I think they took a steamboat down the river last night."

The cop nodded and said, "Lucky for them, then. Somebody here in Manaus didn't like them. The way we put it together, the bomb was set inside the door to go off the moment somebody turned the latch. The poor chambermaid didn't know they'd checked out. So the bomb got her instead of the guys it was intended for."

Captain Gringo nodded, keeping his face casual, and turned to get out of there, his mind in a whirl.

Who the hell had tried to kill him? Not Brazilian Intelligence. Commodore Barboza and Lieutenant Sousa had had him at their mercy if that was their game.

He didn't know anybody else in Manaus. Yet someone had gone to a lot of trouble to wipe him out. He felt a lot better about picking up the little Indian girl, now. Had he gone straight home from the cantina he'd have spent the night on a slab in the morgue instead of in a hammock making nice-nice. So who said virtue was its own reward?

He looked at his watch: he had a little over an hour. Hell, he could take longer if need be. The expedition wasn't going to leave without him and he needed some answers, fast.

As he walked aimlessly away he started checking people off. He hadn't done it; Gaston hadn't done it; the Navy guys made no sense. Those two rough necks he'd had words with? Doubtful. They hadn't had drinking money, so where would they have gotten the makings of a bomb on such short notice? Neither of the ragged bastards could have gotten through the lobby without attracting attention, either. The bomber had to have been well-dressed and familiar with the hotel.

Glynnis Radnor? She had neither the motive nor the brains. He hadn't ditched her. She'd left him to be an opera star or whatever. The whore, Dolores, was an unlikely a suspect. The pimp Gaston had knifed? He might have had friends. But if they'd known who'd knifed Carlos they wouldn't have had to make funny-funny with dynamite. They could have gone to the police. Stabbing people in saloons was considered naughty, even in Manaus. So that exhausted everyone and . . . no it didn't.

He made his way back to the pink stucco house Maureen Mahoney lived in. He had no idea why the Anglo-Irish lady might have wanted him blown up, but she was the only person left to ask about it. She had pointed a gun at him, even if it was empty. She might be miffed because he wouldn't help her look for Dear Old Dad, but that miffed? Okay, redheads were said to have hot tempers. He paused on the deserted street outside her gate and checked his .38. Then he held it in his jacket's side pocket and knocked on the gate with his free hand.

A servant opened the gate. It was Borita. They both stared thunderstruck at one another and then Borita said, "Darling, what are you doing here? Do you wish for me to lose my job?"

"Oboy, I might have known. You said you worked for a rich widow. I didn't expect to find you here, Borita. I came to see La Senhora Mahoney."

"Oh, you like variety?"

"Don't talk silly, kitten. I'm here on business. She tried to hire me the other day. I'm not her boyfriend. Is she in?"

Borita let him in the patio and said, "Wait here, I'll see if she wishes for to speak with you and . . . Dick, about us . . . ?

"Mum's the word. Never saw you before."

Borita smiled a Mona Lisa smile and left him for a moment. When she came back she said demurely, "La Senhora will see you now, Senhor Walker."

As he passed her she goosed him and whispered, "I did not know your last name was Walker."

He found Maureen in the same room he remembered. The contrast between her cameo features and red hair and the duskier charms of the little Indian maid were most intriguing. But Maureen looked sort of annoyed. She didn't offer him a seat on the leather sofa next to her, but he sat down anyway. Maureen said, "That will be all, Borita." And as the Indian girl left them alone Maureen said, "I never expected to see you again, you louse."

"That makes two of us. What did I do so lousy, Doll?"

"Don't Doll me, damn it. You know perfectly well you stole my machinegun last night."

"Somebody lifted that Maxim in the next room?"

"You know damned well they did. I was at the opera with friends. I'd given my maid the night off. So, while the house was empty, you slipped in and carried off the machine gun and ammunition I showed you."

"Hey, that's a lot of carrying."

"All right, you had help. Nobody else knew about that gun and ammo."

"Nobody at all?"

"Oh, heavens, I know Borita didn't do it. I'm not a nosey person, but word gets around. I happen to know for a fact that my naughty little Mission Indian was entertaining a gentleman friend on her houseboat all night."

"Oh? Did you get a description of him?"

"No. What does it matter? Neither Borita nor her waterfront lover could have been here when they were, ah, splashing about down by the river. So my servant has an alibi. Can you say as much for yourself, Captain Walker? What's so funny?"

"Inside joke. Speaking of alibis, I came over here to ask you about a bomb someone planted for me at the hotel. You're talking about a burglary and I'm talking about a murder. The bomb didn't get me, but it sure ended the career of a chambermaid. You say you were at the opera, huh?"

"I was, and I can give you the names of the Brazilians I was with. It was a rather dreadful performance, by the way. One of the knowledgeable Brazilians there said the new soprano was on very good terms with the owner. He must like blonds, and she must be very friendly indeed. She certainly can't sing! Do you want to meet the people I was with?"

"No, I believe you were at the opera. The bomb had to have been placed fairly early in the evening, when the lobby was crowded, too. I didn't think it was you, anyway."

"Right. Let's get back to my stolen Maxim and where you were last night."

"Honey, where I was last night is none of your business. I never kiss and tell. Let's assume I had the opportunity. What the hell motive would I have?"

"Motive? You're a machinegun expert, damn it."

"So what? People who hire me usually have a machinegun already. I don't walk around with one in my pocket. As a matter of fact, I have been hired by somebody and they do have a machinegun for me to make bang-bang with. Before you ask, it ain't yours. I can't tell you who I'm working for, but they are not short of guns and ammo."

"All right, if you didn't take my Maxim, who did?"

"How the hell should I know? Have you asked any other knockaround guys to chase wild geese with you?"

"No, I've only been here in Manaus a short while. I had to tie up some loose ends, make some purchases, and find out more about my father's plans before I contacted anyone to go with me up the Negro. Where's this other expedition of yours headed?"

"Oh, up into the selva someplace," he replied, not exactly lying. She spoke up, "Listen, whatever they've offered you, I'm prepared to match it. I know my plans are dangerous and I really need a man with your reputation to get me up and back in one piece."

He frowned and said, "That's another thing I forgot to ask you. You knew who I was. How come? Who gave you all this information on me?"

She licked her lips and said, "Oh, you know how word gets around."

"No I don't. Gaston and I just got here. We're both wanted, or were wanted, by the law. Knockaround guys know one another's reps, but you say you don't hang out with such ruffians. So who told you I might be just what your doctor ordered, doll?"

She looked away. "I have my sources. If you won't go to work for me you can go to hell."

He looked at his watch and said, "Haven't got time to go quite that far. It's been nice talking to you again, doll."

"Senhora Mahoney to you, you big moose."

He got to his feet and said, "See you around the campus, kid." She didn't rise as he let himself out. Borita had been listening at the door. She escorted him out to the patio and tried to kiss him. He said, "Watch it, she checks up on you."

"I heard. I thought I would choke when she talked about us like that."

"She didn't know it was us. Tell me something. How long have you been working here, Borita?"

"Oh, let me see. A month, maybe three weeks. Why?"

"Nothing. That part of her story checks out. What can you tell me about her other visitors? See any other Anglo types, like me?"

"No, darling. She sends me away when she is expecting visitors. Do you think she likes to screw as much as me? She is very old."

"Yeah, must be pushing thirty, poor thing. I've got to go, Borita. Keep your pretty little lip buttoned."

"Will I ever see you again, my hero?"

"Beats the shit out of me. Something crazy as hell's going on around here."

He reached in his pocket and took out some bills. As he pressed them in the Indian girl's hand she gasped, "Oh, no, I could not take money for last night, Dick!"

"It's not for last night. It's for you, if you need it unexpectedly. I know you think she's a nice boss, and she may be okay, but if you see anything funny going on, don't walk, run for the nearest exit, see?"

"I don't understand, my hero."

"I know. You're a sweet kid, Borita. Take care of yourself, huh?"

So this time it was his turn to walk away without looking back. Borita would be all right—she was smarter than she looked. Anyone had to be. But old Maureen was up to something. He didn't buy that story about a Dear Old Dad lost in the jungle. She was starting to look more and more like somebody's secret agent. She was British and he'd tangled with British Intelligence before. So, okay, what did Queen

Victoria want with Brazil now? They'd already stolen all the rubber trees they needed from Brazil.

"Look," he told himself as he headed for the prison yard, "she doesn't have to be a British agent. The Kaiser's spies are thick as thieves with the Irish Home Rule crowd these days. She could be working for Germany."

But that made no sense, either. Nobody sent agents anywhere unless they wanted to find something out or unless they wanted something . . . Oboy!

Maureen had tried to hire him before the Brazilian Navy could. That meant the people she worked for didn't want the delicate elimination of those unreconstructed Brazilian rebels to take place. Ergo, that meant somebody wanted the rebels to stage a comeback. Barboza was right about the rebels up the river being funded and armed across the border by outsiders.

He'd passed a book store as he ruminated his way along an arcade. He stopped and went back, asking the clerk inside for any books he might have on the current or past political history of Brazil.

The clerk took down four widely-spaced volumes and laid them on the counter, saying, "These books certainly should cover what you wish to read up on, Senhor, but, forgive me, are you not a foreigner? Few people from other lands seem interested in our somewhat confusing history."

Captain Gringo laughed, "I've noticed that. I'm going for a boat ride and I'll have time to take some interest."

"You wish for to know all about our politics, Senhor?"

"Yeah. I'm beginning to wonder if ignorance is bliss when everybody but me knows what's going on."

Captain Gringo was a little tardy, so La Siesta had just started by the time he arrived at the prison yard. He found Lieutenant Sousa and nineteen of the pardoned prisoners. Sousa said, "We warned you there would be desertions if you turned these men loose last night."

Captain Gringo nodded. "Better here than half way up

the river. I figured more than a third would take off on us. These other guys are either stupid or reliable. The deserters didn't get to steal the guns and boat they might have and I'd rather go into a fight with one man I trust than a hundred I don't."

Gringo raised his voice and called out, "All right, Muchachos, we've separated the men from the boys. Let's line up and move it out." Then he turned back to Sousa. "You'll have to lead us to the boats. I haven't any idea where they are. Where's Commodore Barboza, taking his siesta?"

Sousa raised an arm and started out the gate with the column in tow as he told Captain Gringo, "No, he's waiting for us downstream with the arms detail. Naturally we could not leave anything in the launches overnight."

"Wait a minute. You left our vessels downstream for this so-called secret mission?"

"Yes, under guard, of course, with nothing tempting in them. Few Manaus river rats would risk a fire fight for an empty steam launch, but if they had a crack at guns and ammunition . . ."

"That's not the point. We're going *up* stream, damn it."

"So?"

"So how the fuck are we supposed to keep our expedition a secret when we have to cruise the whole length of the Manaus waterfront to go up the Negro? You guys sure think ahead, don't you?"

Sousa shrugged and said defensively, "It was your idea to change the plans and leave by daylight. Nobody would have noticed anything had we left at night as we first intended."

"Oh, shit no, there's only five or six hundred people sleeping on those rafts and houseboats along the shore. But let's skip it. What's done is done and I doubt if a thousand people will notice us during La Siesta."

As they marched along the deserted streets he filled Sousa in on the bombing and asked if the lieutenant had any ideas.

Sousa said they'd already heard about the attempt on his life and that he'd survived it. He added, "Commodore Barboza was very amused. He said it proved what he'd heard about you, Captain Gringo. He said it would take a cat with nine lives to do the job up the Negro."

"Make it eight. They killed me once before I got out of town. Who do you guys figure it was?"

"Probably agents of the rebel party. We've tried to keep this mission a secret, but you know what they say about two men being able to keep a secret if one of them is dead."

"That's the way I see it. So why the hell are we going up the river, Lieutenant?"

Sousa frowned and replied, "Why? To seek out and destroy that rebel encampment, that's why."

"Bullshit. If they know we're coming, why should they be there? Would you sit like a bump on a stump in the selva, waiting for some guys to come along and knock you off?"

Sousa nodded. "I would if I had no choice."

"They have no choice? There's one hell of messy country here to hide out in. If I were in charge of those rebels I'd make a fifty-mile forced march and forget all about anyone looking for me."

Sousa said, "You are not in charge. An ex-navy officer named Fonseca is in command, we think."

"You think? Don't you know?"

"Fonseca escaped up the Negro with other mutinous officers. He's joined forces with a Paulist mestizo called Andrada. Fonseca is used to giving orders. Andrada and his Paulist river-runners have never taken orders from God or their father, the Devil. Commodore Barboza hopes we shall find them divided and bickering among themselves. No matter who is in charge up there, they can't move out of the area."

"Why? What's so special about that particular patch of weeds?"

"Geography. The land lies low between the foothills of the Andes to the west and the Guiana Highlands to the east. Both Brazil and Venezuela claim the vast wooded swamplands up there, although in truth nobody has mapped all of it yet. You see, Brazil claims all the watershed draining into the

Negro. Venezuela claims the headwaters of the Orinoco, to the north."

"That sounds reasonable. But do you mean to say nobody has ever mapped the divide between the two river systems?"

"There does not seem to *be* a divide. Both the Indians and some of the more daring river-runners say both the Orinoco and the Negro issue from the same great maze of channels."

"Hmm, then a guy who knew his way through the swamps could take a boat up the Negro and wind up running down the Orinoco in Venezuela!"

"If he knew the way and wasn't killed by the rather independent Indians who somehow can't seem to grasp that they must be living in Brazil if they are not in Venezuela. The outlaw, Andrada, is part Indian and his four or five wives are pure bloods from various pagan tribes. We think he's using Indians to smuggle arms and other supplies to the combined bands from the other side of the hazy border. As long as the rebels hold the area, nobody else can make the passage, either."

"So that's why they can't afford to move." Captain Gringo nodded as they rounded a corner. He spotted the water's edge at the far end of the block. "Okay," he said, "let's assume the other side has pals here in Manaus and that they planted that bomb. Can you think of any reason outside intelligence agents would be interested in our little outing on the river?"

Sousa frowned and replied, "Of course not. It's an internal political matter. No foreign interests own anything that far up the Negro. There are some American and European companies operating closer to the coast. The interior's timber and rubber are reserved for Brazilian nationals."

"What if somebody found something like a gold mine way up there in the woods? Could one of the international trusts control it?"

"No," Sousa flatly explained. "All minerals are the property of the nation. We are a republic, now, but we still follow the old Iberian mineral laws. It is not like in your United

States. If a prospector finds anything he must report it to the government. He can get a permit to mine his find with the government as his partner."

"What if somebody didn't want a partner?"

"He would be playing with fire for a little gain. Neither Brazil nor Venezuela would demand more than a modest share of the profits. Both would execute anyone trying to smuggle gold, silver, or even copper out of the country. A foolish risk to avoid a small, how you say, pay off?"

They could see the three launches tied up at the water's edge, now. The commodore and a guard detail were standing by, looking wilted in the noon day sun. Sousa pursed his lips and asked, "Why do you ask about mineral rights up where we are going, Captain? We have heard nothing about the rebels shipping bullion out."

Captain Gringo shrugged and said, "Just trying to figure out what interest other folks might have in this expedition. Do you know a Maureen Mahoney, English or Irish widow?"

"I have seen her about town. She is very beautiful. She was at the opera last night as a matter of fact."

"She says she's missing a father, up the Negro."

"Ah, yes, I remember the commodore mentioning that. She has been after him to send a gunboat after the professor. Naturally, we could not tell her why this would be impossible. How did you hear about it?"

"She told me. Tried to hire me before you did. I told her anybody gone a year in a dripping rain forest was gone for good. But that was before I knew about those rebels camped out up there. Think there's any chance they could be holding the old gent?"

"Why would they want to do that?"

"To keep him from telling anyone if he stumbled into their hideout, of course. His daughter says he was looking for some spooky lost city in the jungle. He might have found more than he bargained for. How nasty would you say those rebels are, Lieutenant?"

"Commander Fonseca might be inclined to hold a trespasser prisoner. The bandit, Andrada, would kill him for the fillings in his teeth."

Captain Gringo nodded. So it was fifty-fifty Maureen's father was still alive, if she had a father, and if he'd been captured by more or less white rebels instead of headhunters. He was glad he'd been sensible for once and refused to take her upstream before he'd been told there was a fucking army waiting up there, on the prod.

They joined Commodore Barboza on the quay. He glanced over the men they'd brought with them and asked, "Where are the rest of them?"

Captain Gringo said, "They were afraid of noise. Did you get me that other steam engine guy?"

Barboza shook his head. "No. It seems he hanged himself last night to avoid being executed. He was not a very advanced thinker. But you and the lieutenant know how to run a steam launch, no?"

"Yeah, two of them. That's one left over. Listen, if you gave Gaston back to me, he could take command of the third launch."

"Oh, most certainly," Barboza laughed, "and that would be the last any of them saw of you two again, eh?"

"Aw shit, Lieutenant Sousa is coming along. You expect him to skip out with us?"

"No, I imagine you and these other cuthroats would simply overpower him. The Frenchman stays behind, Captain Gringo. You will get him when you come back and Lieutenant Sousa informs me the mission was carried out to his satisfaction."

"Swell. What if we don't make it?"

"Gaston Verrier will hang in your place, of course."

"Hey, come on, there's a good chance we'll get killed even if we don't desert."

"That would be most unfortunate. I would try to avoid that if I were you. If you don't return, I will know you either deserted or failed. In either case Brazil will be out three steam launches and a junior officer. Your friend will have to even the score with his life."

Captain Gringo stared morosely at the lined up craft. All three were identical. One had a line of dugouts loaded with bags and bales attached in line to its stern. They looked like whaleboats with tea kettle steam engines mounted amidships. The smoke funnels poked up through the flat canvas awnings slung on pipe frames. He saw one had a Maxim mounted on its bow. The gun and ammo had messed up the trim and the launch was down by the bows a few inches. Shifting a few supply cases would fix that. He noted thin wisps of oil smoke drifting from all three funnels, so they'd done something right for a change. The pressure was up in all three boilers indicating they were ready to shove off.

He turned to the ragged band of recruited desperados and pointing at one who looked a little brighter, asked, "You, what's your name?"

"I am Martim Durand, my Captain."

"You just made bos'n. I want the rest of the guys armed and in those first two boats. Where are the guns, Commodore Barboza?"

The officer looked affronted and called out, "Chief, see that this one carries out his captain's orders. Break open a case of rifles."

As the navy non-com and his own appointed strawboss went to work, Captain Gringo turned back to the officers beside him and said, "We'll leave the middle boat. We don't need the room now, even if we had somebody to run it. Sousa, you man the one trailing the dugouts. I'll follow in the one with the machinegun."

Sousa looked puzzled and asked, "Haven't you got that in reverse, Captain? I'd put the heavy weapon out front."

"You would, huh? I can see why you guys put me in command. Haven't you ever been ambushed by Indians, Lieutenant?"

"No, have you?"

"Many many times. Nobody ever hits the lead man, boat, or whatever. They let the point through and fall on Tail End Charlie. It can be kind of confusing. If I was upstream when somebody decided to relieve you of those supply canoes I'd have to make a U-turn and fire with you between me and the target."

Sousa wasn't dumb, just green. He nodded as he caught on and said, "Ah, with me out in front trailing the supplies between us, you would have us covered with the machinegun on your bows. But what if they attack *your* boat from behind?"

"We swing broadside and teach 'em better manners. You'll need our best guide with you up front. Which one of these guys is it?"

Sousa swept his eyes over the motley crew until they stopped on an individual. "The flagelado, José, was among the deserters. That drunken looking Indian, there, is called Bonifacio. He's supposed to know the country up ahead."

Captain Gringo called the Colorado over. Bonifacio didn't just look drunk. He *was* drunk. He smelled like he'd taken a bath in trade rum. Captain Gringo asked him if he thought he could keep them in the main channel and Bonifacio replied, ":Yes, I am going up the Negro for to kill Jivaro. Many Jivaro. Jivaro are no good. They cut off my brother's head and make him little. I like to dance in Jivaro's guts."

Captain Gringo muttered, "Oboy." Then he pointed up the street they'd just come down and said, "Okay, Bonifacio, take a walk. You're excused from class today."

"You don't want for Bonifacio to help you kill Jivaro?"

"You sure catch on quick," sighed Captain Gringo. He reached in his pocket and took out some change, and handing it to the Indian said, "Here, go drink some more on me. Try not to kill anybody and I guess your pardon is still good."

The Indian wandered off, muttering to himself. Barboza asked, "Was that wise, Captain? You'll need a guide when the channels narrow and begin to braid upstream."

"That wasn't a guide," Captain Gringo said. "It was a drunken assassin. I don't want to fight Jivaro along with half the rebels in Brazil."

Barboza shrugged and added, "It has been my experience that the Jivaro seldom give one a choice in such matters and Jivaro have been reported along the river of late."

"Yeah, you swell guys have allowed your slave-raiding rubber barons to chase the poor fucking Indians all over the place until nobody knows where any tribe belongs anymore. I've had a little experience with Indians, too. I've fought

Apache in the States and Gaston and I spent some time with a Jivaro band a while back."

Both Brazilians exchanged glances while Sousa said, dryly, "That's funny. You don't look like you're walking around without a head."

"Maybe that's because I'm not as trigger happy as some of the whites the Jivaro have been running into. The folks we stayed with had some shrunken heads on display. Some of them looked like they might have belonged to white men, once, too. They didn't shrink our heads. We had a party and got drunk together."

"That is astounding. It is my understanding the Jivaro are very primitive."

"They are. They're too dumb to kill a stranger before they decide he's an enemy. Gaston and I were with some refugees from another revolution that didn't work, over on the Colombian Montaña. Some Jivaro kids were scouting us. When we spotted them we offered them some salt instead of taking a shot at them. They must have gone home and told their elders we were okay. The Jivaro cacique invited us to supper and told us about some slavers that were after them. After we smoked up the slave raiding gang for them you couldn't have asked for a nicer bunch of Indians. Their home brew isn't much, but Jivaro gals sure screw good."

Sousa looked at his c.o. with a raised eyebrow. Commodore Barboza nodded and said, "I might have known it was Captain Gringo who destroyed the rubber plantation of Dom Silva. But let bygones be bygones, eh? Dom Silva was a bit of a ruffian in any case."

"All right," Sousa said, "you may have a way with Jivaro, but they are not the only Indians in the selva. What if we run into Colorados, without Bonifacio to speak for us?"

Captain Gringo shrugged. "Same deal. I didn't fancy that particular Colorado, but most folks are reasonable, if you give 'em a chance. Since you'll be in the lead, I want you to promise me you'll think twice when and if you spot someone along the bank. Nobody opens fire on anything that isn't shooting at him, agreed?"

Sousa shrugged and said, "You certainly seem soft-hearted for a man with your reputation, Captain Gringo."

"Try shooting at me some time. We know some of the people we'll be meeting are our enemies, Lieutenant. The idea is not to make any more enemies than you need. I see the guys are about loaded up. Let's get out of here before the town come to life again."

Sousa nodded and took off his cap and uniform jacket to hand to a guard. He saluted Barboza in his short-sleeved undershirt and moved off to board the cargo launch. Captain Gringo nodded at the Commodore and started to do the same. Barboza said, "It is customary to salute when one is taking leave of a superior, Captain."

Captain Gringo raised an eyebrow. "Fuck you. You're not my superior officer. You're a blackmailer. I'd give you the salute you deserve, but what the hell, these sailor boys of yours have guns."

The baroque monstrosity of Manaus dozed in the midday sun as the little armada cruised past it upstream. In the rear launch, Captain Gringo rode for a time in the stern, making sure the man at the tiller knew what he was doing and chatting with the other men he'd taken with him to get a handle on their names and possible I.Q.s. He'd detailed a young black called Thomé to tend the boiler. Thomé said he could read and write and there wasn't a hell of a lot he could lose track of. The boiler was oil fired and you only had to check the gauges and feed from time to time. The engine was designed to run itself more or less. It had a Watt governor to maintain set speed. It had no condenser. You sucked in more river water by cracking a valve when the water in a glass tube on the side of the boiler dropped below mid-level. If you fed it too much cold water, the pressure dropped. If you didn't feed it enough, the boiler blew up. Thomé said he'd try to err on the safe side.

One of the others said, "Hey, Captain, I thought there

was a safety valve." And the tall American tapped a brass plug with his finger and said, "There used to be. Some ass hole replaced it the last time it needed to be repaired. Don't worry. If the boiler blows with us crowded around it like this, we'll never know what hit us." He patted Thomé on the shoulder and said, "Steady as she goes. I'll be up front if you need me."

He made his way around the bulky machinery amidships and joined the four men he'd placed forward. He had nine men all told in his vessel. Sousa had nine upstream in his.

Captain Gringo sat behind the breech of the machinegun and checked the action. The gun had been cleaned and the belt ran neatly enough up from the open metal ammo box wedged in the V of the bowstem. He saw they were passing the boating shanty town where he'd spent the night with Borita. He stared wistfully across the water, trying to pick out her house boat. They all looked much the same at this distance. He saw a group of brown figures diving off the raft where he remembered meeting Borita rather dramatically. He wondered if she was one of those naked swimmers, today. He knew Maureen let her wander off during La Siesta. He wondered who Maureen was spending her siesta with, and who Borita would be spending the night with. He wondered why it bothered him.

One of the men behind him complained, "Hey, this damned rifle is a mess. Some asshole stuffed the bore with shit."

Captain Gringo turned as another man opened the bolt of his Krag and said, "Mine, too. For how do you shoot a gun clogged with shit, eh?"

Captain Gringo held out a hand and said, "Let's see it. I hope I'm wrong."

The nearest man handed his new rifle to him. The tall American opened the bolt action and marveled, "Oh, hell, they never cleaned the kosmoline from these fucking rifles!"

The man who'd been issued the Krag, a civilian albeit a notorious river gunslinger in his own right, asked, "What is kosmoline, My Captain?"

The American handed it back, saying, "I've often wondered. It seems to be a mixture of beeswax and axle grease. They coat the guns with it at the factory. The metal coated with kosmoline will keep forever, but, damn it, you're supposed to clean the crap off before you even think about using the fucking gun!"

One of the men took out a pen knife and dug some of the waxy goo out of his gun's chamber, saying, "It's almost solid. The whole bore is filled with it. How do you get this shit out, Captain Gringo?"

"With naptha," the American said, "if you have it. We don't have it. So you'd better start by field stripping those rifles and wiping a lot. We'll see if we can find some reeds up the river beyond the city limits. When we pull in to camp I'll ask the lieutenant if there are any gun cleaning kits among the supplies. Meanwhile, do the best you can. I doubt if we'll need those guns for a day or so, but it could take a day or so to put them in shape to shoot."

The men grumbled and began to take their weapons apart. One dropped his bolt and Captain Gringo said, "Not in the bilge, you ass hole! Keep the small parts in your laps, or your hats."

"This kosmo shit is getting all over everything, my Captain."

"Good. The more you get on you the less you'll have on your rifle."

He turned his back on them to stare morosely upstream at the train of dugouts between him and Sousa's puffing launch. He might have known the half-ass commodore wouldn't have thought about inspecting the goddam guns before they were issued. They'd probably been lifted, informally, from some navy supply depot. Officially, no military expedition representing the Brazilian government was supposed to be on the river right now.

The machinegun, at least, was cleaned and oiled. He ran an experimental finger over the action to see if the metal was bare anywhere. In this humid tropic air exposed gunmetal rusted while you watched. Whoever had cleaned this gun last had known his business. It was okay. He noticed the maker's mark stamped above the serial number. Then he blinked and

97

read the number over again. Then he muttered, aloud, "Son-of-a-bitch!"

Someone behind him asked, "Did you say something, Captain?" And he replied, "It's nothing. Carry on."

He turned his head to stare back at the gunboat. There was no way to take on a gunboat with a machinegun even if the guys with him went along with the gag. He was stuck with the mission. So, okay, what the hell was the mission?

This was the same Belgian-made Maxim that Maureen Mahoney had shown him the other day. The one she'd said had been stolen. But why in hell would a commodore of the Brazilian Navy rob a poor widow of her one and only machinegun? They didn't have their own guns, for Chrissake?

Okay, machineguns were kind of new and Brazil was off the beaten track and . . . that wouldn't work, either. They imported Russian caviar and French wines to Manaus. You could buy what might pass for a Welsh virgin in Manaus if you had the money. The Brazilian Navy couldn't be broke, could it?

He read the serial number off again, hoping he'd made a mistake. But he hadn't. As a weapons officer he'd trained himself to remember serial numbers and, dammit, this was the same gun he'd examined at Maureen's place. He remembered that scratch through the little crown above the trade mark, too.

It would have made sense if Maureen had bought a hot gun stolen from the Brazilian Navy. This made no sense at all. But there was nobody around here who could answer his questions. So he took out a cigar and lit up. There was nothing else he could do as he steamed up into the unknown. He doubted like hell it would be a lost explorer, and he was having doubts about all the other tall tales they'd been handing him. Nothing about this mission made a bit of sense. But somebody had gone to a lot of trouble to send him on it.

The Amazon had been named by early Spanish explorers who'd reported naked Indian ladies waving spears at them from its red banks. Nobody had reported many Negroes living up the Rio Negro. It got its name from the blackness of its water. A few bends above the Manaus backwaters the river ran the color of diluted India ink. It wasn't dirty water. It was tea. Tannic acid leached from the countless trees of the selva turned the natural iron in the water black and seemed to act as an insecticide. There were far fewer bugs along the Negro despite the natural mosquito breeding swamps along its low marshy shoreline. The water was safe to drink albeit a little acid. It was doubtful one trip up the Negro could corrode the steam engines enough to matter, but God only knew how much acid water had already been fed into them. So Captain Gringo ordered half speed and they moved against the considerable current at a modest pace.

Sunset caught them mid-stream about thirty miles from Manaus in a broad island-studded channel. Lieutenant Sousa hove to in the lee of a sand bar and when Captain Gringo drew abreast he called over to ask about making camp for the night. The American called back, "Keep going. The moon will be rising full in a little while."

"You intend to steam through the night?"

"No, just 'til the moon goes down. What's your problem? You can't take turns sleeping aboard a boat?"

"I thought you were in no hurry, Captain."

"I'm not, but I'd like to get there *someday*. Slow and steady ought to do it. We'll burn less oil in the long run if we keep the engines fired up, and we'll be as comfortable on board as we will on the muddy banks."

"What about eating. Do you expect us to eat our provisions raw?"

"They're not raw. They're canned. Cold canned beans never hurt anybody. Keep going, damn it. We'll stop during the heat of day to boil some water and refill the coffee jugs. I want to get well clear of Manaus before we take a shore break. Too many people already know about this mission and we're still within paddle range of the boat people."

Sousa muttered something and started on upstream again as Captain Gringo waited until the canoe train was straight again and called back, "All right, Thomé. Give the screw some steam."

The banks were black lace against the flamingo sky. He knew anyone watching from the shore had a good shot at them and that they'd be invisible to him save for a rifle flash, if one came. He told himself not to worry about an ambush right outside of town, but some son-of-a-bitch had planted that bomb for him *inside* the town. He knew what Gaston would say if he were here, now. He knew he'd go along with his sidekick's practical suggestions about getting the hell out of this mess, too. He didn't have enough men and too many people knew about the mission. The guys had spent the whole day cleaning their rifles and the rifles were still a mess. They'd told him the men they'd given him were experienced fighters. Not one he'd talked to had ever served in any military unit. They were little more than an armed rabble. They might pan out tough, but Commander Fonseca had escaped up the river with trained navy ratings. They weren't headed into a saloon brawl with a bunch of toughs. They'd facing a gang three or four times their size, including some who'd know how to lay skirmish fire and could be relied on to take orders in a fire fight.

He considered that as he brooded at the breech of the mysterious Maxim he was still wondering about. It would take days to get into the map sector that really mattered. Maybe he could pound some rifle drill into this rag-tag band of river rats along the way. It would be suicide to take on anybody important until he had them shaped up. Some of them seemed a bit brighter than average. If he could pick a few squad leaders and teach them some basics they'd at least be able to take on their own numbers in a skirmish. He'd worry about being outnumbered when the time came the other side might have heavy weapons. They might not. This machinegun could shave the odds a bit if the mutineers only had their rifles. If they had machineguns, too, lots of luck. Neither the commodore nor Sousa knew just how many navy ratings Fonseca had taken up the Negro with him, or how they'd gotten there. The Brazilian navy wasn't missing any gunboats so they'd probably taken off in powered launches, like these. If Commander Fonseca had planned ahead, they'd have swiped all the guns and ammunition they could along the way. Nobody knew how many men and guns the outlaw, Andrada, had. They sure had planned this mission swell for him.

He'd been used as a pawn before, so he could see a couple of ways the government could be suckering him. Barboza hadn't wanted Lieutenant Sousa to come along. And a junior officer could be replaced easily enough. So how did Brazil come out ahead if they were being set up?

He couldn't think of any way. But if was sure beginning to look like Barboza didn't really give a damn if they made it or not. So, how come?

Why send an expedition at all if the results didn't matter one way or the other to you?

He thought about some of the weirder orders he'd been given by his own army back in his Tenth Cav days. The old Tenth had been a colored cav outfit with white officers. He'd thought a couple of times that somebody at headquarters didn't like colored people much. He remembered one suicidal mission into Apacheria that had certainly seemed designed to get him and his troop wiped out. Later, when he'd surprised them by coming back alive with most of his men and some Apache prisoners, he'd been told the strange orders had been a mistake. More than one officer back home still thought the annoying George Armstrong Custer had been sent to his death deliberately, to get rid of him. Custer had been a pain in the ass, but he hadn't been as stupid as it later seemed. The official version, now, was that Custer had been overconfident on the Little Big Horn. Everyone forgot Custer had not been in command that fatal day. He'd been ordered on ahead by Terry, and Terry had been a personal enemy of the flambouyant Custer.

Okay, so why would Commodore Barboza want him and these others dead? The men had been condemned criminals already. Barboza didn't have to let them out of jail to get them killed. He, himself, had been at Barboza's mercy, too. They could have easily shot him on the spot. Why send him up the river to die if that was their game?

You're squirrel caging, he told himself. Think about something else.

But there wasn't a hell of a lot to think about in the middle of the broad Negro. Maureen Mahoney was a prettier piece of puzzle, so he thought about her and how she fit in for a while. He wondered what would have happened if he'd chosen to go up the river with her instead of this gang of petty criminals. He wondered what she looked like with her clothes off—that was twice as much fun and a lot less mysterious. There were only so many ways a woman could look in the buff and he'd already undressed her a couple of times with his eyes. He was still kicking himself for having taken her at first for a lost innocent he didn't want to take advantage of. He could picture her body in detail, but who could say what went on in any woman's mind, and Maureen was more complicated than most.

He knew she would have given herself to him to get him to take her up this same damned stream. He still wasn't sure why. There were some loose ends in her story about the lost explorer. What had happened to her husband if she were a widow? How often did you meet a widow with a machinegun on the premises? And what the hell was the Brazilian Navy doing with the same damned gun?

He turned around to try another way. What if the Navy hadn't gotten the gun from Maureen? What if she'd borrowed the gun from the Navy?

It worked. She wasn't a British agent. She was working for Brazil. The wild story about her long-lost father had been intended to send him up this river. When he'd refused they'd taken off the gloves and approached him more directly. They'd taken the gun back. It hadn't been stolen. She said it had when he arrived unexpectedly, in case he'd wanted to see it. Maureen was quite a little actress, cussing him out like that when all the time she had to know he hadn't swiped her borrowed Navy gun!

Now the sky was getting as dark as the black river water. The moon hadn't risen yet. But the river rolled smooth and the stars above were reflected on the mirror surface. He could make out the distant banks only as dark starless strips and when he looked back toward mid-channel it made for a feeling of vertigo. He seemed to be following the dark forms of the vessels ahead, high in the sky, amid the uncountable lights of the milky way.

A humming something flew into his mouth, restoring him to reality as he spit it out with a curse. There were perhaps a tenth as many bugs up the Negro as over on the mainstream of the Amazon, but a tenth of the Amazon's bugs was still a lot of bugs. Those few who could survive the acid waters of the Negro seemed to come bigger and tougher, too. They hummed, buzzed, and fluttered invisibly over the surrounding waters. The fish had better eyes—from time to time one leaped, unseen, but not unheard. Some of the splashes bespoke big fish indeed, for the eater was often the eaten in Amazonia, so a little fish coming down with a beetle in its mouth sometimes met a bigger fish with a bigger appetite.

The slanting rays of the moon lanced over the eastern horizon, followed by the awesome tropic moon herself. Captain Gringo's jaw dropped as he stared around and realized there was nothing but water all around. The Rio Negro had widened to such an extent that they seemed a sea with both shores beyond the watery horizon.

He looked upstream. Sousa's launch and trailing cargo canoes were plainly visible now. The navy man had a compass and was of course a navy man, so he set a steady course north-west. Nobody expected to get lost here on the lower reaches of the Negro. Manaus was the terminal of ocean-going navigation but there were still a few towns and many plantations or fazendas to pass before they could really say they'd left civilization behind.

So he wasn't surprised, half an hour later, when the Robert E. Lee or a paddle wheeler related to her came over the upstream horizon to bear down on them, funnels shooting crimson sparks and decks lit up like a layered birthday cake. The expedition launches had no running lights, but the bigger crafts pilot could see them well enough to toot his whistle in a benediction or a curse as he churned by them. As the smaller vessels bobbed in the steamboat's wake Captain Gringo frowned as he reconsidered the idea of cruising at night. Then he nodded and decided the time they'd save was worth the slight risk. Both launches had rudders and anything they couldn't survive colliding with ought to have some lights they'd see well ahead of time.

He turned to watch the big steamboat plow on down the Negro. The moonlight betrayed a smudge of smoke from some other vessel farther downstream. As the steamboat lights winked out over the horizon down that way he heard its distant whistle as it greeted or warned the other craft. Captain Gringo shrugged and turned his gaze upstream again. It was a free country. Whoever was coming up the river behind them would show up in a while. They were cruising slower than most Brazilian river pilots seemed to prefer.

He moved to check his own dubious boiler. He found the black Thomé seated on the engine box with a bullseye lantern, staring at the gauges like a gypsy crystal gazer. Captain Gringo didn't insult Thomé by reading over his shoulder. In a low voice he said, "Good thinking." Most of the other men back here had stretched out on the duckboards or side benches to catch some sleep. He told Thomé, "You'd better show one of the other guys how to do that, Thomé. You won't be able to stay awake all the way."

The Black rubbed his face and said, "I know, my Captain. Who do you suggest I teach?"

"You pick him. You know your comrades better than I do."

"You allow me to make such important decisions, Captain Gringo?"

"Why not? I doubt you'd pick an obvious idiot. You're literally in the same boat with me."

The black nodded, soberly, and said, "I, too, can see by a man's eyes if he has a brain behind them or not. I can read and write. I have four years of schooling from the Dominicans. But I was surprised when you chose me for such an important position, my Captain. Most Blancos never look inside my skin."

Captain Gringo figured they'd get around to that sooner or later. He said, "I once led a troop of Black American Cavalry, Thomé. You find out after a while that some of you guys are good soldiers and others are useless bastards, just like the rest of us. I didn't think you folks ran into as much prejudice down here. Brazilians keep telling me how stupid we Yanquis are about color. I thought there was no color bar down here."

Thomé smiled bitterly, then said, "You North Americans say so when you look down on a man. White Brazilians are more polite. They have to be. They are the minority here, since almost everyone is at least part Indian. But you Yanquis don't know what prejudice is. Brazilian Blancos don't just look down on people who are darker than themselves. They look down on anyone who has no power or political pull. The whole country is run by a handful of interbred families."

"I thought it was a democracy."

"Ha. So they say. It is true they hold elections. They even let some poor people vote. But what does it matter who one votes for if a small inside clique picks all the candidates, eh?"

"Reminds me of some towns back home. It's still probably an improvement over the emperor you had down here until recently."

Thomé shook his head. "I mean no disrespect, my Captain, but you have a lot to learn about politics in my country. Do you know why the Republicans threw out Dom Pedro? Do you know why the powerful fazenda owners said he was a tyrant? He enraged them by setting free their slaves, long after your Civil War was over. This is true. I was born a slave. The Emperor Dom Pedro gave me my freedom. He built roads and schools. He gave the country a constitution. While he ruled, the courts were fair and a little man could ask for justice against a bigger man. That is why they threw him out of the country. That is why they called him a tyrant."

Captain Gringo stared thoughtfully as he stored the Black youth's information away for future reference. The smoke smudge far behind still hovered in the moonlight. Why hadn't that other steamboat gained on them?

He asked Thomé, "How did you land in jail, Thomé?"

105

"I killed a man who tried to cheat me. I was a rubber tapper. Do you know how hard it is to make a living tapping rubber?"

"I imagine it's tough."

"It is. The rubber barons are too stupid or lazy to plant rubber, like the British in their East Indian colonies. Despite the great Brazil ships' tonnage, it is all from wild trees, growing scattered in the selva. They give you a tapping route, like a trapper's line through the northern woodlands. You carry the heavy buckets with you for a great distance. The trees you tap stand far apart. You walk all day to fill your buckets. At night you make the latex hard by smoking it over your campfire. It takes forever to make one small bale on your dip stick. In a month or so you have enough to take to the trading post. They weigh and credit the rubber to your account. If you work very hard you sometimes make a few cruzeiros more than you owe the rubber baron."

"He charges you for supplies and such while you're out in the selva, eh?"

"He charges you for to tap the trees on his fazenda, too. No matter how far you go and no matter what you say, he says you were still on his land when you tapped the latex. They are most greedy men, the rubber barons."

"You said you killed one."

"Oh, not the baron. We flagelados never see the owner. He lives in a big house and drinks all day to relieve his fatigue. The man I fought with was a rubber checker from the docks. He, too, thought people used their skin to think with and tried to tell me a dozen was a ten. Such mistakes add up when one brings in a dugout full of rubber. When I said he was trying to cheat me he mentioned my mother. So I never got paid for any rubber that day, but he will never cheat anybody again."

Captain Gringo nodded and said, "They told me you were good with a gun, too."

"I am all right." Thomé shrugged. "One carries a gun for to tap rubber far from the river. Sometimes the Indians become confused and do not know they are on someone's azenda either. I was arrowed by a Colorado once. He won't o that anymore, either."

The tall American nodded and said, "I'm going forward. Vake somebody up and show them the ropes. I want somebody back here to keep an eye on that vessel behind us. It's ot gaining. It's not falling back."

"You think someone is trailing us in another boat, my aptain?"

"Don't know. We'll wait a while and see."

He moved forward again and sat down in the bows with is elbow on the machinegun breech as he lit a fresh cigar ith his free hand. The moon was higher, now, and they were o longer among the stars. The river was a shimmering sheet f tarnished silver under the star-spangled vault of the tropic y. Black things, either slow clumsy bats or moths too g to believe fluttered over the water all around. Every nce in a while a fish leaped like a silver shuttle to snap one ut of the air. He blinked in surprise when one salmon-sized sh leaped high in the air, arced down, and landed in the aping jaws of a surfacing something as big as a shark. It was bering to think what might be lurking under the surface of e Negro. The only fresh water sharks he'd ever run into had een on Lake Nicaragua that time. He knew there were aymans closer to the distant banks. He'd heard there were olphins on the Amazon, funny, pink, fresh water dolphins at the locals could eat on Friday with the approval of the lerant Brazilian priesthood. There were manatees one could so eat on Friday, even though they tasted a lot like pork. e'd seen a catfish in the fish market at Manaus that he still idn't believe. The one he'd seen had been bigger than a rpon and the natives said they came a lot bigger.

He noticed they were overtaking the supply dugouts and as about to call back to the tillerman. But the bow swung port and he saw they were okay, but why was Sousa slowing own?

His own launch slowly overtook the lieutenant's and ousa called over to him, "We're being followed."

"I noticed," Captain Gringo called back. "Let's both slow own and see what happens."

Sousa agreed and said something to the men in his own craft. As his bows dropped abeam Captain Gringo moved as far back as the boiler amidships and said, "Thomé, throttle back and stay abreast of the others. You at the tiller. What's your name?"

"I am called Deodoro, my Captain."

"Good enough. Stay alert and if I yell back that I want a hard right rudder, I'll expect a hard right rudder. Thomé you stop the engine if we heave to."

"Very well, my Captain. But won't we drift downstream?"

"Yeah, broadside with my gun trained on the mother fuckers. Steady as she goes for now. It may be just an innocent steamboat. We'll find out as they overtake us."

. He resumed his position by the machinegun, but swung the muzzle starboard so it would be pointing downstream when they hove to. Lieutenant Sousa swung away, staying abeam but giving him elbow room, for he'd heard the shouted commands. Sousa was all right. He might be a little green, but he didn't have to be led to the toilet by the hand.

Captain Gringo leaned against the starboard bulwarks, elbow on the rail as he stared downstream. They were barely moving against the current, now. The mysterious smoke plume following them stayed just where it had been, over the horizon. How the hell had they caught on so fast? Oh, right, they could see *his* smoke, too.

Okay, they were being followed. Since the others didn't seem interested in overtaking them there was nothing much they could do about it.

He waited half an hour. Then he called across to Sousa, "Fuck 'em. They don't want to fight. Let's try three quarters speed and make up for lost time. You take the point and I'll still cover your ass."

Sousa's launch moved forward as his engine began to throb harder. As the last trailing canoe passed, Captain Gringo was about to call back to Thomé, but the duckboards quivered under his boots as the Black cracked open the throttle without waiting for the command. Captain Gringo let it go. The guy was smart and sometimes it paid to ride with a oose rein. No officer could hope to be everywhere at once and so you concentrated on the dumb guys in your command and let the bright ones carry the ball on their own.

The man he'd made bos'n back in Manaus was in Sousa's launch. Deodoro at the tiller seemed worth considering. Thomé was a bit brighter. Had this been the Tenth Cav he wouldn't have hesitated to make Thomé a non-com. But the negro had told him the color bar wasn't as blurred as they said it was down here. So some of the others might resent a Black over them. He'd have to think about that. Thomé would feel insulted if he were passed over. Thomé killed people who annoyed him.

He craned his neck to see if the other boat had picked up speed. It had. So what the fuck did they want? Anybody tailing them already knew where they were going. They obviously didn't want to come close enough to swap shots. It was pretty spooky.

The odd chase continued for several hours and Captain Gringo's mouth was rancid from smoking too much to stay awake. He put the fresh cigar he'd just taken out back where it belonged, unsmoked, and decided to stretch out on the duckboards and catch forty winks. The two men awake in the stern would tell him if the other boat was gaining on them.

He hauled his bedroll from under the bench and unrolled it on the duck boards to lay atop the covers. The night was a balmy seventy degrees or so. He hadn't known how tired he was until he had stretched out on the firm surface. It had been an exciting day after a back-breaking night with little Borita. He told himself not to think about Borita. It was over. He'd probably never see her again. It was funny, but a man never missed the ones he'd spent a lot of time with. It was the ships passing in the night he remembered with longing. He'd lost track of how many women he'd had in his time. Yet there were still a couple of girls from High School Days that he often had a hard on over. He remembered a little shy brunette who sat next to him in Latin. He'd never kissed her. He'd never taken her out. He still remembered how for a whole semester he'd wanted to lean over and kiss the nape of her neck below her upswept pile of jet black hair and he could picture her dark apron of pubic hair as if he'd seen it a hundred times, even though he'd never seen her bare ankle.

Who had that blond been, that weekend at The Point? She'd been the sister of a fellow cadet and he'd strolled along Flirtation Walk with her, trying to get up the nerve to kiss her. He never had. He'd forgotten her name. Yet he could still smell her perfume as they leaned against the rail above the Hudson, both too shy to exchange addresses. He'd never seen her again. He'd made love to her in his dreams a thousand times or more. She was probably married and a mother by now. If he ever found out who the son-of-a-bitch was he'd kill him.

He didn't remember falling asleep, but he must have, because he woke up with a start as the boat slowed down under him. He sat up and rubbed a hand across his face. He needed a shave and his mouth tasted like fly paper, flies and all. Looking around he saw the moon was setting. They were near a tree-covered island in mid-stream and Sousa had hove to in it's lee. His own vessel had once more pulled abeam. He called out, "What's up, Sousa?" And the officer called back, "It's going to be dark again in a few minutes and the channel is starting to braid. If we tie up here, it will soon be dawn and, meanwhile, that other boat may be thrown off if we kill our smoke."

The American nodded and called, "Good idea. We'll let the guys stretch their legs ashore before we move on again. Nobody moves into those trees before daybreak, though. It's probably an uninhabited island but let's not take any chances."

It took the better part of twenty minutes to run the bows into the shallows and tie up to some exposed roots at the water's edge. By then the moon was setting and it was getting black as a bitch. Captain Gringo looked down the river to see if he could spot the other smoke in the slanting rays of the moon. He couldn't. They'd either fallen back, meaning they hadn't been trailing them after all, or they'd killed their own smoke and dropped anchor as soon as they couldn't take out the two plumes from the upstream expedition's tunnels, which meant they were annoyingly smart.

The two launches lay side by side close together, so the men in both could talk back and forth in a conversational tone, now. Everyone was of course awake. Captain Gringo started to shout an order to keep it down to a roar. Then he decided to let them loosen up. He climbed over into Sousa's launch to be able to converse with the lieutenant more comfortably. He said, "Commodore Barboza might have sent someone after us to make sure we didn't overpower you and turn river pirate."

Sousa shook his head and said, "It's not our guys. The whole point of this undertaking is to leave the navy out of it, *officially*."

"Yeah, if he wanted a patrol boat this far up he wouldn't have screwed around with recruiting me and these convicts. I've been mulling over this mess, Sousa. Has it occurred to you, yet, that none of this makes a bit of sense?"

"I thought the commodore explained it all to you. I was here when he told you the political situation was delicate. You must understand that the Brazilian family ties are very extensive and the new government has all the enemies it needs. Commander Fonseca, the rebel leader, has a brother in the national assembly in Rio. There are Fonsecas all over the place, on both sides. Some, loyal to the new administration, have been petitioning President Barros for a full pardon for their erring cousin."

"Wouldn't it be simpler to pardon the silly bastard?"

"His friends and relations think so. Alas, Commander Fonseca is a very stubborn man. He is most bitter that the rest of the navy did not join him in his mutiny and he keeps saying silly things about the fairness of the last election."

"So if he was given a full pardon he'd be free to run for president on his own, eh? I see the picture. The government wants him eliminated, but they don't want to be blamed for his demise by his powerful clan. What about the other guy, Andrada?"

Sousa shrugged and said, "He has no friends in high

places. I doubt if he has many in low places. He is, how you say, a robber baron."

"Don't you mean *rubber* baron?"

"No, he does not sell rubber. He sells nothing. He takes tribute from everyone in his part of the selva. He claims to hold his fazendas as a land grant from the Emperor Dom Pedro. He has no papers to prove this, just a gun. It is he and his Indios, of course, who smuggle across the poorly mapped border. Alone, Andrada is just a pest. He would never dare to move down the river where our gunboats could have him in range. He has been declared an outlaw. Every man's hand is against him if he chooses to expand his operations. But Commander Fonseca as a partner makes things more complicated. Some people might consider the combined force a legitimate revolutionary army."

"Think anybody closer to Rio might change sides if they came busting out?"

"Of course. That is why we must make sure he does not do so."

Captain Gringo reached for a water bag and rinsed his mouth out before lighting up another smoke. "Like I said, no sense. But try her this way. Suppose they have us down on paper as some sory of innocent expedition. Maybe we're looking for long lost cities or gold or something."

"That is ridiculous. You heard Commodore Barboza's orders."

"To *us,* yeah. He could easily say it another way to the newspapers. Maureen Mahoney is on record as wanting to look for a missing father up the Negro. Commodore Barboza issues permits to foreign expeditions and I don't come from Brazil."

"Did the commodore issue you any such thing, Captain Gringo?"

"No, but he might have a carbon copy in his files anyway. Let's assume that other boat behind us is one of your river monitors with a four-inch gun. Maybe a detachment of marines, including a heavy weapons squad."

"That's ridiculous. I just explained why we can't openly attack the rebel stronghold with navy vessels."

"I know. It would be a massacre. Unless, of course, the navy had to rescue somebody. Namely us! Don't you see how it would work, kid? We're the bait. The rebels have friends in Manaus. They have to know we're on our way. So we move in on them, a handful of half-ass guerrillas with one lousy machinegun that's not listed as Brazilian property in the first place and probably won't be enough to do the job in the second. We tangle with the rebels. It gets very noisy. A navy gunboat on a routine patrol moves in to investigate and what do you know, banditos are shooting up a civilian expedition! The government can't stand for that, can it? Of course not. Let's lob a few shells into the bastards to restore law and order and, what do you know, one of the wiped out banditos was the late Commander Fonesca! We're sorry, guys, we didn't know your crazy cousin was hiding out with those vicious outlaws."

Sousa's jaw dropped. He shook his head and started to object, but Captain Gringo saw he'd made the young officer think. Gringo continued, "Right out of *The Prince*, by Machiavelli. It was a favorite chess move of the Borgia clan. They'd send in an advance party to take a town and execute all the important people. Then a higher officer would arrive to inspect the new conquest and hold court to hear complaints, smiling a lot. Sooner or later the surviving relatives of the dead former leaders would mention the executions. The Borgia would look surprised and call for the hatchet men he'd sent in ahead. Then he'd chew them out good in front of everybody and hang them for having exceeded their authority. So everybody was happy. The Borgias owned the town, the people who might argue about it were dead. The people who might want revenge were satisfied that the new rulers weren't such bad guys after all. It's kind of obvious, but it must work. They've been doing it ever since in one damned country or another."

Sousa frowned and said, "I read Machiavelli in school. What you suggest is monstrous."

"Look, I never said it was nice. I just said it would work! Fonesca's family and friends would be mad as hell if he went down in a standup fight between military units. But they could hardly bitch if it seemed he'd turned out-and-out bandito and was shooting up innocent travelers like us. Even his brother in the central government would expect the navy to do it's duty, right?"

Sousa looked around and said, "It's too complicated. These men all know we are not on an innocent expedition."

"Yeah, that's why the commodore sent so many guys and armed us so well. These guys are all poor river rats with not too many people likely to ever ask about them. You're the only guy along who might have his name on file somewhere."

"But there are twenty-one of us. Somebody might talk."

"Yeah, if any of us got out alive. Makes one wonder, doesn't it?"

Apparently it did. Sousa sat silently for a time and then he said, "If what you say is true, I can see why he tried to discourage me from coming along. But I can't believe Commodore Barboza could be so ruthless, and, even if he is, what can we do about it?"

"Good question. If that's a gunboat trailing us, turning around might be more fatal than pressing on. They've got us by the short hairs, kid. For now there's nothing to do but keep on going and maybe I'll turn out to be wrong. I've won a few times against odds. The odds right now are lousy, but what the hell."

"You have some plan to take the rebels, Captain Gringo?"

"No. But I sure have to think one up pretty damned quick."

Captain Gringo had just gotten back to sleep when Thomé woke him up, saying, "I am sorry to disturb you, my Captain."

The weary American sat up, muttering, "Why the hell did you do it, then?"

He saw the sun was rising. Thome said, "You told the men they could go ashore as soon as it was light. But I have not been sleeping. I have been listening. There is somebody on the island. I heard them moving through the brush along the water's edge."

Captain Gringo put on his gun, jacket, and Panama hat as he considered the Black's words. Now that he could see it, the island was a big one. You couldn't see it all from any one spot. He looked around and saw they were still on the broad lake-like channel of the lower Negro. The island was as isolated as if it had been in the South Seas. He called to Sousa and said, "My guy here thinks the island is inhabited. Know anything about it?"

"No," Sousa said. "There are hundreds of islands along the river. Some are fazendas in their own right. Others are only owned by the parrots and monkeys. Why don't we just move on and forget the shore leave?"

Captain Gringo knew that was the smartest move. On the other hand the men had heard him give an order. It wasn't a good idea to change orders without a good reason. And being a sissy wasn't a good one.

He spoke loud enough for all to hear as he said. "Lieutenant, you move over here to the machinegun. Keep our people with you until I come back from my patrol. Thomé, Durand, Deodoro, pick up your rifles and come with me."

He leaped overboard into the shin-deep shallows to wade ashore as the three followed. He bulled through the tangled brush growing at the water's edge and, as expected, found that under the overhead canopy the underbrush was shaded out. The sandy earth was partly covered by fallen leaves and creepers, but he could see well into the cathedral gloom between the butressed tree trunks. He spotted a scuff mark where a boot heel had slid on some slick rotten leaves to expose fresh soil. He said, "All right, Martim Durand out front on point. Move slow and stay in sight. Do you know how to signal silently with your rifle when you see anything, Bos'n?"

Durand looked puzzled. Captain Gringo held his own rifle and said, "Watch me. If you see something and you're not sure what we should do about it you hold your rifle over

115

your head like so and stay put until I join you. If it looks dangerous you pump the rifle up and down like this. Then take cover or run, depending."

He turned to Deodoro and said, "You'll be the getaway man. Stay well behind me. If I signal enemy ahead or if I suddenly fall down boom, you run like hell and warn Lieutenant Sousa. He'll take it from there. Thomé, you stay with me. You know this country better than me."

Nobody moved. He snapped, "What the fuck are you waiting for, my blessings? Move it out, Durand!"

The bos'n nodded and headed deeper into the forest. Captain Gringo let him take a good lead before he nodded to the Black and said, "Let's go." As they walked side by side Thomé said, "I did not know it was done this way. I thought the leader was always out in front."

"That's why I'm a pro and you're not. You can't command a line of men from one end. You do it from the middle. I've got all sorts of neat tricks to teach you guys. But let's make sure of this landing first."

They passed a smooth barked tree. Captain Gringo said, "That's a rubber tree, isn't it?" And the Black nodded and said, "Yes, it has never been tapped, and it is a good one."

"Okay, so anybody we meet is growing something else, or else they'll be river pirates."

The island kept getting bigger as they explored it. They were at least a mile from where they'd left the boats when Captain Gringo saw his point man had stopped, raised his rifle, and stepped behind a tree. Captain Gringo looked back to see Deodoro was still tailing him. He and Thomé moved up to join Durand. He didn't have to tell them what he'd seen. They could see the trees ended just ahead and that a big white house lay on the far side of a big sugar cane field. Captain Gringo said, "Okay, Durand, you stay here and cover us. Thomé and I will go over and ask permission to land the boys on the far end."

"They will see you coming, no?"

"They already know we're here. Somebody from that fazenda was pussy footing too. Thomé, sling your rifle. We'll make them less uneasy if we just walk up to the front door politely."

Slinging his own Krag, Captain Gringo moved out into the morning sunlight with the Black at his side. They found a trail through the shoulder high cane. He could see the crop had a ways to go before harvest. He said, "That explains the untapped rubber. There probably aren't enough wild rubber trees on the island to make it worth their while. We're close enough to Manaus for them to sell their sugar locally. Funny, it's a pretty big house for such a small fazenda."

"I agree, My Captain," Thomé said. "Sugar is cheap in Brazil and there is hardly enough here to matter."

As they neared the house, Captain Gringo could see both the house and sugar field were exposed to views from boats passing on the river. He glanced to the west where the sky line was blocked by a wall of trees running along the far shore behind the house and grounds. It was only a thin screen, though. There were other fields over that way. They were either fallow or growing a crop lower than cane. As they passed a cross lane through the sugar he spotted closely packed flower beds, nodded, and kept going. He asked Thomé, "Is opium legal in Brazil?"

The Black said, "Anything is legal in Brazil if you know the right people, why?"

"They planted this cane to screen their opium crop from passing river boats. It makes you wonder. It explains the luxurious house, too."

"There is much opium smoking in Manaus, my Captain."

"That's what I mean. The cops don't seem too interested. So why are they hiding their cash crop?"

"Perhaps they are ashamed?"

"Or it offers a tempting prize to passing flagelados. The poppies have gone to flower, so the crop should be ready to harvest, soon. You gather the gum from the seed pods. Don't mention any of this when we get to the house, by the way. It wouldn't be polite."

As they rounded the last of the cane Captain Gringo

spotted two men and a woman on the veranda of the tin roofed house. He waved as they approached but nobody waved back.

Captain Gringo stopped near the steps and removed his hat to say, "Good morning. My name is Walker and this is my man, Thomé."

Nobody answered for a moment. The woman was about thirty and not bad. She wore a black lace dress and was twisting the handkerchief in her lap nervously with white knuckled hands. The two men were dressed more roughly and both could have used a shave. They had gunbelts slung on their hips. One of them said, "You are on private property, Senhor."

Captain Gringo nodded pleasantly and said, "I know. We tied up for the night downstream. We didn't know anybody lived here."

"You know it now, eh? What are you waiting for? Shove off."

Captain Gringo's eyes narrowed thoughtfully. They didn't look that brave. Then he spotted the rifle barrel trained on him from between the slats of a window up the veranda and so he shrugged and said, "Well, it's your island. I'm sorry if we upset you. Like I said, we were just looking around. Come on, Thomé. Let's go back and tell the others it's time to shove off."

They turned to retrace their steps. Captain Gringo's shoulder blades tingled all the way back to the tree line, but if they'd wanted a fight they'd have started one down by the boats by now. As they got out of sight, Thomé said, "They had us covered from the house. They must be growing a lot of opium, eh?"

"Maybe. They scouted us first. So there can't be that many of them or they'd have tried to ambush us. Let's get the guys and find out what the hell is going on."

Thomé grinned and said, "Ah, you mean they did not frighten you after all?"

"Oh, I damned near shit my britches when I spotted that rifle winking out at me. But if your asking how easy it is to run me off, it ain't that easy."

"I found them most rude, too. Even Blancas have better manners to passing strangers at isolated fazendas. I am a Negro, but you are a Blanco and a gentleman. I expected that fancy lady to invite you in for coffee, at least."

"I don't think she had anything to say about it. Don't you see it yet?"

"What is there to see, my Captain? The woman did not speak. It is the place of the man of the house to speak to strangers."

"That wasn't the man of the house. Nobody with a wife like that wanders around barefoot and needing a shave. Those guys are highjackers. They've moved in on the opium growers to help them harvest their crop. I don't know what happened to the real man of the house, but his wife back there was their prisoner. Couldn't you see how she was trying to tell us what was going on with her eyes?"

"Ah, I noticed she seemed nervous. Now the poor thing thinks we are leaving her to the mercy of those ruffians, eh?"

"Yeah, let's see if we can make them think so, too."

It was a pretty simple ruse, but the highjackers were pretty simple. So when they saw the two launches steam past them up the river with Lieutenant Sousa's few men aboard they naturally assumed their bluff had worked. Meanwhile, of course, Captain Gringo led most of their party up the far shore of the island to take them from the rear.

Trees grew close to the rear of the house and nobody was on guard back there. One of the five outlaws stood guard on the front steps, watching the river landing with his rifle across his knees while the other four took the woman inside to rape her some more. They had her naked across a mattress on the floor when Captain Gringo kicked open the door with his machinegun braced against his hips.

The man holding the woman's arms froze, thunderstruck, as the man who'd been about to mount her rolled away to grope for the gunbelt he'd dropped nearby. The two who'd been waiting their turn still wore their guns so Captain Gringo opened up and shread a deadly fan of hot lead at waist level, blowing them off their feet and dropping the muzzle to cover the naked rapist crawling away on his hands and knees. His second burst blew the highjacker's bare ass to rassberry jam as the one who'd been holding the woman let go and raised his hands, shouting, "Please, I beg of you, Senhor!"

Captain Gringo looked at the woman and asked, "Ma'am?"

She covered her nakedness with her hands as she said, in a venomous voice, "Kill him, please." So Captain Gringo said, "You heard what the lady said," and blew his head off with a short savage burst.

One of the men behind him made the sign of the cross and murmured, "Ay, my Captain is most good with that weapon." And Captain Gringo said, "Get something to cover the lady, and remember you didn't see her any other way." Then he ran forward, leaping over one of the bodies to tear out the front, gun leveled. The last outlaw wasn't sure just what was going on and wasn't hanging around to find out. He was half way to his dugout down by the shore when Captain Gringo dropped him on the lawn with plunging fire.

He saw he'd used up half the belt. He stepped back inside to find the woman wrapped in her dress without taking time to put it on. He nodded at the gaping men around her and said, "Out. Wait in back for me."

The woman turned to him when they were alone, save for the dead, and stammered, "Thank God you understood what was happening. They were waiting here to ambush my husband and some of our men. He went down to Manaus. He should be back any time, now, and, oh, Mother of God, what am I to say to him?"

"Let's figure that out. Did you have any other servants here?"

"Yes, but these flagelados killed them all. They are out in the cane, they have been dead since yesterday. My husband is such a proud man. How can I ever face him, now?"

"You can start by putting on some clothes. My men and I will clean up the mess. We'll be gone by the time your husband returns. You'll have to tell him part of what happened, of course, but . . ."

"They had their way with me, all five of them!"

"No they didn't. We got here just as they attacked your fazenda, see? You hid out while the fighting was going on. Your servants died bravely defending you. The outlaws never saw you. Where were you, in the attic?"

She started to say something stupid. Then her eyes filled with new-found hope and she nodded and said, "I was up at the far end of the island. I went for a morning walk. When I heard the shooting I was frightened and I hid in the woods, no?"

"That ought to do it. I'd get rid of that dress and freshen up before I put on a clean one. We'd better throw this mattress in the river. It's, ah, sort of messy."

"I know, they abused me on it many times and . . . but you are right, it never happened. How are you called, Senhor?"

"I'm Dick Walker. I don't want to know your name. My men and I were never here. You were saved by some rubber tappers going down the river, not up."

She looked puzzled and then she nodded and said, "Yes, my husband would insist on following after you to thank you properly. You are wise as well as most gallant, Senhor Walker. I shall never forget what you did for me."

"Hell, they deserved a good killing, Ma'am."

She glanced down at the dead bodies at her feet, grimaced, and said, "I am not speaking of your killing them. My husband would have done that if their ambush failed. I thank you from the bottom of my heart, for your greater favor. Many men are brave. A hero who does not talk about it is less easy to find. Go with God, Senhor Walker, and if one woman's prayers can get a man into heaven, you are assured safe entry."

"Thank you. If it's all the same, though, I'd like to wait a while before I go knocking on any pearly gates, Ma'am."

Lieutenant Sousa had of course circled the island and put in at the fazenda's landing when signaled. The men made short work of the bodies while the rescued woman enjoyed a long, hot soak. Both the outlaws and her somewhat soggy dead servants were shoved in the river without consulting her about formalities. They were gone by the time she came out to thank them in her fresh clothing and underwear.

Sousa informed Captain Gringo that it was indeed legal to grow opium there, albeit damned foolish to have anything that valuable at an isolated small fazenda. The screen of sugar cane hadn't hidden the poppy fields from the river traffic as planned, or, just as likely, the highjackers had been tipped off by a disgruntled employee or a treacherous dealer. When Captain Gringo commented on the casual drug regulations, Sousa shrugged and added, "I, myself, would not smoke opium at gunpoint. But aside from it's legitimate medical uses it helps a lot of useless people mark time until they die."

"Don't you think they might live longer if they weren't on opium?"

"No, they'd probably die in a fight, or do something the state would have to execute them for. Nine out of ten people are immune to whatever it takes to make a dedicated addict. That tenth pobrecito is going to ruin his life, one way or the other, no matter what he uses to do it with. If all the opium on Earth were sunk in the deep blue sea, he would find some other weapon to use against himself. There are legitimate reasons to grow opium. There are legitimate reasons to manufacture guns. Neither the man who sells you opium nor the man who sells you a gun is responsible if you use one or the other foolishly, eh?"

Captain Gringo had a few reservations, but it was Sousa's country and none of his men had found any refined opium in or about the house, so who cared?

Their shake down skirmish had shown him his men were willing to fight, but little more than an armed mob when it came to carrying out orders. He'd had to yell too much and even so they'd crowded in and bunched up like raw recruits. He'd sent details to swing around either side of the house and nail anybody running out the front, but they hadn't swung worth shit and he'd had to finish the last outlaw on the lawn himself. They desperately needed some basic training. The island wasn't the place to give it to them. They had to be on their way. So they went. Sousa in the lead boat said he'd pull in if he spotted a well-wooded smaller island by siesta time It was only mid-morning and the humid heat out on the exposed surface of the Negro was already getting brutal. Captain Gringo rode in the bow, stripped to his waist and under the shade of the overhead awning. He still felt like he was in a steam bath and the sunlight glinting on the water was a bitch on the eyes.

The mystery smoke plume still haunted them far downstream and barely noticeable in the shimmering haze of the horizon. It was getting to be a real pain in the ass. There were other crafts moving up and down the Negro by day light, of course. It was easy to separate their smoke from the sneak's. They didn't maintain one constant position relative to the two plumes they were ghosting. They went down toward Manaus or they came up to pass the two slow cruising little launches.

They kept meeting or were overhauled by a mixed bag of things that floated. A lot of the downstream traffic was thrown together for a one way trip. Log rafts, dugouts, timber simply branded with an owner's mark and allowed to drift downstream on it's own. They met steam launches much like their own. There were larger craft in all stages of repair from spic-and-span to rusty bucket. Some of the paddle wheelers looked like they were left over from the earlier times on the Mississippi. Captain Gringo had no idea how they'd wound up down here.

La Siesta caught them out in the middle of a broad stretch with no place to put in, so they kept going as it just got hotter. An hour later Sousa waved back to him and pointed to a grove of trees coming at them over the horizon. Captain Gringo signaled assent and Sousa picked up speed, anxious to get ashore to the cool of the forest shade. Thomé at the throttle did the same without having to be told.

Captain Gringo leaned out to see how their shadower was doing. They were still being followed. But now two faster craft were in sight. A one-funnel converted harbor tug was leading a two-stacker stern wheeler up the river by a nose. It looked like they were racing. They probably were. Few river pilots could resist the temptation to vary the monotony of a long watch with a spot of sport. Both craft were making good time and the mild north-east trades were blowing the three thick smoke clouds broadside to the current. Captain Gringo grimaced. That was all they needed. He knew the wakes of the two bigger craft were going to bob the hell out of his own small craft, and the smoke and cinders would settle on the sweaty skins of himself and everyone else. The racing steamboats were both burning wood, which seemed reasonable on the Negro, but it looked as if both skippers had thrown coal oil in their fireboxes to increase the heat, which didn't. Aside from risking a boiler explosion they were stinking up the neighborhood.

But the approaching racers gave Gringo an idea. He yelled back, "Thomé, full speed ahead. Tiller man, swing our stern in line with Sousa's bow as we pass him."

The men with him brightened as the launch started moving faster, cooling things a bit under the canopy. One of the men in the bow with him said, "We are having a race with those other boats, no?"

"Not exactly," Captain Gringo said, as he stood to hail Sousa as his own launch drew abreast of the other. He called over, "Line up on my stern and follow at full!" And then they were upstream beyond Sousa and swinging starboard. Captain Gringo made his way aft and told the tiller man he'd take over. He sat down, backward, with the rudder bar held like a fishing pole. Deodoro frowned and asked, "Don't you want to see where we are going, my Captain?" And the tall American answered, "No, I'm more interested in where we've been."

He saw they were almost lined up with the two racers from the position of the mystery smudge far downstream. Almost wasn't good enough. He moved the tiller and swung alee until the mystery vessel's smoke was hidden by the thicker smoke of the bigger boats between them. Sousa of course did the same as he stayed in line with Captain Gringo. Deodoro said, "Excuse me, my Captain, but if we don't get out of the way those racers are going to run us down."

"No they won't. They should pass us on either side."

Deodoro licked his lips as he stared downstream. "They are neck and neck and only a few meters apart."

"I noticed. Everybody secure loose cargo and get ready for some bumps."

Sitting in the stern he was facing Sousa in the bow of the boat behind. He yelled back, "Cut your oil jet when you see me do it and follow on the pressure in your boiler, okay?"

"We can only run a short time with the steam on hand," Sousa yelled back.

"That's okay, we're not going far. Better keep an eye behind you. Try to keep your towed canoes in line."

The pilots of the racing steamboats were tooting arrogantly as they bore down on the smaller flotilla. Neither wanted to lose way by swerving. Captain Gringo could only hope they didn't want dented bows, either, as he held his position midstream.

The converted tug came up aport; the bigger sternwheeler had a bone in her teeth as she chuffed to starboard, starting to gain on the one-stacker. Passengers and crewmen stared down at the smaller launches as the two bigger vessels passed on either side, the water between them solid foam. Captain Gringo was momentarily blinded as the spray from the bigger boats enveloped him. The rudder bar fought him like a snake trying to get away as the launch rose sickeningly, waving her ass in a corkscrew dance. And then they were downstream from the racers, albeit still bobbing like corks in the cross wakes. He yelled, "Thomé, kill the fire!" And as the Black turned off the oil jet he swung the rudder hard over to swing them toward the island just upstream. He saw Sousa's smoke plume die and grunted in satisfaction as he turned to steer properly. They were slowing down, even with the throttle at full speed, but the engine was still turning over as the pressure dropped. He knew the others following, way down the river, were waiting to separate the confusion of smoke they must be watching on their own north-west horiozn, so he was grinning wolfishly as he rounded the upstream tip of the small island and hove to in the shallows. Sousa pulled alongside and called over with a grin, "I see what you mean!

Look up the river! The stern wheeler is ahead, trailing two plumes. The one-stacker has given up and is slowing down. Those bastards following us will have to figure out which smoke belongs to whomsoever and they couldn't have seen us moving broadside so . . ."

"Screw telling me what I already know!" the American cut in, adding, "Let's haul these tubs in and camouflage them, fast!"

It only took a few minutes. They tied up to shoreside roots and sent men ashore with machetes to hack a few tree limbs. They dropped the butts in the water to tipi the leafy branches over the canvas awnings. Then, fairly safe from a casual glance, Captain Gringo swung his Maxim to cover the main channel as they waited.

A million years seemed to go by. The smoke of the steamboats who'd passed them were mere smudges upstream when they spotted a smaller steam-powered cabin cruiser coming gingerly up the river. Captain Gringo knew its smoke funnel's pattern all too well after watching it for so many hours. But he'd been expecting a gunboat. Who the hell were they?

The cruiser passed them, picking up speed as its confused pilot lost the scent. Captain Gringo couldn't see the people aboard because of the cabin. Nobody was in the exposed rear cockpit because of the searing noon-day sun. He waited until the mahogany transome was out of his vision and said, "Okay, Thomé, fire up the engine. Rest of you guys toss these branches out of the way."

As his men moved to obey, Sousa called over to ask what they were doing. He yelled back, "Going after them, of course."

"I thought the idea was to hide and let them pass."

"It was. We did. And now we have the mother fuckers out in the open at last. I want to settle it here and now, before they figure out what happened and set up their *own* ambush for *us,* God damn it!"

Upstream, the people aboard the cruiser must have noticed the new smoke plume from Captain Gringo's funnel. The cruiser slowed, as if undecided, then started moving up the river again at wary speed. Captain Gringo waited until he'd gotten rid of his camouflage and built some pressure before he swung the machinegun muzzle in line with his keel and called back, "Okay, muchachos, everybody with a free hand, one round ball ammunition in your chambers and await my signal to fire. Thomé, full speed. Deodoro, line us up on their stern as we overtake them."

The duckboards shuddered under him as the screw clawed them forward again. Somebody on the cruiser must have been worried about the sight, for they started moving faster as the launch chased them. To the rear, Lieutenant Sousa was trying, but taking more time to get underway. It didn't matter. Captain Gringo had the only machinegun, mounted where it could do the most good.

The steam cruiser started throwing a creamy wake as she moved faster, but she moved oddly, from side to side, as if the people aboard were having trouble making up their minds about something. His own navy launch was as fast and so, moving straighter, began to gain. He was just out of range, but what the hell. He elevated the muzzle and fired a burst of plunging fire, tap dancing slugs across the mystery boat's superstructure. A man popped out of the cabin to shake a fist at him. Captain Gringo put both hands to his face and bellowed, "Heave to, or I'll blow you out of the water, you son-of-a-bitch!"

The cruiser slowed, then started to pick up speed after all. He grimaced and lowered the muzzle slightly as he saw they were almost in killing range.

Then someone waved a white kerchief and the cruiser swung broadside as another crewman ran up to the bow to drop the mud hook. Captain Gringo ordered reduced speed as he drew abreast and told one of his men to do the same. A minute later the two craft bobbed side by side at anchor just at pistol range. He covered them with the machinegun and yelled, "Let's have a look at you. Everybody on deck, and your fucking hands had better be empty!"

Two women and four men moved out into the cockpit. He blinked in surprise as her recognized Maureen Mahoney and her maid, Borita. Maureen said, "Don't shoot, Dick!"

And he called back, "What in the hell do you think you're doing up here, doll?"

She called back, "Following you, of course. You wouldn't take me with you, but my father is still missing and I won't take no for an answer."

He muttered, "Oh, for Chrisake." Then he yelled, "Okay, we're shading back there on that island. Follow me and we'll chat about it out of this damned sun."

Both crafts weighed anchor and as Maureen's craft followed his they met the confused Lieutenant Sousa, just getting under way. Captain Gringo called, "It's okay, she's with me. We'll sort it out ashore."

All three vessels ran their bows up on the soft mud and everyone piled out to move into the trees. A quick check showed the island was deserted and it was a good ten degrees cooler in the leafy shade. Captain Gringo sat Maureen on a fallen log as Borita stood behind her, looking like butter wouldn't melt in her mouth. He put a boot up on the log and said, "Okay, give. Who are those guys with you and how many guns have you between you?"

Maureen smoothed her wilted whipcord skirts, took off her pith helmet, and wiped her flushed face with her kerchief before she said, "I chartered the cruiser from Brazilian friends in Manaus, of course. The crew came with it. They are simple sailors, not desperados. That's why my pilot didn't want to stop until I made him. We have four shotguns and two rifles on board. I of course have this."

She raised her skirt to reveal a familiar nickel plated Virtue in the holster strapped to her laced boot. He shook his head in wonder and said, "Great. You were headed into uncharted wilds with common seamen and a whore pistol. It's no wonder your dad got lost up there if his daughter takes after him."

She smiled and said, "I intended to overtake and join you once we were too far from Manaus for you to send us back."

"Honey, we'll *never* be that far from Manaus! Trip's over. When it cools off a bit my men and me are going on and

128

you kiddies are going back to Manaus. Like the Injun said, I have spoken."

"Dick, that's not fair. You can see I have my own boat and crew, so I'd hardly be a burden to you."

He shook his head and said, "I'm not supposed to tell you about the job I've taken on, but I'll tell you this. We're not hunting for lost explorers or ancient ruins. We're hunting men, a lot of men, and the last thing I need in a guerrilla war is a boatload of tourists to worry about."

"I promise we'll keep out of your way," she insisted as, behind her, Borita sent him smoke signals with her smouldering Indian eyes. He wanted some more of what she was offering, too. He could see down the front of the redhead's khaki shirt and he wanted some of that, too. War sure was hell. He shook his head and told them, "You're already in the way. Make yourselves comfy and figure on heading home when we're ready to leave. I have to get back to work."

He left them there and found Sousa, explaining, "The guys were pretty lousy when we hit those highjackers down the river. If there'd been more of them and they'd known their asses from their elbows we'd have been in a peck of trouble. Before we get to the major leagues I think we'd better pound some basics into them. Do you like to give close order drill?"

"Nobody *likes* to give close order drill, but I know how, naturally."

"Good, we'll divide 'em into three watches. One bunch stays on guard. You teach your watch to stomp and salute. I'll give a quick course in basic infantry tactics to mine. Then we'll switch around each time we stop."

"I see the value of lecturing them," Sousa said, "but what's the point of drilling them? We're not likely to ever be on parade with this bunch."

"There's method in my chicken shit. Nobody ever uses close order drill in combat, but it does get them used to moving fast, without discussing it, when an officer snaps an order at them. There's another reason. Recruits hate drill and don't see why they have to do it, but it makes them feel like soldiers. We've got to convince these ragamuffins that they're no longer a street gang but an infantry platoon."

"Don't you mean Marines?"

"Whatever, just so they shape up a bit. That Black guy, Thomé, is bright and eager. You know your people. Do you think they'd be steamed if I made him a squad leader?"

"Probably. But with only eighteen men, you and I can form two squads and lead them ourselves, no?"

"What if one of us is hit? Who'll take over?"

Sousa shrugged and said, "What does it matter, if we're not here? They'll probably just run."

"Yeah, and get slaughtered. On the other hand, if we start them bickering about their complexions and who gets to be teacher's pet we could have some troubles with them while we were still alive. Two squads it'll have to be for now. On the river at least. I want to mix the training details up so they get used to taking commands from the both of us."

Sousa nodded and said, "I like your plan. What about those people from the other boat?"

"I just told them they couldn't come along."

"What if they follow us anyway?"

Captain Gringo frowned and said, "I wish you hadn't asked that. I'm hoping they haven't figured out that I can't shoot them to save their dumb necks. We'll cross that bridge when we get to it. Let's worry about our own necks, right now."

He called Bos'n Durand over and told him to divide the men into three details. A few minutes later he led his own half dozen off to a clearing and sat them on the sand to listen up.

He hooked his left rump over a stump in the shady glade. "You bastards were terrible in that first fight. Starting alphabetically, you bunched. It's the most common mistake green troops make. Honest, guys, you can't avoid a bullet by standing closer to your buddies. But a clump of men draws more fire than one guy alone. When you move in, spread out—the enemy has to make a choice of targets, so the odds against any one man being his first one are pretty good. Even a rattled rifleman fires first into a clump of targets. So, Jesus, do I have to draw you a picture?"

One of the men protested, "I stayed close to you because you were our leader, Captain Gringo."

The tall American nodded and said, "I noticed. Don't do that no more, Oswaldo. You, Nilo, you were right in Oswaldo's hip pocket when we charged in. One bullet could have bought the farm for all three of us. Besides that, neither of you could shoot with me out in front of you, so what the fuck good were you? When I order a line of skirmish I expect a line, God damn your eyes! No man should ever be close enough to a comrade in a gun fight to be hit by the same burst. Next time, I want you at least two full paces apart, pointing your guns at the other guys, not each other's asses."

They exchanged worried glances. He knew how they felt. He'd been there. He said, "Look, battle tactics are designed to knock-off people doing what comes naturally. An old soldier never dies because he never does what his natural instincts tell him to do. Let me give you another example. They may have some field guns up the river where we're going. Let's say we're moving in line through heavy cover and a shell slams down near you. What's the first natural thing to do?"

A man called Rosas raised a hand and said, "You fall flat and try for to crawl away, no?"

"No. That's what the gunners ranging on you are expecting you to do! The usual pattern is to lay a line of shells to stop an advance. Then they elevate and drop others behind you so you can walk or run right into them. It sounds dumb, but the military cliche is always: when in doubt, advance on the guns. Move toward the sound of the enemy cannon. Sounds crazy? Think. The other side will have at least a few scouts out between his big stuff and you. He won't want to drop shells on his own and you face an even fight with his riflemen when you meet them. He can't hear you. You can hear him, so guess who has the better idea where the likely line is? I just told you what happens if you move the other way. Is it starting to make a little sense?"

131

A few men nodded. Most looked pretty bewildered. Commodore Barboza sure had picked him some great recruits, the son-of-a-bitch. Captain Gringo said, "It gets worse. You have to trust your officers. Sometimes they turn out to be assholes. That's tough, but there's nothing any old soldier can do about it. Two out of three leaders know what they're doing. So when you hear an order you don't understand, just do it. The officer almost certainly knows more than you do about battle tactics and, as you see, they're sort of tricky. Men in battle are ordered to make unusual moves because if they make usual moves they get *killed* a lot! Your leader's job is to mix up the other side's leader. There's no time for a bull session in a fire fight, so, even if you think you've got a better idea, keep it to yourself and just do as you're told." He pointed at a pale mestizo and said, "You, Salvador, what you do if the guy next to you get's hit?"

"I stop and see if I can save him, no?"

"Wrong. You keep going. We worry about our dead and wounded when the fight is over. It sounds cruel. It is. It's a cruel business, but it's simple math. If one guy stops to help a wounded buddy the enemy has put two men out of action with one bullet. We don't have the numbers to spare. I'll promise, now, never to leave a wounded man behind if we have to pull back. But that's the best you can hope for. Nobody, repeat, *nobody* falls out of line for any reason unless Lieutenant Sousa or myself tells him to. If you see your mother on the ground with a bullet in her, leave her there and let *us* worry about her! Let's talk about markmanship. They told me all you guys knew how to handle your guns and that some of you are supposed to be good shots. We don't have the ammo to spare on target practice, so I'll just have to hope and pray a lot. If you're average, half of you can hit the broad side of a barn and the other half couldn't if they were inside it. You may have done some hunting. It ain't the same. I noticed the way some of you held your guns back there at the fazenda. It was pitiful."

Captain Gringo got off the stump and borrowed a rifle. He braced the action against his right hip and held the muzzle out at waist level with his stiff left arm. He said, "This is the standard combat position, with or without bayonet, which you don't have to worry about. Watch as I advance on that palmetto over there."

He walked toward the tree, calling out, "See how the muzzle moves with my line of sight? Never swivel your neck around like this when you're on a skirmish line. Turn your whole trunk in line with your head and the muzzle will be looking the same way you are. You spot something, you just have to pull the trigger. Swing a rifle at a guy and the son-of-a-bitch will duck every time. Sometimes he might think he's hidden from you if you don't give the show away by gawking at him. Never stop to take aim if you spot a guy behind a bush. He'll know he's spotted and pot a stationary target. Just keep walking and fire from the hip. Then fire some more as you move in. When in doubt, fire *low*. A bullet over a guy's head doesn't rattle him much. A low round spattering him with crud can put him off his feed, even if you miss. If you're the one taking cover, remember to roll aside the moment you fire at anybody. Don't be there anymore if you miss and he fires at your muzzle flash. Don't wait to *see* if you missed or not. Take your second look from other cover. You'll find it a lot easier on your body if the bullets go somewhere you ain't."

He twirled the rifle in a Queen's salute as he gounded it, letting them see he knew the fancy shit, too. He handed it back to its owner and said, "Lieutenant Sousa will show you that sort of stuff. Any questions about tactics?"

Oswaldo said, "I have always sighted along my barrel when I shot at something. I don't think I know how to aim from the hip, my Captain."

The tall American nodded and said, "You can't. I shoot as close as possible on the rifle range and they gave me a medal one time to prove it. Nobody can hope to hit a bullseye firing off hand. But in a battle you don't shoot at bulls. The idea's not to put a round between the bastard's eyes. The idea is to hit him some damned place, or come close enough so that he's too rattled to hit *you!* It's surprising how the muzzle lines up if you just point the damned thing like a stick at somebody. Most men fire high, so think low. Your target is

133

the guy's crotch. I told you it was a cruel business. You'll probably miss his balls a foot either way. But a man's crotch is exactly half his height from the ground, so if you aim there, the odds on hitting him some damned place go up. Most shots aimed at a man's heart go over his head. You can imagine what happens if you aim at his head. He won't even know you're shooting at him nine times out of ten."

He saw some nodding. Some of it was getting through. One man hesitated, raised his hand, and asked, "What if the guys on the other side have heard all these things, Captain Gringo?"

The tall American said, "Some of them must have. There's a navy officer in charge of them. Most of 'em will be banditos, not used to taking orders. That's why we're trying to pound it into you that we have to think and act like soldiers. One trained man is worth at least three in a fire fight."

"But, my Captain, the flagelado leader, Andrada, has many men and they have tough reputations, trained or not."

Captain Gringo nodded and said, "Sorry, guys, but here comes the history lesson anyway. The ancient Greeks had a tough rep. They'd kicked the shit out of everyone from the Trojans to the Persians. They ran around in fireman's hats and fig leaves, scaring everybody until they ran into the Roman Legion. The Greek hoplites were aristocratic warriors, trained from the cradle up in razzle-dazzle sword play. You couldn't join their army unless you were built like a marble statue. The Romans drafted farm boys and street sweepers. They recruited unwashed Germans and Slavs. They didn't give a shit who you were as long as you could carry your pack and take orders without staging a debate like the heroic Greeks. So the two sides met. The Romans kicked the shit out of all those beautiful athletes in a series of dull, set-piece, slugging matches. They never had clever ideas like the Trojan Horse. They just bulled into anybody they met and stabbed and slashed by rote until their commanders ordered them to stop. The Greeks were brave and tough. The Romans were *soldiers*. Put your money on the soldiers every time."

He took out his watch and said, "History lesson's over.

134

On your feet and line up. We're going to form a skirmish line and move against those gumbo limbo trees over there. I want those rifles on your hips and, so help me, if you bunch up again you can give your souls to Jesus, for your asses will be kicked by me!"

They left the little island about three-thirty. It was still hot as hell but at least endurable under the canvas awnings. Lieutenant Sousa resumed the lead with Captain Gringo covering his stern again. The crazy lady in the cruiser followed them at hailing distance, but Captain Gringo didn't yell at Maureen. He didn't want to let his men get the idea there was anyone around who didn't have to obey his commands, and he knew Maureen would tag along if he shouted himself blue in the face.

He didn't know what she was up to. He still didn't buy that wild story about a long-lost explorer, captive of some primitive tribe or maybe distributed in little morsels among the army ants. He'd checked her cruiser out. She'd been telling the truth about her arms, or, rather, the lack of them. Some of his guys had been talking to Maureen's crew. They seemed indeed to be the hired hands of a rubber baron who must have liked the redhead a lot. Maybe little Borita would tell him more about that if he could get her alone. The idea of getting Borita alone gave him other ideas. But where could he be alone with the Indian girl? Maureen would have a fit if she caught them tearing off a piece, or . . . would she?

Captain Gringo grinned to himself as he began to see a way to get rid of the pestiferous, determined redhead. Her Brazilian boyfriend wasn't going to like it, either.

They steamed through the long, hot afternoon to sundown, and kept going. The Negro was beginning to narrow, which wasn't saying much. You could see the shore lines, now, but they were still on a river that made the mighty Mississippi look like a trout stream. They encountered fewer boats and saw many more islands by nightfall. Again they steamed among the stars a while before the moon rose. The

135

stars had company. Fireflies. Millions of fireflies. Some hovered over the water and the fish were going wild. Others clung to the brush of passing islands and pretended to be Christmas tree lights. In some stretches the whole bank seemed to flash on and off in unison, illuminating the shoreline for as much as a mile in flashing pale green light. The moon rose, adding to the fairy land quality of the night with its big orange pumpkin smile. Once in a while something whined in his ear and a couple of times he had to slap a mosquito who seemed ignorant of the fact it wasn't supposed to be on the Negro. But as it began to cool it seemed romantic as hell. He wished he were aboard a big paddle wheeler, watching all this from a dark stateroom with some lady who liked poetry. Heading into a battle against unknown odds, against an enemy he wasn't too clear about, put a damper on the pretty scenery.

He'd been reading the books he'd bought in Manaus during the lazier day-time hours on the river. Brazilian politics made even less sense once you tried to take them seriously. He couldn't figure out what the outlawed navy officer up the river was fighting for. Commander Fonseca was a member of the Paulist Party. The rough interior frontier types. The big mutiny everyone was talking about had taken place a couple of years ago. They'd rebelled against the previous administration under President Peixoto.

That seemed reasonable. Marshal Floriano Peixoto had been a military dictator who'd sort of grabbed his office informally while the guys who'd thrown the Emperor Dom Pedro out were still working on a constitution.

Fonseca and other officers, who must have thought they'd make better military dictators, had risen against Peixoto, and the civil war had lasted a year or so. As the rebels were losing, another clique, led by the Paulist Party, tossed Peixoto out and put the present President Barros in the cat bird seat.

So here they were, steaming into unexplored territory to wipe out a Paulist Party rebel, for the Paulist Party. It seemed pretty Alice in Wonderland, even for Latin America.

Captain Gringo was used to weird political views. In Nicaragua the rebels had called themselves the Conservatives and the dictatorship in power called itself the Liberal Party. The Mexican dictator who'd helped launch Captain Gringo's career as a soldier of fortune kept insisting he was going to give the people of Mexico a true democracy if he had to bust their dusty asses.

He didn't like Commodore Barboza's explanation, much. He doubted that the rebel leader, Fonseca, wanted to take the time to explain his odd position, either. If only they didn't have Gaston as a hostage the best bet would be to skip the whole mess. But they did have Gaston. He'd have to think some more about it. Meanwhile they had a few more days before he had to make any hard choices.

He stretched out and caught a few winks, lulled by the throbbing engine as others did the same. A man slept efficiently on a bed of duckboards. As soon as your body was half-way rested, they woke you up.

He hauled himself up beside the Maxim and dipped a hand in the river to rinse his face. As he withdrew his hand, something snapped in the water where it had just been. That did more to make him fully alert than the water on his face. He ran a thumbnail along his jaw line. Now he really needed a shave or a violin. A bath would have helped, too. A change of clothes was too much to even dream about.

The moon was sinking again; it was later than he'd thought. He lit a smoke, belly-growling with hunger, as they passed another island outlined by fireflies. He ordered Thomé to give them more speed and as they overtook Sousa he called out, "We'll put in over there. We've got to give the guys some warm cooked food and a chance to wash up."

So they nudged into shore. When he looked downstream he saw Maureen's cruiser doing the same. She landed about three hundred yards down.

Captain Gringo leaped ashore, rifle in hand, and when Sousa joined him, he said, "It seems clear of trees up at this end. It's cool enough to build a fire. Detail some guys to build a second one and heat up some water. There's soap among the supplies and I want everyone to scrub off their crud before we all come down with tropical crotch. I'll scout downstream and make sure we have it to ourselves."

"Aren't you going to take a patrol with you?"

"No, it's a small island and the guys are pretty useless even in broad daylight. Those others landed well down. If anybody was planning an ambush we should have heard about it by now."

As the others got to work Captain Gringo moved into the trees. The low moon's slanting rays gave him a good view between the trunks holding the solid canopy overhead. The forest floor was bare clean sand, for the island lay low and a recent flood had scoured it. That meant no snakes. Probably no army ants, either. The branches overhead twinkled as the fireflies winked on and off at him. He scouted down the south-west shore and swung around to approach his and Maureen's boats from downstream. As he spotted a distant fire through the trees a voice called out, "Who's there? I warn you, I have a gun!"

He grounded his rifle and growled, "For God's sake, Maureen, would a river pirate or wild Indian understand English?"

She moved into sight, her khaki a pale blue against the darkness as she said, "Oh, is that you, Dick? I was going up to your camp when I heard you. What are you doing down at this end of the island?"

"Looking for spooks. Where are your friends?"

"Aboard my cruiser, of course. I told them to wait for me there while I tried to make you see reason."

He moved closer, leaned the rifle against a tree, and said, "Well, as long as you're here." Then he took her in his arms and kissed her.

She stiffened in surprise, then she loosened up and responded as he held her tight, putting some heart into his effort as well as his tongue.

When they came up for air, she gasped and said, "My, that was a surprise. Does this mean we can go up the river with you?"

He made his voice deliberately brutal as he replied, "Don't know. Let's see how you fuck, first."

Naturally, he expected her to run like hell. She didn't but sighed and said, "Oh, all right, but I wish you'd wash off a bit, first. You smell sort of gamey, Dick."

"I need a shave, too. But that's the way I come. Take it or leave it."

"Are you always this romantic? What are you doing with that hand and, *stop* it, you're popping my shirt buttons!"

He pulled her down to the sand with him, putting a hand inside her shirt to roll her turgid nipple like a ball of gum rubber between his thumb and fingers as he kissed her roughly again. He really wanted her, now. But he was still trying to scare her off with his deliberately rough foreplay. It didn't work. She moaned softly and said, "I said you *could*, but can't we move farther into the jungle? What if someone *sees* us?"

"They'll think we're friends." He grinned and pulled her skirt up. She tried to cross her thighs as he slid his hand between them. Then, as he discovered she wasn't wearing pantaloons, she went limp and said, "Please be gentle, I haven't done this for some time."

He wasn't. He ripped off his gunbelt and unbuttoned everything to mount her with no further ceremony. Her hips were planted firmly against the sand under the tail of her skirt as he guided his erection into her unseen red thatch. She gasped as he drove it to the hilt with a jar as she spread her white thighs in the dappled moonlight. Then she wrapped herself around him and met his rough and ready lovemaking with passion to match it. He climaxed and kept going, working on her remaining buttons with his free hand as she giggled and said, "Oh, I felt that! I think I'm almost there, too!" Then, as he exposed her naked torso to his own she dug her nails into his bounding buttocks and crooned in mindless ecstacy. This was great, but it wasn't working out the way he'd planned at all! She *liked* it rough and ready! What was he supposed to do, now?

This was obviously not the way one got rid of the

stubborn redhead, but it sure was fun. He kept hammering her as she climaxed and she sobbed, "Stop, let me catch my breath. You have me too excited and . . . oh, never mind, don't stop. Don't ever stop, it's happening again!"

He came with her. Now it was his turn to beg for mercy as she kept moving and growled, "I think you've created a monster, darling. My God, you're even better than Borita said you were!"

That acted as a dash of cold water. He stiffened, still in her, and said, "Oh? I thought some secrets were safe."

Maureen moved her hips teasingly as she giggled and said, "I can be very motherly when I find a young girl crying in her pillow. That *was* you she spent the night with, wasn't it?"

He sighed and said, "I cannot tell a lie. I did it with my little hatchet."

"That's hardly a *little* hatchet, you brute. You're really an awful person, you know." Then she raised her knees to take him deeper as she added, "I'm so glad." So he started pounding her again. He'd cross Borita's bridge when he came to it. Her employer obviously didn't mind. He hadn't expected this snooty-looking redhead to be such a salty broad. But that was one of the reasons he found women interesting. A guy just never knew. One dame would swap dirty stories with the boys and then go all fluttery and faint when you got her alone. The quiet shy looking gals more often turned out to be the man-eaters. Maybe thinking a lot about sex was what made them blush so easily.

Maureen suggested more privacy. He couldn't think why, but he helped her to her feet and, carrying their clothes, they walked hand in hand deeper into the trees. She picked out a glade she liked and spread her skirt on the sand, removing her open shirt to use as a pillow. He asked where her hat was and she replied, "Who cares? Take everything off, darling. It's barbarous to make love half-dressed, like the working classes."

He could see her better, now, and the view was fantastic as she stood there naked save for her high laced boots. A firefly landed in her hair to wink on and off and since green

140

meant go, he finished stripping and they lay down together on her improvised bed. As he entered her hospitable flesh again she said, "We really have to consider more comfortable quarters for this, dear. I have a shower as well as a private room aboard my cruiser."

He said, "I have to keep an eye on my men, and besides, what will Borita think about this?"

"Pooh, who cares what she thinks? She works for me. Besides, I don't think she's jealous."

"I see you're not."

Maureen giggled and replied, "I know I'm prettier. Am I as good a lay?"

He answered by thrusting deeper as he tried to decide. She responded, but insisted, "Well?"

He said, "It's a tough question, as long as we're being truthful. You never learned to screw like this from one husband, so you probably know how it is. Whoever you're doing it with always seems the best in the world at the time."

She moved her hips judiciously and mused, "You're right. I must have done this with someone as good, once or twice, but right now it does feel as if you were tailor-made for me. I wouldn't want it an inch longer and I certainly wouldn't want it shorter."

"Jesus, do we have to be so clinical, doll? Why can't we just enjoy it? Tonight we're the only two people on Earth and this would be perfect if you didn't keep reminding me of other people."

"Oh, my, are you one of those possessive types? Your approach was pretty crude if you took me for a virgin."

"Hey, neither one of us just hatched out of an egg. But I've got a vivid imagination and it's sort of depressing to see you doing this with other guys."

She playfully clawed his spine with her nails as she said, conversationally, "A lot of men are like that. You all want an experienced virgin, preferably oversexed."

He grinned sheepishly and said, "Well, two out of three ain't bad. Do you want to talk or do you want to come?"

"Both. Now that we're getting used to each other's

bodies. My husband and I used to have quite nice chats while . . . Oh, sorry. I'll behave. It's funny, though, I don't mind picturing you like this with my serving wench. The idea is rather piquant, when I think of the contrasting complexions. I wonder if she'd let me watch."

"Good grief, would you want to?"

"It might be fun. We could have a party and settle once and for all which of us you thought was best."

"What if I couldn't decide?"

"We'd just have to keep going, wouldn't we? I'll ask her, later. She's a little old-fashioned, but she might go along with the idea."

He frowned and tried to ignore her prattle as he rutted, trying to fire his load again. But although she still had him excited enough to maintain his erection, the weird conversation distracted him. He could see, now, that Maureen thought no more of casual sex than many a man. So he didn't have to feel guilty about his foiled plot to scare her off and he didn't really owe her, if only he could figure out how to *ditch* her! He thought about the wild night he'd spent with little Borita and couldn't for the life of him figure out how Maureen had gotten the idea Borita was more sedate than she was. Neither of them seemed to know how to say no to anything. They compared notes, too. Women could be as bad about kissing and telling as men. But that could mean Borita knew who Maureen had literally screwed out of her cruiser. A man was a man, but if Borita could identify some politico Sousa might know about, he'd get some answers to play with.

He started to climax again and Maureen, feeling his renewed passion, began to respond in kind, locking her booted ankles over his rump. The butt of the holstered pistol strapped to her ankle felt cold under his tail bone. She knew where it was and started to tease him by running it up and down the groove between his cheeks as he let himself go. He knew she was using him, too, and it felt good to pound her as a beautiful plaything until he once more exploded inside her.

She came with him, or said she had. As they paused to sit up and share a cigar she sighed and said, "I like uncomplicated sex, don't you?"

"It sure beats pissing."

"Don't be vulgar. I only like dirty talk when I'm doing it. Why did you rape me, Dick? Not that I have any complaints, but I'd like to know."

He took a drag of smoke, handed the claro to her, and said, "I wasn't trying to rape you. I was trying to scare you."

"Oh, that's what I thought. I was planning a more seemly seduction aboard my cruiser. That stubble on your chin is sort of exciting, in a cave man way, and there's a lot to be said for body odor when one is feeling earthy. But I don't think I'd like to really have an orgy with you before we've had a chance to shower together."

"What we had wasn't an orgy?"

"Silly, we've barely scratched the surface. Once the ice is broken I'd like to get more, oh, intimate."

He didn't ask what she meant. Life sure was full of surprises, lately. He knew she must be enjoying him as well, even though he suspected she'd have laid the Hunchback of Notre Dame if it meant coming along on the expedition.

She handed him back the cigar, exhaling sensuously through her nose. She was ravishing in the dim light, but she was all moonlight and shadow. He couldn't wait to see her in full color. If that dark V between her trim thighs was as red as her other hair and if, Sweet Jesus, he could get the tawny Borita in the same bunk with her . . .

Maureen apparently numbered mind reading among her other skills. She placed a hand in his lap and said, "I'll have to approach my little Indian delicately, but I think she'll go along with it. It's not as if you and she are strangers, after all. We could have a lot of fun going up the river with you. We *are* going up the river with you, aren't we, Dick Dear?"

He took a drag on the cigar and said, "Maybe. We're going to have to play this very cool, Maureen. Borita might not be the only one who's inclined to be jealous.

"Doesn't rank have it's privileges, dear?"

"That's what Captain Bligh thought. Men don't mind sharing privations. But they can get to muttering pretty good about somebody keeping all the goodies for himself."

She grimaced and said, "Well, fun is fun, but I don't really think I'd like to service your whole crew, even if they were all white. But we can be *discreet,* can't we?"

He handed her the cigar to shut her up. Who was shitting whom around here? He'd already figured out how he'd work it. She was going to be sore as hell, but she was too pretty to die, no matter what the hell she was up to, and Borita would be in danger, too, if he took them all the way along.

He said, "I'd better get back to my bunch before someone comes looking for me." She nodded and conceded, "I'm looking forward to the next time we stop."

He was, too. He figured he wouldn't have a chance to ditch them for a few more days and if his back held out he had to keep her from catching on that she hadn't conned him. It figured to be more fun than chess, but winning would be more important for all concerned. When you lose at chess you could simply clear the board and start all over. This game was for keeps.

They got an early start the next morning. The river was still one hell of a stream but it was running darker and narrower now. They encountered more islands, if you wanted to call them islands, as they steamed up the Negro. It was as easy to say the Negro was braiding into multiple channels. Some were smaller and shallower than others and Lieutenant Sousa spent more time consulting his map. The upper river wasn't mapped too well, or the islands, sandbars or whatever shifted every rainy season, or both. There were still other vessels on the river, albeit fewer big ones. There were still some villages and trading posts ahead before they reached totally untamed wilderness, but the few they passed were widely spaced and the main channel wasn't marked. Sousa wanted to put in at a landing and ask the natives some questions about what lay ahead. Captain Gringo vetoed the idea for now. The fewer people they talked to the better. He and his followers knew where the river was. He didn't want the people of the river chatting about the three strange boats steaming past any more than he could help it.

He could see they'd have to consider changing their routine as the channel got trickier. He'd favored traveling mostly at night because most traffic moved up and downstream during the daylight hours. The few they passed in the night could only report three dark blurs to anybody they ran into. Night running also avoided the afternoon heat. But they were too far from civilization, now, to risk running aground in the dark. There were fewer strange vessels to avoid, and by hugging the sunward banks they could stay in the shade of the huge trees leaning out over the water. Sousa, as a navy man and occasional river pilot, knew enough to swing wide of bends that were convex and hug the shore in the deeper waters of the concave bends. They'd both agreed that if the antique boilers seriously intended to explode they'd have done so by now. Sousa ordered more steam and they started bucking the current at increased speed. Captain Gringo glanced back each time they rounded a bend to see if Maureen's cruiser was able to keep up. It was, damn it. The newer and more luxurious craft had a good engine and a shallower draft than he'd expected when they barely made it over a shallow stretch and he grinned in expectation, only to see Maureen's tagalong vessel glide its flat bottom over it with no trouble.

He mulled over his devious designs as they passed a sunny mud bank covered with basking caymans. One of his river rats commented that you seldom met piranha where the big reptiles ruled the banks. That was just swell. The caymans ate the piranha, but who the hell ate the caymans? He had to make sure that Maureen and her servants had a safe drift down the river when he got a chance to put them out of business.

The day was not without interest if one liked to look at flora and fauna while taking a steam bath. But it was still one long hot day. Captain Gringo finished the books he'd brought along and as he tossed the last one overboard, something big pulled it under with a silent swirl in the inky surface. He grimaced and lit another smoke. He hadn't been planning on a swim anyway. He'd been puzzled when someone had told him few of the river people knew how to swim, despite spending most of their lives on the water. The reason was becoming obvious. As he'd seen when he shot that cayman after Borita, it wasn't really safe to swim right off the docks of Manaus. Up here in the *wilder* country nobody would last long enough in the river to *learn* to swim. When people fell overboard, up here, something ate them before they could drown, so what the hell.

A million years later the sun was low above the west bank and the river ran blood red. Sousa signaled back and Captain Gringo pulled around the supply canoes and moved up to shout, "Yeah, we'd better start thinking of a place to tie up. See if we can make a few more kilometers before the light fails, but keep your eye out for an island with high banks. I don't want anyone waking up with a cayman in bed with them!"

Sousa agreed and Captain Gringo dropped back to let him lead. They came to a fork where the water on either side could just as well be the main channel. Sousa picked the left one to have more light. But long before the sky grew really dark, they found themselves in a dark tunnel of branches meeting overhead as the channel rapidly narrowed. Sousa hove to. When the American rejoined him, Sousa shouted across, "We're up a blind alley. This is an old oxbow cut off. The passage ahead is blocked by floating timber and slit."

Captain Gringo wondered what else was new. He said, "It'll be buggy in here, too. Let's move back to open water and tie up near the point. The banks are high and the ground looks solid."

"It's not an island, is it?"

"No. But we're *almost* surrounded by water. What do you want, an egg in your cerveza?"

There was no current, once they'd shut their throttles. Captain Gringo ordered dead slow and took the lead going back the way they'd come. He met Maureen's boat coming up the false channel. The redhead was up on the flying bridge, conning her pilot from her better visual position. She waved and he waved back, shouting, "Dead end. We're camping down on the point."

Maureen called something down to her pilot and the cruiser turned to lead by a cable length. She sure was a pushy dame, considering she hadn't been invited to this party.

As Maureen dropped anchor near the point, Captain Gringo spotted the smoke of something bigger than usual moving up the other true channel. It was nice to see somebody knew the way up here. He was just as happy, now, that they'd moved into the cutoff. The other steamboat's crew wouldn't mention them when they got wherever they were headed, further up the Negro. If the map meant anything, there were only a couple of trading posts left between them and the outlaw-rebel empire of Fonseca and Andrada.

When all three vessels had nosed in and the cargo canoes were secured Captain Gringo led a shore patrol to make sure of the landing site. He'd been right about the soil between the massive trees being high and reasonably dry. There was a paper thin layer of black leaf mold that felt underfoot like vomited banana skins, but it was easy to scuff it away to expose the clean red sandy loam. He found a narrow neck where a couple of posted guards could see the water on both sides. He went back and told the others to set up. He chose a guard detail and as long as they had to do it, he decided to teach 'em to do it right. A regulation guard mount was pretty chicken, especially when the men you drilled were ragged guerrillas, but, like the other seemingly pointless drill, it had a psychology behind it. A man posted formally on guard felt more like a guard than if you just told him, off hand, to go over there and sit on a log for Chrissake.

He and Sousa were never going to make real soldiers out of these river rats, but he noticed there was a slight trace of military bearing as they went about their chores. The Bos'n, Durand, detailed some men to gather wood and tend the fire in a surprisingly military tone and, more important, they just did what he told them to, without the former slack-jawed, hang-dog attitude.

Captain Gringo took advantage of the remaining light to take aside a few men who hadn't heard his lecture yet, as

147

Sousa gathered a small group and drilled the hell out of them with their rifles on their shoulders. When supper was ready and all joined in around the fire, the men were joking and seemed more confident. He noticed the four crewmen from Maureen's boat had wandered over to join his men. Captain Gringo asked them where the girls were and one said, "La Senhora and her maid said they would eat aboard, but she told us to take the break and stretch the legs. La Senhora's cabin is large enough for four people, but the crew's compartment in the bow leaves much to be desired. They built the bunks for us with dwarves in mind, I think."

Captain Gringo nodded soberly and said, "You're welcome to spread your bedding out here with us. I see you left your guns on board the cruiser."

"Do you think we may need our guns, Captain?"

"I doubt it. Nobody seems to live around here and we have the point well guarded in any case. Help yourselves to some coffee and beans."

He ate a pan himself and washed it down with three cups of coffee—strong coffee. Then he eased away from the fire, moved down to the supply dugouts, and broke open a case of "medical supplies." Sousa had told him the Brazilian Navy felt rum would cure most anything, so he helped himself to a couple of pints.

Maureen Mahoney was waiting for him on a cushioned bench in her cruiser's cockpit. She had on a green silk kimono, but she hadn't bothered to close it, so her own cockpit was exposed as she rose to greet him. In the light from the open hatchway he saw her hair was indeed red all over.

As he climbed aboard with a bottle in both hands she plastered herself against him to kiss him and say, "I thought you'd take a hint when I sent my men away for the night. I see you brought refreshments, too."

"You said you wanted to have a party."

She laughed and said, "I've been looking forward to it all day. I somehow feel you must have been, too. Is that a gun in your pocket or are you glad to see me?"

He laughed. It was an old joke, but she pumped her pelvis against the bulge teasingly as she said it. His real gun, of course, was on his hip.

She led him inside, saying in a less teasing tone, "I'm afraid we'll have to start without poor little Borita. It seems she's shy."

They were in the main salon; Borita sat in a corner, looking down at the deck stubbornly. He said, "Evening, Borita." The Indian girl didn't look up as she blushed.

Maureen led him on to her smaller, private cabin. He could see she was smiling rather smugly. He could see everything, many many times. The cabin walls were covered with mirrors. He felt like blushing himself. He sure looked silly standing there with a silly smirk and a bottle in each hand, over and over again. He hadn't noticed the grass stains on the seat of his pants before. He looked sort of like a stranger to himself in profile, too. He said, "Well, we know you're not a vampire."

Maureen didn't get it, but she smiled anyway as she let her open kimono slide off her shoulders and crumple to the rug around her bare feet. She turned to face him in the lamplight to ask, "How do you like it so far?"

He looked beyond her, far indeed, as he stared at the hundreds of naked redheads fading off into the distance. They all looked great, frontways, sideways, or from the rear. Maureen's creamy white skin was stretched without blemish over her junoesque curves. He saw she'd henna stained her perky nipples to match her red hair exactly. He put the bottles down and started to unbutton his shirt as he said, "I like all of you." She lay down on the pale green satin sheets of her built-in bed as a hundred other redheads did the same.

He could see why Borita had found the idea too rich for her blood. He knew he was just as raunchy as the little Indian girl, but it made him feel silly as he watched all of himselves undress. He considered asking her to turn out the light, but he didn't want her to think he was a sissy and in truth, the idea was sort of interesting.

It got more interesting as he stepped over to the bed. Maureen sat up to grasp his erection and kiss it. As he watched her do it from every angle it stood straighter to attention. He shook his head, rolled her on her back, and mounted her with no further foreplay as, all around him, a lot of other people seemed to be doing the same thing. He laughed, hooked one of her knees over each of his elbows, and proceeded to enjoy the view as well as her sensuous body. He was too polite to ask if the mirrors had been her idea, but whoever owned this tub had a great imagination.

Safe in her own quarters, Maureen made love with more noise as well as passion. He suspected she was showing off as she began to sob and moan. There was only a thin plywood door between them and her servant girl in the other compartment. That made him feel silly, too. He knew Borita knew how big he was and it seemed sort of dumb for Maureen to keep yelling about the way he filled her love muscles.

She had him almost there when she said, "I want to see, too. Let's do it like the doggies do."

He said, "Anything to oblige a lady," as he helped her roll over onto her hands and knees. As he remounted her from the rear with a palm on each white hemisphere Maureen raised her head to stare into the mirrors with a roguish grin and marvel, "Oh, my, we look just like dirty French postcards. A *lot* of dirty French postcards!"

He had to agree she had a point. But the sideshow was distracting so he closed his eyes and started humping harder as she gasped and groaned for more. He exploded in her and she pleaded, "Don't stop! For Christ's sake don't leave me hanging!" So he kept moving as well as he was able. He opened his eyes for inspiration—it worked. The shock of all those other naked bodies rutting hard and dirty was sort of exciting, albeit hardly very romantic. Like most men, Captain Gringo imagined his sex wild, and liked it sweet and soft when he was getting it. Maureen was beautiful, and Gringo knew she screwed like a mink, but he felt like a schoolboy in a whorehouse and something was missing.

But he'd come for more than sex, so they were going at it hot and heavy when the door suddenly opened and Borita came in, stark naked and brown as a berry to sob, "I can't stand it. I want for him to do it to *me* again, too!"

Maureen patted the sheets and said, "Join the party, then, you silly child. Why are you stopping, Dick? We're all friends here, you bashful thing."

He moved experimentally, not looking at Borita but seeing her from a hundred angles as the trim younger girl climbed on the bed, closer to the headboards, eyes downcast. He started moving in and out of Maureen again as the redhead reached forward to place her white hand on Borita's dark thigh and say, "Move down this way, dear."

"Senhora, I told you I only like for to do things with *men*."

"You don't know what you're missing, then. Are you hot, Borita? I'm almost coming. Let's all come together, eh?"

He didn't believe this. Borita was confused, too, as Maureen pulled her closer, parted her brown thighs, and lowered her red head between them. The Indian girl's eyes met his as she stared wide-eyed over the redhead's creamy spine toward him. Then she hissed and closed her eyes, biting her own lip as Maureen began to tongue her. She pleaded, "Please, this is most embarrassing, Senhora!" as Maureen began to eat her out, wig-wagging her pale rump as the man giving it to her at the other end went a little crazy himself. Borita sobbed and threw her head back to arch her pelvis up to meet her mistress's lesbian advances and when Captain Gringo shot a long side glance at the mirrored wall the view was French postcard indeed. The redhead stiffened and suddenly rolled off and on her side, moaning, "Oh, Jesus, that was wonderful!" as Captain Gringo, on his knees, faced the excited Borita with nothing but his raging erection between them. Borita's eyes were still closed but her thighs were wide open as she fingered herself in confusion. He moved forward, dropped into her love saddle and felt her climaxing as he entered her. She wrapped her arms and legs around him, panting with passion as she had a second and then a third orgasm before he exploded in her darker flesh and collapsed atop her, panting some himself. Beside him, Maureen sat up on one elbow and said, brightly, "My turn."

He laughed and said, "Hey, ladies, have mercy! Let's have a drink and get our second winds before we draw straws or something."

He dismounted and sat up. Borita turned over and began to cry as he reached for the rum. Maureen stroked her tawny little rump and smoothed, "Come on, you know you liked it. Next time you can do me while he screws you, eh?"

"Never!" protested Borita. "I am not that kind of girl."

Captain Gringo wondered what kind of a girl Borita was as he pulled the cork with his teeth and went through the motions of taking a healthy slug. He hadn't known Borita spoke such good English; although, now that he thought about it, she'd have to, if she worked for Maureen. The redhead spoke almost no Portuguese or Spanish. They'd obviously been talking a lot, of late. Maureen was more an anything-for-a-thrill gal than a bi-sexual. The more primitive Borita wasn't as sophisticated, but he could see Maureen had been trying to educate her.

He got between them and passed the bottle, muttering, "Decisions, decisions," as he put an arm around each to wink at himself several hundred fold in the mirrors. Maureen took a man-sized jolt of straight rum and passed the bottle to Borita, saying, "Here, this will loosen you up."

Borita swallowed, giggled, and swallowed some more. Maureen said, "I want to screw some more, Dick." So he rolled aboard and did his best to please her. Borita shot them a jealous look and swallowed some more rum. Maureen didn't miss the dirty look. It was hard to miss anything in a room walled with mirrors. She said, "Wait, I have a cute idea. Get off a minute."

He did. She took the bottle from Borita and said, "Now, you lay across the bed like so, you silly." Then, when she had the little Indian in place she swung her own derriere around so they were head to hips. She told her male lover, "See how it works?" He looked blank and she added, "We're going to play Musical Cunts. Start with me and as soon as I tell you ..." But he nodded and said, "Gotcha," as he placed his hips between her thighs. He lay atop Maureen to kiss her as

152

he ran a hand over the darker curves of their next door neighbor and Maureen said, "Don't kiss me, silly. Kiss *her!*"

He saw what she meant. Borita's little box was right by Maureen's ear. It was a little less fastidious than he preferred, but he had to keep them happy and, more important, drinking. So he took a deep breath, parted Borita's coal black thatch with his fingers and began to French her as he laid Maureen. It felt wildly exciting as well as dirty. Maureen's laugh was dirty as she husked, "Time to change! Time to change!" just as Borita was responding to his oral sex. He moved to his hands and knees and swapped ends to enter Borita right as the redhead grabbed his hair and raised her pelvis to meet his face. It was even better this way. Borita was tighter and Maureen wasn't as salty between her legs. He felt Borita clamping down as she climaxed with her already stimulated vaginal muscles. He tongued Maureen's engorged clit and fingered her as he came in Borita. Maureen came with them, if his fingers were any judge. But then she demanded he change partners again. He did, allowing her to enjoy her afterglow around his shaft as he soothed the excited Borita with gentle kisses. But he called another halt for refreshments and this time as he was so hot and thirsty, it was all he could do not to swallow as he put the bottle to his lips again. The flushed girls shared the bottle, taking deep swallows as Maureen held the little Indian against her and caressed her smaller brown breasts, saying, "There, that was fun, wasn't it?"

Borita suddenly laughed and kissed Maureen full on the mouth as the redhead ran her hands over her. They fell back together, giggling like school girls. The rum was partly the reason. But he could see the notion of forbidden desires had them both excited. They wrestled playfully, Borita saying La Senhora was most naughty as she rolled atop Maureen with her little brown tail up. Captain Gringo stood up, took Borita by the hips, and pulled her on like a sock as she giggled in mock dismay. Maureen laughed, too, as he started to dog her maid. She moved up until her creamy thighs rose to either side of Borita's brunette head. Then she smoothed the Indian girl's long black hair and hugged her to her crotch. Borita started to protest, then giggled, and started moving her tail wildly as she took care of them both. He was getting tired and although the bizarre scene kept him up to snuff, he knew he was starting to show off for those other guys in the mirrors. He wished he had a camera. He knew he wasn't going to believe this night himself, in the cold gray light of dawn.

They took another break. He passed the bottle again, noting it was a third empty, now. He said he had to rest when Maureen suggested something even more outrageous. So the next thing he knew they were going at each other sixty nine. For a shy young thing, Borita converted fast. He stood and stretched. Maureen asked what he was doing and he said, "Got to take a leak," and stepped out of the cabin before Maureen could suggest a dirty place to tinkle.

He did have to go, but that wasn't why he'd ducked out. Stark naked he let himself into the engine room just down the companionway. The damned safety valve was rusted in good, but he put his back into it and it suddenly gave, so he twisted it off. He put the cork he'd palmed in the hole in the boiler. Then he stepped out on deck, took a piss over the rail and dropped the safety valve after it. Nobody ever looked at the safety valve until it acted up. The cork would pop out once they built up a head of steam. The room would fill with vapor and the crew would go nuts looking for the missing valve on the deck. If they noticed the cork at all they'd think it was left over from another party or something. They'd have to kill the flame and let the whole rig cool before they tried to improvise repairs. If they fashioned a plug, the engines would be able to turn over again, just, at dead slow. It wouldn't matter if Maureen insisted on following or not. They wouldn't be able to. She'd be mad as hell, but if she had any sense at all she'd know it was time to go back down with the current to Manaus. He still didn't know what she was up to, but it hardly mattered, now.

He went back to the party. It was some party. Borita was on her back, legs spread as the redhead straddled her face resting on her own knees. Maureen was using some sort of dildo on Borita as the Indian girl ate her. It looked like a big brown sausage. Maureen looked up owlishly as Gringo came back in and said, "Oh, there you are. We got tired of waiting, so we started without you."

She was drunk as a skunk, but it hadn't slowed her down much. She rolled off Borita to offer her all to him as she went on abusing the Indian girl with her improvised tool. He repressed a grimace as he mounted her. But as he saw she was still diddling Borita wth that rather oversized whatever he said, "Hey, take it easy. You'll hurt her. What the hell *is* that thing, anyway?"

Maureen giggled and said, "Oops, it's a secret." She withdrew the mysterious object and shoved it out of sight between the mattress and the mirrored wall. Borita moaned, "Hey, why did you stop? That felt good."

Maureen shook her tousled red hair as if to clear her head and said, "Take care of her, Dick. I want another drink."

So he did, and Borita said she liked the real thing better as Maureen swilled rum and offered suggestions. He didn't think he could last much longer. But, mercifully, as he was coming in Borita and wondering what the hell he was going to do to satisfy Maureen, the redhead keeled over and began to snore softly. He let himself go in Borita and by the time he'd finished, she was out, too. They made strong rum in Brazil.

He sat up, panting for breath. It was getting late and he'd done what he'd come to do. Got to come a lot while doing it, too. He grinned and started to dress. He managed to do so without waking either of them as they sprawled across the mattress, sated. It was nice to know they'd made friends. They had a long trip back to Manaus ahead of them. He rose to his feet and started to leave. Then he moved back to the bed, reached over Maureen's hips, and groped between the mattress and the wall until he had the funny love tool. He held it up to the light. Aside from smelling a lot like Borita it seemed to be a long leather bag, like a gold miner's poke filled with sand or gravel. He was about to open it when he heard a distant gunshot. He put the poke in his hip pocket and let himself out. As he got outside he heard a second shot. He leaped ashore and landed running in the direction of the sounds, wide awake despite the orgy he'd just lived through. Gunshots had that effect on him.

The moonbeams lanced down through the forest canopy from the west. He had no idea he'd shot so much of the night with the bimbo broads on the boat back there. But at least he could see where he was going.

He spotted his campfire ahead. Some figures were between the glow and himself. They were running his way. He drew his revolver and stepped behind a buttress-rooted quinine tree. They tore past without spotting him. It was the crew from Maureen's boat. That made sense. He wondered if they were trained to knock. Maybe it didn't matter, considering Maureen's sexual appetites.

He moved on to find the fireside deserted. He kept going until he found everyone up at the narrow neck of land, waving their guns and running around like chickens with their heads cut off. He shouted for silence and demanded, "What the hell is going on? Who's that ass hole out there to the north with the bullseye lantern?"

Oswaldo presented arms and said, "I was on guard, walking my post in a military manner like my Captain said. I heard something. I yelled halt and fired, like I was supposed to. Lieutenant Sousa is out there trying to see if I hit anyone."

The tall American stared morosely at the bobbing light winking on and off between the tree trunks and muttered, "If anybody's mad at us out there, right now, they'd have nailed the guy with the light by now."

He looked around for Durand, assumed the Bos'n must be with Sousa, and called out, "Thomé, detail four helpers and let's have some light on the subject. I want a line of picket fires across the neck, here. One in the middle, one near each shore."

Thomé saluted and said he'd see to it. Nearby, the one called Cruz muttered something about Negroes to Campos. Captain Gringo said, "Cruz, run back and get my machinegun. Campos and Salles, carry the ammo boxes, and let's see some asses moving."

He did. They'd brought the Maxim up to him and the others were lighting the second fire when Lieutenant Sousa and his three man patrol came back to report, "Nothing. If anyone was scouting us, the rifle fire drove them off. Why are we setting up camp here?"

The American said, "We're not. I'm going to cover this neck from here, with my back to the dark and anybody headed our way crossing through the illuminated zone. No offense, Lieutenant, but it's not a good idea to move against a possible enemy in the dark holding a fucking light in your *hand!*"

Sousa looked down at the bullseye lantern he was holding and said, "I had to see, didn't I?"

Captain Gringo let it go. The trouble with gunboat guys was that they got arrogant shining lights along the shoreline at night with a couple of inches of steel in front of them.

He wondered if Commodore Barboza knew how little Sousa knew about shore patroling. It was a safe bet he did. The picture was starting to clear a bit.

He sent Sousa and most of the others back to the main campfire to catch some shut-eye while he held the neck. Had they had the leeway of the lower river he'd have shoved off at once, but hitting a sand bar or snag in the tricky light seemed a greater danger than the whatever they'd scared off.

He hunkered down behind the Maxim's tripod mount. He was keyed-up and full of coffee when he started. A million years later the fucking sun hadn't risen and his eyes were full of sand. He caught himself starting to doze off behind the gun. So he stood up, stomping up and down to move his blood around. It didn't wake him up, but he'd never fallen asleep on his feet yet, so what the hell. He saw it was time to replenish the wood on his picket fires and was about to order one of the men with him to do so when he noticed the sky above seemed a little less black. He took out his watch and nodded. Then he called out, "Rosas, go wake the Lieutenant. Tell him to coffee everybody and have them aboard the boats in one hour."

Then he lit a smoke, screening the cigar tip's treacherous red glow in his cupped hand as he paced back and forth near the squatting gun. An hour was such a little time when you were enjoying yourself. Why was an hour so long when you weren't?

But everything must end, if you wait long enough, and the dawn finally came up like thunder, just like the poet said it did in the tropics. He waited until he could see colors in the woods across the fire line before he drew his revolver again and moved in gingerly for a closer look by dim daylight.

He spotted the white patch where Oswaldo's blind shot had torn away the bark of a balsa tree and spotted something else at it's base. A line of almost dried blood spatters led from the tree in one wide wild loop and then bee-lined into the selva to the north-west. Oswaldo had hit something or somebody, sure as hell.

He went back by the Maxim and called out to the guards along his picket line. "Okay, Muchachos, the show's over. You three lug the gun and ammo back to my launch and mount it for me. Salvador, stay here for a few minutes just in case. I'll send for you when we're about to shove off. If you spot anything, fire your rifle and take cover. Don't come to us—we'll come to you."

He walked back to the fire, stiff and chilled by the water's morning coolness. Someone handed him a tin cup of black coffee which he drank without sitting down. He then ordered the men to board the launches. One of the supply canoes were nearly empty, so he had the few supplies in it loaded in another and cast the empty one adrift. When they had the steam up in both launches and were set to go, he sent a runner to fetch Salvador and told Sousa to wait for them and then follow. Sousa asked if he was taking the lead this morning and he replied, "Just back to the point and main channel. Got to tidy some things up on the way."

He ordered slow speed and when they got down to Maureen's cruiser he hove to and hailed it. A crew member came out in the cockpit. Captain Gringo called, "Toss me your stern painter and we'll tow you off."

"La Senhora is still sleeping and we have no steam up, Captain."

"That's what I just said. We're pulling out and it looks like there are some Indians in the neighborhood. You want to throw me that painter or hang around here on your own a while?"

The crewman reached down, picked up a coiled stern line, and threw it across. One of Captain Gringo's men, back near the tiller, caught it and the tall American said, "Full steam, Thomé," as the painter was made fast. It twanged taut and they sucked Maureen's craft off the mud to pull it stern-first after them as they moved back to the main channel. By the time they got there, Maureen was out in the cockpit, fully dressed in her safari outfit, trying to talk to him across the open water. He didn't answer from the bow of his own craft. They rounded the point and as the current tried to sweep them downstream, Captain Gringo ordered, "Hard left rudder. Cast off that line."

As his own launch swung its bows upstream he saw Maureen was shaking her fist at him as her own cruiser drifted sideways in the general direction of Manaus. He grinned as he saw a gout of oily smoke rise from her funnel. He could see they'd just fired her boiler and that she was determined to keep tagging along. He'd figured she would be. The cork stuck in her boiler would blow any minute now.

He saw Sousa rounding the point. He ordered his own crew to pull over and allow the officer and the supply canoes to take the lead again. A few minutes later they were around a slight bend and all seemed right with the world. They'd fallen smoothly into their usual morning routine and Maureen was off their tail.

He still wondered what the hell she'd really wanted, though. So as he sat in the bow he took out the funny leather sausage for a better look in the morning light. It was shaped exactly like a hell of a big prick. He knew Maureen could hide it where a customs officer would have to be very rude indeed to search. Maureen liked big pricks.

The thongs holding one end shut had been cut short and

159

were knotted too tight to open with his thumb nails. He took out a pen knife and worked the whatever open. He spilled some of the contents in his open palm. He frowned and muttered, "What the hell?"

It looked like gravel. He held a small pebble up to the light between thumb and forefinger. It seemed to be quartz and he knew gold occurred in quartz. But there wasn't any gold in it. The stone was transparent enough to see through. He tried a few more. Nothing. The pebbles were greasy feeling and he remembered where the girls had been shoving the poke. The leather had been oiled or greased for comfort. He grimaced. Maybe it was just a dildo for the rare occasional night old Maureen found herself with only herself on her hands. He decided not to throw it overboard anyway, just yet. She'd been drunk and sexually charged when he'd caught her using it on Borita. But even then she'd decided she'd better hide it from him. Ergo she hadn't wanted him to ask questions about it. Because she was embarrassed about owning a love toy? Doubtful. A lady who ate out another while she screwed with the lights on didn't embarrass easy.

He reknotted the poke and stuck it in his hip pocket. If nothing else, it made a handy black jack, and one never knew.

He saw Sousa, out front, was rounding another bend into a wider stretch of river ahead. He gave no orders. Deodoro at the tiller could see and was trained, now, to follow the last canoe at pistol range.

The morning sun had risen high enough to be blinding as its rays lanced off the water at a low angle. Sousa swung starboard to hug the shade on that side of the channel. It turned out to be a lousy idea.

Captain Gringo blinked as something thunked into the log side of the canoe in front of him. It was a feathered six-foot arrow of black reed. He yelled, "Hard aport!" as he swung his machinegun muzzle the other way and opened up on the wooded bank the arrows were coming from. He fired blindly into the trees. The sons-of-bitches shooting the long arrows had the launched river party in plain view. They were sending volley after volley of the silent feathered shafts. One thunked into the gun'l near Captain Gringo, as a man on the far side of the boiler screamed in pain. Another arrow lanced down through the canvas awning to imbed itself in the duckboards near the American's hip as he ceased fire, looking for a target in the wall of spinach green. He shouted, "Deodoro, swing our ass broadside to the river to give them less of a target."

Thomé called back, "Deodoro's hit, my Captain." The American snapped, "Somebody else, then. Get me and the boiler between you guys and that fucking shore!"

He glanced to his left: Sousa's launch was moving at an angle for the far side. That seemed reasonable. But then Captain Gringo saw they weren't up against a handful of pissed off Indians after all. He swore as he saw he'd been outgeneralled by a jungle Napoleon, when the bank they'd been driven toward by the harrassing fire exploded into a skirmish line of howling, blood-red, naked figures!

Someone shouted, "Colorados!" as he yelled, "Strike that last order and try to hold us midstream at full speed."

He swung his muzzle the other way as he saw the literally red Indians were launching dugouts to attack them on the water. Apparently they weren't impressed by modern weaponry. He'd heard they painted themselves with ocher like that because it made them brave and bullet proof. He could see they were brave. Crazy brave. A big red bastard wearing nothing but a gold ring in his nose was standing in the lead canoe, shaking a feathered spear in one hand and beating himseelf on the chest with the other. Captain Gringo trained the Maxim on him and opened up to blow the war chief, his dugout, and the others in it into cayman bait and bloody froth.

That should have done it. It would have stopped Apache or even Sioux, but the Colorados were made of sterner stuff. He made it fifteen or sixteen canoes coming across the water at them, with a bigger bunch on shore shooting plunging arrows over them like an artillery barrage. The Colorados paddled like unfeeling machines and seemed inhuman in their garish red-devil paint. Their mushroom hairdos were painted with the same red clay and it looked like they were wearing helmets. Their faces were red masks with eyebrows shaved and all sorts of sharp things stuck through their noses and lower lips. But Captain Gringo knew they were human beings, and that they thought they were in the right after one of their hunters or scouts had been shot for no good reason that they could see. He stitched a line of machinegun fire across the black water between them to see if it would change their minds. It didn't. It just seemed to make them madder. So he sighed, adjusted the elevation, and proceeded to show them the true advantages of civilization.

They died magnificently as he hosed hot lead back and forth into them. The proud primitive warriors didn't know the word retreat. It had never occurred to a Colorado that a man in battle had any choice but to do or die, so they died, paddle or spear in hand, as he knocked them overboard like ducks in a shooting gallery. The water began to froth pink all around as piranha or some other river creatures attracted by the blood in the water began to feed. He saw one lone Indian in a shot up canoe still doggedly trying to paddle his way. The Colorado had been hit in the chest and the blood against his war paint ran down it glinting in the sunlight. Captain Gringo saw that the brave fool couldn't reach them as his dugout began to fill with water. He held his fire and threw the Colorado a West Point salute. He knew the Indian glaring dully at him didn't understand, but it was all he could do as they left him behind.

The ones on shore began to launch a second line of dugouts, but the steam launches were moving at a pace against the current no men with paddles could match. So it was over, and Captain Gringo gagged, leaned over the rail, and threw up his morning coffee.

He wiped his face, sheepishly, and ordered his crew to overtake Sousa's launch, now once more on course in mid-stream, but moving slower with its dragging canoe train. As they pulled alongside, he called over to Sousa. Martim Durand replied to his hail, explaining, "The lieutenant is dead,

Captain Gringo. He took an arrow in the ear and it came out his mouth. We lost Nilo and Floriano, too. I took an arrow in the arm but it is nothing."

"Carry on, Bos'n. We'll pull in to compare notes a few kilometers up."

He moved aft to see how his own crew had made out. It hadn't made out so good. Deodoro was dead on the duckboards wearing a silly grin and an arrow shaft broken off in his chest. Alvarez and the kid called José were wounded. They had either minor flesh wounds or they were dead, depending on what the Colorados had smeared on the arrow tips. He knew the Jivaro used curare and that the wounded men would have been down by now if they were full of curare. No arrow poison made much sense if it didn't stop you soon. So they probably only had infection to worry about. Infection in the tropics was enough to worry about. A splinter in the heel could kill you, messy, if it festered in this damp heat.

They steamed on ten miles or so before they tied up at a small midstream bar to restudy their options. Neither launch was damaged. Captain Gringo assigned a burial detail and told them to plant their dead deep. Durand, naked to the waist with a gauze bandage around his upper left arm, objected that the next flood would probably shift this bar and float the bodies down the river in any case. Captain Gringo said, "We'll bury them anyway. What happens to a corpse in its grave is not our responsibility. Giving our dead a proper burial is."

While he waited for them to finish he got Sousa's map and studied it. There was one last river port upstream. Beyond, the Negro braided into a multi-channeled mess. Sousa had traced a pencil line in a ragged V to the north-east. With a penciled little question mark beside it. He ran his finger along it. The map had a lot of dotted lines, which meant the streams indicated were more or less a guess. A maybe-river called the Brazo Casiquiare entered the Negro's headwaters a few days beyond the last outpost of civilization. He followed it north-east to where, near a high massif called the Cerro Duida, it forked, maybe. There was a printed

163

question mark on the map. The north fork of the mountain stream ran here, there, around another question mark and through a big swamp and what do you know, it ran into the *Orinoco!* The Orinoco, of course, emptied into the sea near Trinidad on the Caribbean after traversing most of the plains of Venezuela. Swell. There was just one more detail. Sousa had drawn a circle around the area where the Brazo Casiquiare fed into the Negro's swampy birthplace. It was marked, "Lands claimed by the rebels."

He folded the map and put it away realizing why they wanted Commander Fonseca and his Paulist sidekick, Andrada, eliminated. Or did he?

Brazil and Venezuela weren't on such good terms, but they weren't at war this season. Such lawful trade as there was between the two countries made more sense by sea. The mouth of the Amazon and Orinoco were just around the north-east shoulder of South America from one another. An ocean steamer could make its way faster than anyone screwing around up here in the headwaters, even if you *could* float a boat through from one river valley to the other. No honest merchant needed to go to so much effort. But a *smuggler* would! Sure, Brazil didn't care what you brought *up* the Amazon, but they had a stiff export duty on natural resources, and were said to be really pissed about those Englishmen smuggling rubber seeds out. Maureen would look English enough to a Brazilian customs officer and they'd find anything she had on her as she left via Para or Macapa, up her snatch or not. That was why she wanted to come up here to the smuggle-smuggle swamplands. To make it over to the Orinoco. The Trinidad Brits off the mouth of the Orinoco attracted less interest from Venezuelan officials in the first place, and the Brits hadn't stolen anything from Venezuela in the second. He started to reach for the funny poke she'd been trying to use him for. He left it where it was for now as he grinned in sudden understanding. It wasn't rubber seeds, this time. There was another natural resource Brazil was famous for. The tricky green-eyed hellion had tried to con him into getting her safely up and over the inland passage carrying a cuntfull of *uncut diamonds.*

Leaving their fallen comrades in their unmarked graves the little party moved on. It took them four days to reach the last river port marked on Sousa's map. By the time they got there the wounded men were in bad shape. As he'd feared, the seemingly mild arrow wounds had festered, and although he tried jack knife surgery around the campfire one night, he saw they had to have a doctor, soon. Assuming the Colorados downstream had faded back into the scenery, the wounded still needed sound hands to help them make it. So when they reached the river port he put in, this time.

The village hardly rated its dot on Sousa's map. It consisted of thatched shacks around a tin-roofed trading post above the one timber ramp running up the red bank to a clearing little bigger than a football field back home. The trader and post-master was a fat creole of mixed White, Black, and Red ancestry. The villagers were nominally Christian Indians. The trader had lots of rum and a little quinine: that was the full extent of medicine on the upper Negro. Captain Gringo had rum, he bought the quinine.

As he was walking back to his boats along the shore he heard a familiar voice call his name. He turned, thunderstruck, to see Gaston Verrier coming out of a palm-thatched hut with his arm around two giggling Indian girls. Gaston said, "This one is Rosa and the fat one is Mariposa. She's the best lay."

Captain Gringo shook his head wearily and said, "I figured you'd know. What in blue blazes are you doing up here, Gaston? The last I saw of you they were holding you aboard that fucking gunboat down in Manaus!"

Gaston said, "Oui, it was trés fatigué. I escaped a few nights ago and made my way down here on a raft I improvised trés cleverly. I was hoping you had not yet made it up this far. My little friends, here, have been most hospitable, but I have been afraid I was wearing out my welcome."

"Wait a minute. You say you came *down* the river? Don't you mean *up?*"

"Mes non. I may be getting old, but I still know up from down, non? The gunboat steamed upstream right after you people left, with me aboard, of course. I was at my charming best and after a time they neglected to guard me as closely. One imagines they did not think I would be mad enough to leap overboard at night into cayman infested waters, hein?"

"Jesus, is that how you got away?"

"But of course. Nobody ever said the life of a soldier of fortune is all wine and roses. Between the bullets bouncing off the water and possible company in the murky liquid, you should have seen me swim, my old and rare! They failed to send a shore party after me, so one assumes they must have thought the river got me, hein?"

"Yeah. Tell me more about it on the way. We've got to get back to my guys."

Gaston patted the two Indian girls on their bottoms and told them to wait for him in the shade. As he fell in with Captain Gringo, the tall American filled him in on his own adventures. By the time he'd made it short, they were moving down the planks to the river's edge. He asked Gaston, "How far up is the gunboat?" The Frenchman said, "It's near the rebel stronghold, but up a side stream, why?"

"I thought that was their plan. We don't have to worry about 'em right now. Get yourself a gun and some grub while I reshuffle the deck."

His men were waiting expectantly. He tossed the bottle of quinine to Durand and said, "Okay, here's the plan. We're splitting up. I'll take Thomé and five other sound men with me and Senhor Verrier, here. We'll divide the supply canoes. Durand, you and everybody else will take the other launch and head back to Manaus. You ought to make better time going downstream. Try to find a town with a doctor in residence along the river anyway. How's that arm coming?"

Durand shrugged and said, "It is swollen, but your lancing helped, my Captain. I am willing to press on. I am not a baby."

The American said, "I know. You've been a good man, Durand. That's why I'm counting on you to get these guys safely back to Manaus. Keep taking quinine and if that arm swells up again you know what to do."

One of the other wounded asked, "What about you,

Captain? How can you possibly hope to fight all those rebels with so few men?"

It was a good question. Captain Gringo didn't have the answer. He said, "I'll worry about that bridge when it's time to cross it. Let's get cracking, guys. Commodore Barboza won't be in Manaus when you arrive, so you ought to be able to fade into the scenery and forget his deal. It was a double cross anyway. Go with God, and, for Chrissake, if you can't stay out of more trouble, be a little more *careful!*"

He turned his back on them as they talked it over in some confusion. He joined Gaston, who sat on a mooring post enjoying a smoke as he watched with one sardonic eyebrow raised. As Captain Gringo took out a cigar for himself, Gaston said, "Once more you are not thinking, Dick."

"What's wrong, now? I thought it was a pretty good idea. There's no sense in moving on upstream with a mess of wounded and we don't have the manpower to handle both launches if things get hairy."

"True, but I fail to see why we still have to go on. Barboza no longer holds me as a hostage. Sousa is not in any position to argue if you turn back, either. We could *all* go back to Manaus and fade into the scenery, non?"

"Hang some crepe on your nose. Your brain just died. It's true Barboza and his gunboat are up ahead of us. We'll have to be careful about that. But, aside from being strangers who stand out in Manaus, we have one very pissed-off redhead and her smuggler friends. Some political pals of the rebels also know us well enough to plant bombs in our vicinity, and I told you about the diamonds. I'll show 'em to you later. But if you don't mind an educated guess, I'm packing a king's ransom in my hip pocket. So, I'm not about to try and leave the country by way of it's front door. Two can play at old Maureen's game and even if we only fence them for a fraction of their value we ought to make a profit on this deal for once."

Gaston shrugged and said, "I doubt Barboza intended to pay us as much as he promised. You do see his plan, don't you, Dick?"

"Sure, he wants us to try to get through the rebels. Then,

as soon as they start acting rude, he aims to move in with his gunboat and start lobbing four-inch shells on everybody. The only mystery left is why."

"Barboza doesn't want to start the fight because Commander Fonesca still has powerful political connections?"

"That's *his* story. It's as full of holes as swiss cheese. I sense more than the usual double-cross, here. It's some kind of triple-cross. Commodore Barboza's superiors may buy it when he tells them he was trying to rescue us poor wayfaring strangers and, Gee Boss, how was he to know the late Commander Fonesca was among the banditos? But there's more to it than that. Commander Fonesca has a brother in the national assembly. He's never fired a shot in anger since the new president took over. His friends in the new administration are trying to get him a pardon for his messy misunderstandings with the last one."

Gaston nodded and said, "Ah, perhaps his political enemies, or the enemies of his brother, wish to assure he remains a Robin Hood, preferably a dead one?"

"That's the way I see it. A book I read said the Fonsecas are one of the more powerful Paulist clans."

"Ergo Commodore Barboza is not a Paulist, hein?"

"Ergo he wouldn't be a Navy Commodore under the new Paulist Party rule if he wasn't a Paulist in good standing. I checked that out, too. The Barboza clan is another pack of Paulists. They have fazendas and mines all over Brazil. They own half the coffee in Sao Paulo, Paulist headquarters. Sort of weird, when you think about it."

Gaston said, "Merde alors, it is more than weird, it is mad! The two navy men are supposed to be on the *same* side. Yet, most obviously they are not. Perhaps it is a family feud, like your unfortunate Hatfields and McCoys in the States?"

"It's starting to look that way. Barboza would never dare attack one of the paid-up Fonsecas; but a black sheep of the family might make a tempting target for a guy who hates good."

"Hmm, I got the impression Commodore Barboza was more rational."

"So did I. He doesn't want to wipe out a classmate who

took his steady to the Senior Prom. He's playing a tricky and deadly game. The stakes have to be high, if only we could figure out what they *were*."

One of the men at the water's edge called to him. Captain Gringo turned and saw the launch he was sending back was loaded and ready to shove off. He turned to Thomé and the five men staying behind with him and snapped, "Present arms." Then he raised his own hand in salute as the wounded and their attendents moved out to mid-channel and caught the current. As they headed downstream one of the men aboard waved his hat and shouted, "Viva Captain Gringo!" So he held his salute until they rounded the bend, then dropped his hand wearily, swallowed the lump in his throat, and said, "Order arms. Let's get ourselves aboard, Thomé. I want to get out of here before the runner reaches the bandits upstream."

"You think these villagers sent someone for to warn the rebels, my Captain?"

"Think? Shit, I know they did. This village couldn't exist without staying on good terms with Robin Hood and his Merry Men of the Greenwood, Thomé."

"Robin who, my Captain?"

"Never mind. Let's just get out of here, muy pronto."

The next few days on the river went smoothly enough, and then things got tricky. The headwaters of the Rio Negro were wildly braided even if they were still in the main channel, and they were sort of guessing about that. The late Lieutenant Sousa's map was large scale and hopelessly inaccurate. They kept coming to forks where streams of the same size poured out of the unknown from more or less north-west, so Captain Gringo got to climb a lot of trees. Comparing the view with the crumpled map in his shirt pocket was better than flipping a coin; but they still had to retrace their route every once in a while when they wound up in a dead end or came to rapids the map said didn't belong on the Negro this far south.

Late one afternoon he hauled himself up the vine-laced bole of a forest giant for a peek across a wide bend. A monkey eating an eagle eyed him curiously from another part of the crown as he told it not to be silly and craned his neck for a better view up the river. The main channel did indeed circle around in a big S, like the map said it should. There was an oxbow off to one side of the main channel. He couldn't see much of the surface, but he saw the conning tower and funnel of the navy gunboat well enough. He cursed and gingerly lowered himself to the ground where Gaston and the others waited with interest. He said, "Barboza's anchored a couple of miles up, tucked in a backwater."

Gaston said, "Ah, that must mean we are nearing the rebel lines, non?"

Captain Gringo nodded and said, "Yeah, they're expecting us and Barboza would let us pass, since he aims to follow behind and join in later. But let's fuck him up anyway. There's another channel, on our side of the main one. It's little more than a ditch, but I think we can get through."

"Won't they see out funnel smoke, Dick?"

"In daylight, yeah. We'll sit tight here and move up the river some more after dark."

Thomé had been listening. He asked, "Don't we want the gunboat on our side when we meet the rebels, my Captain?"

The American smiled thinly and said, "We would if we could be sure it was on our side. I think once we get into a fight the Commodore intends to just start lobbing shells in the direction of the gunfire. A four-incher down the back of your neck could smart."

Gaston said, "Oui, I have heard it said that getting hit by cannon fire can take fifty years off a man's life."

"Okay, there's a couple of hours of daylight left," Captain Gringo began. "Oswaldo, you and Cruz break out some rations we can eat cold. Thomé, lower the flame in the launch but keep a head of steam up. Salles and Campos, you two clear some of this forest muck and we'll have a dry place to lay out our groundcloths. May as well relax and get comfortable while we wait for it to get dark."

Gaston asked, "What about Barboza's shore patrols, Dick?" The tall American shrugged and said, "He's a couple of miles and across the main channel besides. I doubt we'll have company. But since you brought it up, guess who's going to stand the first guard."

"Merde alors, I thought I was an officer."

"We don't have enough men for two officers, Pal. Just stay close enough to the water to keep an eye on our boats. I'll watch the landward trees."

It only took them a short while to make camp on the bare, red sand in sight of the rolling, black river. They opened cans and ate cold rations, washed down with canteen coffee. It was safe to smoke, of course.

Captain Gringo stretched out on his canvas groundcloth and tried to relax, but he couldn't. He had too much on his mind. He tried to tell himself he'd get some answers soon enough, but he wanted some answers now. He wondered if it would be possible to make a deal.

Commander Fonseca up the river was a pro and maybe a gentleman as well as an officer. There was damned little sense in the coming fight. Captain Gringo didn't give a hoot what happened to the rebels, now that he had Gaston under his wing, safe and sound. He didn't see what danger he and his handful of men were to the rebels, and they ought to find Barboza's plan worth hearing about, if they didn't shoot first and ask questions later. Okay, how did you approach an armed guerrilla band deep in the selva without having them shoot at you on sight?

You laid down your arms and went in waving a white flag, that was how. Then they'd either listen to you or blow your head off, depending on how they felt about it. He presented only a small danger to them armed and ready to fight. He had nothing to offer them that they couldn't just *take,* if he tried to parley his way through! He and his handful of men would be placing their lives in the rebel leader's hands and at least one of them was said to be pretty savage.

He got up and wandered over to the water's edge to tell Gaston, "Get some rest. I'll keep an eye on the boats."

171

Gaston nodded and started to join the others. Then both men turned to stare as they heard a cry in some unknown tongue. The current was sweeping a dark human head around the bend, and since it was yelling a lot they could safely assume a human being was still attached to it, caymans or piranhas notwithstanding.

Gaston said, "It seems to be an Indian child. What on earth do you think you are doing, Dick?"

Captain Gringo didn't answer as he dropped his gunbelt to the ground, tossed his hat aside, and dove in. As the black water closed around him he wondered, "What the fuck *am* I doing here?" but kept swimming as his head broke the surface. The Indian was a lousy swimmer, barely able to keep afloat, so he gained on him or her, shouting, "Hang on, I'm trying."

As he neared the half drowned native he saw it was a girl of ten or twelve. Her eyes were filled with terror as she splashed and floundered, coughing and sputtering. He reached her and she wrapped herself around him as if to drown them both. She was stark naked. He tried to pry her loose, saw he could side stroke with his free arm and legs and started to do so as she sobbed and clung to him like a limpet. Gaston waded out waist deep as he made it into the shallows, and the two of them hauled the little Indian girl ashore as Gaston muttered, "I must be insane. I saw that damned cayman on the far side sliding off the bank. Apparently it felt we were more than it could chew, hein?"

The others had risen to move toward them as they steadied the naked girl between them, patting her back to help her cough up the water she'd inhaled. She was still sobbing and bewildered, but as she got her bearings she eyed the men around her dubiously and without another word started to run into the selva. One of the men started after her and Captain Gringo snapped, "Let her go. Can't you see she's afraid of us?"

Gaston took off a boot to drain it as he muttered, "That is what I like, gratitude. Why did we just do that, Dick?"

"Beats the shit out of me. I was half way to her before I

172

thought about the pretty little fishies they grow up here. But, what the hell, it's over and no harm done. Any of you guys know what tribe she might belong to?"

Oswaldo said, "Not Colorado, not Jivaro. I noticed tribal markings tattooed on her chin, but they were unfamiliar to me."

Captain Gringo frowned as he realized Oswaldo was one up on him. He'd been too intent on hauling her out of the river to take a close look at her. As he took off his wet shirt and checked to make sure he hadn't lost the contents of his pants pockets he said, "By God, that explains something that's been eating me. An Indian girl in the water is an Indian girl in the water."

He was unfolding Sousa's soggy map to dry it on his groundcloth as Gaston said, "That sounds most profound, my old and rare. But what the devil are you talking about?"

"Borita. I now know she and Maureen were working closer together than they let on. Borita speaks English with a West Indian accent, too. So she's probably from Trinidad instead of Brazil. She acted as the Anglo-Irish dame's translator and confederate. Probably her lover, when their not conning some poor male."

"Ah, Borita is the Indian girl you saved from the cayman back in Manaus, right?"

"Wrong. The odds against me saving the servant girl of the redhead that had just tried to hire me was bothering the hell out of me. But now I see how they worked it. The girl the cayman was chasing was just a river kid, like I thought. A wet and naked Indian is a wet and naked Indian, and I only exchanged a few words with the one I saved from the cayman. The other gals heard about it from the kids. Maureen sent her own Indian sidekick to seduce me, later. I was sitting in the dark and she said how grateful she was, so what the hell."

"But, Dick, you saw her later in the light, non?"

"Shit, I saw her reflected in a mess of mirrors, screwing like a mink. Of course I saw her later in the light, after spending a night making love to her. It never occurred to me

173

until just now, that the girl I saved in the river was a bit younger and skinnier. We must all look a lot alike to them, too."

Gaston shrugged and said, "Well, you said they were pretty brazen, and one sees the advantages. Borita's shy act was designed to make you confide in her if you suspected what they were up to together, hein?"

"I guess so. But we have the rocks and they're on their way back to Manaus to tell the guys they work with that things didn't work out the way they planned."

"Ah, one suspects confederates among the Brazilian gentry?"

"Of course. Those two bimbos never dug the uncut diamonds on their own. Some bigger muggy-mucks want to smuggle them out without paying the export duties on them. Maureen said she'd been to the opera and that cruiser was one expensive little tub."

Gaston laughed and said, "Eh bien, so now we know why she wanted to hire strong arm boys to get her through this bandit infested country. Now, if we could only figure out what Barboza and *his* friends are up to, hein?"

Before Captain Gringo could answer, one of his men called to him in a worried tone. He looked up and said, "Okay, everybody stay put!" as a quartet of stark naked ladies walked out of the selva toward them.

All four women were tall for Indians. The one in the lead looked part white and carried no arms. The three gals with her made up for it by packing spears and leather shields trimmed with what looked suspiciously like human hair. He rose, saying, "Everybody as you are. I'll do the talking."

The leader of the odd-looking women stopped and raised her hand in the universal peace sign. So he did the same and stepped closer as he smiled and asked if she spoke Spanish. She was almost beautiful, if one ignored the fact she and her friends had beard-like tattoos on their chins and wore their hair in the soup-bowl cut favored by most Indian warriors.

She said, in Spanish, "I am called Brujo. I am cacique of Los Mujeros. For why did you just save my niece from drowning?"

Captain Gringo said, "I didn't know who's niece she was. I only saw she was in trouble."

"She was. She tells us she had almost given up her life to the river spirits when you jumped in to save her. Do you not know there are dangerous creatures in the black waters, strange person?"

He shrugged and said, "I did what I had to. I'm sorry if you folks feel insulted about it."

Brujo smiled, showing perfect pearly teeth as she stepped closer and reached out to feel his bare arm. She said, "You look strong as well as brave. We Mujeros are not used to meeting friends with yellow hair. How are you called?"

"My name is Ricardo. My friends call me Dick."

"Deek? It is a funny name, but it does not mean anything, so it can not carry a curse. You and your friends must come with us. The river spirits will be angry. We must purify you all with proper ceremonies to make them forgive you for depriving them of a chosen one."

She turned, imperiously, and though they didn't seem to be under guard, he got the distinct impression she was used to having her orders obeyed.

Her rear view was very interesting. She had a fantastic figure and without the tattooed beard and plucked eyebrows she looked even more female. He looked at the sky and said, "Let's go along with her for now, guys. We might be able to enlist some of her men as scouts."

"Her *men,* Captain Gringo?" asked Oswaldo in a low tone as he moved up beside him. Captain Gringo nodded thoughtfully. Spanish was an inflected language, so an O on the end of a word made it masculine. A Bruja was a female witch. A Brujo was a male. Mujeres meant women. Mujeros didn't exist as a Spanish word, since it meant male woman, which wouldn't work, when you thought about it. Oswaldo made the sign of the cross and said, "I have always believed they were a myth, even though Orillano said he fought with them, many years ago."

Captain Gringo said, "They look real enough to me," as he followed the statuesque Brujo and her shapely tall companions deeper into the selva. He'd always thought the

Amazons of Amazonia were a myth, too. But if the female witch-chief and her warrior girls weren't Amazons, he didn't know what else you could call them.

Los Mujeros lived well back from the river banks, apparently to avoid the river spirits, rubber tappers, and other evil creatures that had bothered them in the past. Brujo's village was in a clearing surrounded by a stockade with armed females posted all around as guards. Most Indians who built such elaborate set-ups were slash and burn agricultural tribes. But when he commented on the lack of manioc milpas, Brujo laughed and lightly explained, "We plant no crops. Our subject tribes pay tribute to us. Grubbing in the earth for roots is work fit only for mere men. My people are warriors."

That would have seemed more reasonable if there'd been any men around. But as she led them into her compound he saw nothing but women and girls. It was sort of spooky, when you remembered all the legends.

He said, "It's going to be dark, soon, and nobody is guarding our boats."

"Don't worry. Nobody is allowed to steal in this part of the selva. Come, that big house over there is mine."

She led him into a peaked, thatch hut the size of a Cape Cod cottage. A fire was burning on the central hearth and mats were spread on the earth floor all around. As he and his men ducked inside he noticed only a few of the tougher-looking women followed. Brujo indicated a seat and as Captain Gringo sat down she joined him on the mat, clapped her hands, and said, "We shall drink together and see if we wish to make children together, no?"

He didn't answer as he stared upward to get his bearings. His jaw dropped as he saw the human heads staring back down at him from the smokey beams above them. Los Mujeros didn't shrink heads as the Jivaro did. These were full sized, with the skulls inside. All were black from being smoked. But he noticed a few had lighter hair and caucasian features. Brujo saw what he was looking at and asked, "Do you like my trophies?"

"They're, ah, very interesting. Do you just collect heads or were those guys all enemies?"

She said, "Of course they were all enemies. Do you take us for barbarians?" Another woman knelt to hand her a calabash full of native manioc beer and Brujo took a deep draft before she passed it to her guest, saying, "Here, if we are to be friends we should get good and drunk together."

He swallowed some and passed it on, noting that the woman had taken up alternate positions around the fire so that each man had a woman between himself and the next. The numbers came out even and the warrior women had made no move to disarm them. If they weren't being poisoned things might work out. In English he told Gaston, "Easygay on the oozebay." And Gaston said, "Great minds run in the same channels, non?" There was no way either could warn the others without the Spanish speaking cacique overhearing. He could only hope their knockaround lives had educated them a bit.

As the bowl went around, Brujo said, "The girl you saved wanted to mate with you, but I told her she was too young, yet."

"That sounds reasonable. Who was that guy up there with the big moustache?"

Brujo looked up casually and said, "Oh, him? His name was Andrada. He had a fazenda up the river, a day's journey. He enslaved some other Indians and when they complained to us about it we took care of him for them. Those seven in a row next to him were other flagelados. Very nasty fellows."

Captain Gringo frowned and said, "Wait a minute, Brujo, are you saying you and your girls wiped out Andrada's gang?"

"Not all of them. Some of them got away down river when we burned the house and landing. Why do you ask? Did you know this Andrada?"

"We were sent up the river to fight him."

She slugged him on the shoulder with her fist and said, "Good, I knew you had a good heart when you saved that little girl." She said something to the other Mujeros and they all smiled and started beating their drinking companions on the back. They were big tough gals and they hit hard as many a man might have. Brujo said, "We admire men who like to fight. After we get drunk we shall all wrestle, eh?"

Captain Gringo raised an eyebow and said, "I'm not sure I want to brawl with you, Brujo."

She looked hurt and asked, "Why? Don't you like me? I knew as soon as I saw you that I wanted to be impregnated by you. But, of course, you will have to whip me, first."

He laughed, incredulously, and asked, "Is that how your men court you, Brujo?"

She said, "We have no men, if you mean male Mujeros. Our tribe is all female."

"I noticed that. But how do you have children if you don't have any men?"

"We mate with guests, like you and your men, of course. If we like a youth from among the tribes paying tribute to us we allow him to wrestle with us and if he beats us we give ourselves to him, as women, for a night or so. No man is allowed to live among us permanently. It gives men odd notions of superiority to stay long with a woman as her husband."

Oswaldo had been listening. He murmured. "Just as in the old legends. They *are* the Amazons!"

Brujo nodded and said, "Some people call us that. But our Indian name translates best as Los Mujeros, the he-shes. It has always been so. Some say that many years ago a band of women had had enough of their husband's lazy brutal ways and decided to change things by killing them all and taking up the warrior life we lead. But I think that is a myth, too. Look at me and my girls. Do we look like we Mujeros were ever as small and weak as the women of other tribes?"

He shook his head and muttered, "Selective breeding." Gaston nodded and said, "But of course. If one only makes la zig-zig with a very strong man all the children that result tend to be strong, too, hein?"

He asked Brujo what happened to the little boys they had by accident, afraid he knew the answer. But Brujo laughed and said, "We are not as cruel as our enemies would have it. The boys we bear are sent to the tribes of their fathers, to act as our agents. They are usually very big and strong, too, so most of them become caciques. I was related on my mother's side to the cacique who asked for our help against the slave raiders of Andrada."

Captain Gringo looked relieved and said, "We understood that others had joined Andrada and his outlaws. Brazilian Navy men, perhaps in uniforms?"

Brujo shrugged and passed him the drinking bowl again as she replied, "There are some soldados with big guns up the river near the burned out-fazenda. We know little about the so-called government's business. Every time they talk to us they say we must put clothes on and go to their silly church. They are very tiresome people. We try to avoid them."

Gaston had heard. Speaking Spanish to avoid insulting their hostess, he said, "Barboza had his facts confused if Commander Fonseca had not indeed joined forces with the border ruffians, hein?"

Captain Gringo glanced up at the smoked head of the man they were discussing and said, "He may have been confused. He may have smeared a political enemy's name by linking him up with a known bastard."

He turned to the female witch-chief and asked her, "Could you say how many military men came up the river with Fonseca, Brujo?"

She said, "No. We did not see them. They were just *there*, one day. They are holding the mouth of the Brazo Casiquiare well above the lands I rule. If they do not bother my subjects, I see no reason to bother them." Then she took a healthy swig of joy juice, wiped her tattooed chin, and asked, "Why, Deek? Do you wish for to fight them?"

"I'll have to, if they won't let me up the Casiquiare channel. You say they have big guns?"

"Yes, like the one on your boat. The ones that go poof poor poof. It is getting dark. Let us all take off our clothes and grease our skins for to wrestle. If you beat me fair and square and manage to rape me I will help you fight the soldados if you wish it."

"Uh, we're supposed to wrestle greased and naked?"

"Yes, it makes it more fair. If I grabbed you by the crotch of your pants I would have an unfair advantage, since you see I wear none."

He grinned and looked around at the others as he said, "You heard her, guys. You boys are supposed to be the toughest river rats in Brazil. Do I have any volunteers?"

Gaston said, "Mine is a trés big bitch, but one must uphold the honor of the legion, non?" None of the others looked too worried as they started to unbutton and unbuckle. Brujo spoke in her own dialect and two women started shoving sand on the fire to put it out, either because they were bashful or, more likely, didn't want to roll on the hot coals. The sun was setting outside and it was pretty dark inside, but they could see more or less what they were doing. Brujo rose and said, "Each man pairs off with the woman next to him. Nobody must help another. It is considered rude to kick or bite and my girls will repay in kind. But first, we must all get properly oiled."

One of the naked women produced another calabash of vegetable oil. Brujo dipped her hands in it and began to slather it all over her bare flesh. She saw Captain Gringo hesitating as he dropped his pants. She stepped closer and began to oil his body, all over. When she took his virile member in her oily hands she murmured, "Oh, I hope you win."

It only took a few moments and a lot of giggling before both sides were ready. Then Brujo said something in her own dialect and the eight girls piled on them, growling like hungry animals!

Captain Gringo had no idea how the others were making out in the semi-darkness, as he had his own hands full. Brujo's body was well muscled but smooth and feminine as they slithered against each other, trying to get a grip on something. His hands slid over her greasy curves as she stepped in and hooked an ankle behind his to trip him. That didn't work, so she grabbed his erection and hung on as she tried to stiff-arm him the other way. He growled, "Jee-zuss!" and repaying her in kind, grabbed her with one hand by the hair and inserted the other, or two fingers of it at any rate, in her crotch to hook her pubic bone like a bowling ball and lift her off her feet. As he dropped her on the mat and fell atop her he thought the battle was about over, but Brujo clamped her thighs together and twisted off his slippery fingers, giggling. So they wound up with her face down and him on top with his virile member between her greased buttocks as he twisted one arm up into the small of her back. She tried to buck him off and his shaft entered her. She protested, "That's the wrong place, damn it!" and when he tried to let her roll over she played him false by grabbing his hair with both hands and trying to knee him.

The next thing he knew she was on top, a thigh on either side of his naked flanks as she tried to pin him. He moved down a bit, felt the tip of his shaft in the oiled groove between her strong brown thighs, and thrust up into her. She gasped and bit down hard with her internal muscles, but she really wanted to wrestle and Brujo was one tough lady. She slid off just as it was starting to feel really nice in there and as she lay across him, sideways, to pin him, he decided he'd had about enough of this shit. He wedged an elbow under himself to rise, despite her best efforts, and then he grabbed her by the crotch with a thumb up her rectum and the other fingers inside to the knuckles as she tried to call a foul. He rolled on top again as she flailed her legs to fight free of his unseemly hold, but it was distracting her and he easily pinned her on her back, his chest against her oiled hard breasts, and then he slid and slithered into the right position, forced her thighs apart with his knee, and replaced his hand with what she really wanted. There was little doubt he'd convinced her of that, as he started raping, laying, or whatever the hell they called this wild business. Brujo wrapped her oily limbs around him and when he kissed her, she asked what he was doing, so he taught her about kissing, too, as he proceeded to pound the hell out of her. She liked to learn new tricks and pounded back pretty good, with the strength of a grown man. That and the beard tattooed on her otherwise pretty face might have put him off his feed, had she not been built in a way nobody could possibly mistake for male, no matter what they called themselves. She was all woman inside as well as out, although he couldn't help wondering how the hell she exercised those muscles to make them so solid. Had it not been for the oil all over them both he'd have never been able to enter her against her will. But, then, maybe that was the idea of the oil, once you thought about it. It wasn't that Brujo didn't like to make love. She loved it, when a man was strong enough to do it her primitive way.

The whole party was getting primitive by Roman orgy standards. One other couple wound up against a post supporting the roof and, as the male partner humped the female he'd pinned against it, the thatch roof threatened to come down on them as the dried heads hanging from the rafters rattled together in the dark, like coconuts. A living head wound up cushioned on Captain Gringo's rump as another man pinned an Amazon between his bare legs. She giggled coyly as her head bobbed up and down back there while somebody worked her over good at the other end. He heard Gaston's crow of triumph as he called out in the dark, "Regardez, science triumphs over brute force every time, hein?" and another man grunted, "Got you, you little minx, oops, sorry, amigo!"

The husky American came fast, exited by the tussle despite a certain distaste. The unventilated hut was rank with the musky odor of unwashed greasy flesh and the codfish and chestnuts reek of human rut. Brujo was probably as clean as average, but she'd never heard of toilet water or perfume, and she didn't shave under her arms or douche. She felt his ejaculation and that triggered her own orgasm, which, on the hard matting rather resembled an earthquake. As the incredibly athletic girl clamped even tighter she ejected him like a watermelon seed. He braced himself for more dirty tricks as he fumbled to get it back in, but apparently she'd given up the struggle for dominance and was enjoying her rough version of submission. She sighed and said, "You have conquered me." Then she rolled him off and body slammed him on his back to leap on top of him and show him how licked she felt. She held his shoulders with her greasy palms as she squatted on him like a cossack taking a crap and bobbed up and down on his shaft, literally milking it with her muscular body. He really had no complaints, because it felt fantastic, but if this was how Los Mujeros treated people they were *fond* of, he wondered what they'd do when they were *mad* at somebody!

It was too dark to see the dried heads above them, but they made a lot more sense, now, than they had when he'd first pictured Brujo and her girls attacking an armed fazenda. Captain Gringo was bigger and stronger than most men, but he'd fought enough to have a pretty good grasp on just how powerful the average man was. Brujo could have taken three quarters of the men he'd met in a barroom brawl. She was the boss of this outfit, but he'd noticed some of the other girls were bigger. He assumed that as in most Indian tribes, Brujo led by common consent because they considered her wise or she had good medicine. All Indian warriors knew how to *fight*. Brujo's knowledge of Spanish and the outside world, meager as it was, gave her the edge at a war council.

The new position inspired but exhausted even the strong-thighed Brujo, so as she neared another climax she grabbed him by the hair and fell backward, damned near busting off his erection as he tried to follow her wherever the hell she was going. It turned out she wanted to come on her side with him in a bone wrenching position sitting on one doubled under leg as he managed to stay in long enough to help her climax. She moaned and rolled off and over on her belly, pleading, "No more, I am too excited."

He growled, "Bullshit. What am I supposed to do about *my* excitement?"

Brujo called out in her own dialect and the next thing he knew a softer, total stranger was wrapped around him in the dark, giggling girlishy as she pulled him down next to Brujo. He didn't know if the guerrilla matched with her had failed or if she'd worn him out. She obviously wanted to screw. So what the hell, and the contrast was delightful. He could feel hard muscles under the soft layer of subcutaneous tissue under her oily smooth skin, but she was all girl where it counted. Her invisible breasts were bigger than Brujos and softer, save for the hard nipples she teased back and forth across his greasy chest. Her thighs cradled him as she moved her hips from side to side instead of up and down. The new motion inspired him to renewed passion as he entered totally different proving grounds. Brujo had clasped the length of his shaft firmly. This one had a tight opening that felt like pursed lips holding in a mouthful of marshmallow. She must have liked what he was doing, because she groaned and whimpered and said something to Brujo in her own lingo. Brujo sat up to play his spine like piano as she explained, "She says you are almost too much for her. Hurry and satisfy her. I am getting hot again."

"*Getting* hot?" he marveled as he ground his pubic bone into the soft cushion of his partner's fleshy mons and let go inside her. He collapsed atop her, panting for breath as she stiffened and enjoyed her own shuddering orgasm. She murmured softly to Brujo and the witch-chief laughed and said, "She says to thank you. Now I want you to do *me* again!"

He wasn't sure he could, but he was willing to try, and this time, as he rejoined the firmer flesh of Brujo she welcomed his, willingly, and that inspired him, too. He'd thought he liked that other love box he'd just been in, but now he could see Brujo's was the best in the universe, after all.

No matter how many you had or what they looked like, each one was the best there was, while you were in her. He and Brujo settled down to a friendly old-fashioned lay, and that was sort of a novelty, too. Especially to Brujo. He taught her more about kissing as he made it last. She said she liked it and wondered if the tribes who allowed men and women to live together all the time did it like this. He said he imagined so. She said she found this slow gentle stuff sort of perverse, but interesting. He wondered if he was starting a trend. None of the old tribal customs could last much longer, as the march of civilization made the world less interesting. The Amazon habits of Los Mujeros had given a good name to a river, but he doubted it would turn out practical in the long run. Even the once savage Navajo back home had given up raiding as a way of life in favor of sheep herding. It was kind of a shame, he thought, as he ran a caressing hand over Brujo's firm young body; but he doubted Los Mujeros would last far into

184

the dawning twentieth century as he'd found them. In another generation they'd be wearing mother hubbards and working in some mill, at the rate his world was changing. But meanwhile, it would be great while it lasted and he moved slowly in and out of her, trying to make it last.

The sounds of the orgy around them were dying down, too, as other couples settled down and either made love quieter or just held hands. Someone in the darkness was snoring. He chuckled and said, "This would be a dumb time to call the roll. But did any of you guys get left out?"

There was a lazy chorus of contented grunts and Gaston called back, "I knew mine was bluffing. She fought me like a tigress, but somehow she wound up on top."

Thomé said, "I think I have had three, or maybe four. I seem to be a novelty, and they have been fighting over my poor black ass."

Captain Gringo didn't think ass was the right word, but he let it go. He was coming and he moved his own rump faster as Brujo held him in her oily arms and husked, "Oh, yes, me too!"

It took more effort this time and while they enjoyed it he knew it was time to take a break. He rolled off Brujo and groped in the dark for his clothes. He found his shirt nearby and took out a cigar and a waterproof match. As he sat up on Brujo's mat and thumbed a light, he looked around, muttered, "Jesus!" and shook it out after lighting his smoke.

Gaston laughed and said, "Oui, we present a picture one could sell for a fortune in Place Pigalle. But it is good to know the natives are friendly. But now that we know we won't have to fight any more Indians, what are we to do about those other *whites* ahead?"

Captain Gringo held the claro out to Brujo and as the witch-chief took a drag he asked her about that. She said she liked him a lot and that his enemies would always be her enemies. So he nodded and told Gaston, "I think we just evened the odds a bit. Aside from these tough ladies, Brujo has other tribes tributary to her and her Amazons."

"Mon Dieu! Does that mean we recruit the Indians to fight the rebels with us, Dick?"

"Shit, as long as we've got an army, let's fight *all* the motherfuckers!"

The moonlit selva echoed to the distant calling-drums of Los Mujeros as Captain Gringo and Gaston scouted far from Brujo's village with the witch-chief herself and another warrior girl who said she liked Frenchmen. The two white men wore their gun rigs but were naked as their savage companions, partly because they didn't want to put their clothes on until they'd had a chance to wash the grease off, and partly because Captain Gringo hoped anyone who spotted their naked hides in the moonlight would take them for Indians. Neither Barboza and his gunboat crew nor the mystery rebels further north would be likely to want to stir up local Indians, while either would shoot at a strange white on sight.

They knew where the gunboat was, so he'd asked Brujo and her scout to show them where the other outfit was. Brujo knew the local selva like the palm of her hand, of course, and despite being thoroughly and recently ravaged she set a rapid pace along the maze of forest trails. The two men had a time keeping up, and despite the cooler night air and nudity they were sweating by the time Brujo led them to a tangle of gumbo limbo and said, "We must move through this brush silently. They are on the far side of an oxbow lagoon. The fools build big fires at night."

He followed her, leaving Gaston and the other Amazon behind as they made their way through the thicket. Captain Gringo knew the thick brush was a perfect place to meet a bushmaster, but he didn't want to sound like a sissy. So he didn't ask Brujo how she avoided snakes. She obviously had, up to now, and she was over twenty or so. That was old for an Indian unless they were smart.

Brujo crouched in front of him and parted gumbo limbo stems as he dropped down behind her. His knee was between her bare greasy buttocks and she settled back on it, sighing, "Oh, nice."

"Never mind that, where are the . . . oh, yeah."

He had a perfect view across the ink black quiet waters of the lagoon. Brujo scouted good, too. The camp fire reflected in the water and lit up the clearing in orange light as far back as the tree line. He saw tents set in a semi-circle, facing the ink pool of the oxbow. He started wishing he'd brought his machinegun after all. From here he could rake the whole dumb set-up. Didn't the clowns know anything about soldiering? He wouldn't even need the Indians to help and . . . yeah, and then the gunboat a couple of miles away would start lobbing shells and make matchsticks out of the trees all around as they fired indiscriminately at the sounds of a fire-fight. Barboza had known these chumps would be duck soup for professionals, the son-of-a-bitch. So what was all this bullshit about? A longboat of Brazilian marines should have taken care of the matter months ago.

He spotted a man across the lagoon moving to the fire with an armload of wood. As he dropped it on the already wasteful fire Captain Gringo gave his uniform the once over. He didn't look like a Brazilian Navy man. He wore khaki, cut like an infantryman's tropic kit. Commander Fonseca had some Brazilian marines with him?

He leaned forward, his chest against Brujo's back, to whisper, "You said they had machineguns. I don't see any."

She snuggled back against him and purred, "We are at the rear of their position, lover. Beyond those trees runs the channel of the Brazo Casiquiare. They have sand bags and guns over there to keep people from moving between the Negro and Orinoco without their permission, eh?"

"Hmm, they left this side unguarded because they don't expect Indian trouble and nobody but an Indian could get through this spinach. I take back what I just thought about them not knowing their trade. It's sort of sloppy, but if they mean to control all the smuggling trade between Brazil and Venezuela they're going about it right enough."

Another man stepped out of a tent, wearing the same outfit. He walked into the woods to take a leak, apparently, leaving the tent flap partly open. There was a flag staff stuck in the sand by his tent, so that made it Commander Fonseca's headquarters tent, if that had been Commander Fonseca, but the guy had been wearing khaki, not the tropic whites of the navy. An aide, perhaps?

The light was dim and the colors on the flag staff were furled and tied with a string. But he could just make out the wide bands of . . . red, blue and gold?

The Brazilian flag was green.

The penny dropped and he muttered, "Son of a bitch, that's it!"

Brujo moved her tail-bone up and reached back to fondle him, rubbing the tip of his shaft up and down the oiled groove between her buttocks as she giggled and said, "They can't see us. Isn't this fun?"

He said, "For God's sake, you sure pick funny times and places, doll." But it did feel interesting as he rose to the occasion and so as she moved forward on her hands and knees he started giving it to her dog style as he watched the camp across the water. Brujo was amused and he was interested as the officer came back, entered the tent, and closed the flap to blot out the colors of his flag. She bit her lip to keep from sounding off as she came. He pulled her back, letting the gumbo limbo branches snap together again as he finished with her on her back in the mud. Then he helped her to her feet and they moved back to join Gaston and the other girl, who were doing it standing up against a tree. Running around bare-ass in the moonlight seemed to have that effect on everyone.

Since it seemed impolite to break in on them, he took Brujo around to the other side of the tree and did the same. But Gaston had noticed them and he humped on his side he asked, conversationally, "See anything, Dick?"

Captain Gringo leaned against the tall Brujo's oiled flesh as he teased her with his shaft and replied, "Yeah, it's not a rebel camp. It's a Venezuelan army outpost. They told us this was disputed territory. Venezuela must have gotten tired of the smuggling. So they've grabbed the old sneaky waterway and they're holding it with at least a full troop and heavy weapons."

"But, Dick, what about Commander Fonseca? Ouch, watch those teeth, you little tigress."

Captain Gringo noticed Brujo's nails were sharp, too, as she dug them into his bare buttocks to pull him deeper. He said, "If Fonseca and his mutineers were ever up here they left about the time their own Paulist Party took over down in Rio. If the new president hasn't issued Fonseca a full pardon by now he will any day now. I imagine the commander is hiding out on one of his family's many fazendas, waiting word."

"But this is madness, my old and rare! Barboza must have known this long before he sent you up here."

"Of course he did. He's a Paulist in good standing. Remember how that Colombian officer used us one time instead of his own troops to avoid a border incident?"

"Oui, but that was another time and another border. Are you saying Commodore Barboza is up to the same sort of tricks?"

"No, just the opposite. He *wants* a border incident with Venezuela. Uh, I'll explain it later, right now I'm coming."

He hammered Brujo's butt against the tree trunk and from the way the limbs above were shaking Gaston was doing pretty good on his own side.

Later, as they strolled away with the two girls clinging to them, he told Gaston, "I've now figured out who Maureen Mahoney's smuggling partners in Manaus were. It was Barboza's crowd of frontier gut and gitters. They must have been using the smuggling route up here for years to avoid the export duties on minerals. Things started going wrong for them when the Indians wiped out their outlaw confederates who controlled the passage. The Venezuelans didn't help by deciding it was about time they patrolled the disputed border. Not even Barboza's Paulist pals in Rio would go for an open attack on the Venezuelan Army. I doubt like hell they know the Commodore's reason for wanting to wipe them out. So he hired us as pawns, feeding us a few fibs. He expected us to come up here and tangle with the Venezuelan border guards. Then he aimed to restore order a lot with his gunboat. How was *he* to know the guys smoking up a Brazilian-approved expedition was the Venezuelan army, right?"

"Ah, one sees the method in his madness at last. A lot of

bonbons could move duty-free through the general confusion of a frontier war. As the ranking officer in these parts he would of course be charged with seeing everyone paid duties, too, should anyone in Rio even think of it. But I fail to see how the redhead that liked you so much fit in."

"The left hand didn't know what the right hand was doing. Maureen was a mere smuggler, not a co-conspirator. She only knew she'd heard it was getting tough to get through these days. So she wanted some muscle to help her make it to Trinidad with her uncut stones. If Barboza knew what she was doing he didn't care. Maureen or the people she works for had already paid for the rocks. It didn't matter if she got through or not to the big boys. The big boys play sort of rough."

"One begins to notice that after a time. So, now that we know where we fit on the chess board, what do you think we ought to do about it, Dick? With Indian guides, it ought to be quite simple to get around the border post on foot and simply raft down the Orinoco, non?"

Captain Gringo nodded and said, "I've thought of that and you're right for once. We can abandon the steam launches and portage our supplies through with a little help from our new friends. We don't need power to go *down* any river and it's no big deal to build rafts in a rain forest. Hell, we can even have a houseboat like Borita's. There's all the balsa, thatch and cordage we'd ever need, free for the gathering in the selva."

Gaston laughed and said, "Eh, bien, let us gather our weary lads and be on our way before we are all screwed to death, hein?"

But Captain Gringo said, "Not so fast. Have you forgotten. Barboza and his gunboat?"

"Mais non, but what can he do to us if he does not see us slipping past him, hein?"

"It's not what he *can* do. It's what he *did* do! We lost some good men on this wild goose chase, and even if we hadn't, I don't like being used and I don't like crooks. Those Venezuelan border guards don't know it, and I guess they'd shoot us if they spotted us. But I think I'd like to give.'em a hand anyway."

"Merde alors, don't tell me you intend to attack that gunboat, Dick?"

"We've got to. If Barboza can't get his border incident one way he'll just find another."

Gaston sighed and said, "I asked you not to tell me that, Dick."

Back at the Mujero village, Brujo had a powwow with her women warriors and they thought a war with Brazil sounded like a swell idea, but Brujo said they still hadn't purified Captain Gringo and his men for the river spirits they'd stolen the little girl from. When he asked her how come she hadn't gotten around to that by now she giggled and said it had slipped her mind. But now that they were all friends and he wanted them to attack an enemy on the river it was time they made up with the river spirits.

He found their religion less interesting than their other customs. As the sun rose, he and his men were still sitting around painted red and black while Brujo shook a rattle at them and a circle of naked ladies shuffled around them in a monotonous side step, singing the same three notes over and over for what seemed like hours.

As it got light, Brujo said it was time to test their medicine. She led them, bare-ass and covered with sticky paint, back to the bend where they'd left their launches. She pointed out to the stretch he'd fished the child from and said, "If the spirits are pleased with you, it will be safe for you to enter the water."

He frowned at her and asked, "You want me to jump in the river, when I don't *have* to?"

"You have to, Deek. My warriors are watching. Since only you entered the water to steal the child from the spirits, your friends can wait with us to see if the creatures eat you or not."

She read the look in his eyes and added in a low urgent tone, *"Do it, Querido. I told you I am a witch, no?"*

He smiled crookedly at Gaston and the others and said, "It's been nice knowing you, guys."

Then he decided to get it over with fast. So he dove in head first as the assembled Indians shouted with approval. The water was like stale tea as he opened his eyes under the surface. He'd heard, somewhere, that sharks and such were attracted to a swimmer splashing on the surface. So he stayed near the bottom as he breast stroked out to mid-stream before surfacing to call out, "Can I come home now?"

Brujo clapped her hands and said yes, so he ducked under and started back, navigating by watching the muddy bottom. That's when he noticed the piranha. A whole school of piranha, circling him like Sioux around a forted-up wagon train, only, no Indian tribe ever came in such numbers! There were *hundreds* of the little bastards. Whoever had said the little man-eaters looked like sunfish was full of shit. Each was about the size and shape of a small-mouth bass, but their mouths weren't small. They were filled with needle sharp teeth, way too big for fish that size. He hung above the muddy bottom, wondering what he did now. Breathing seemed like a hell of a good idea, but he was afraid to move, let alone surface. Then he noticed none of the piranha were moving closer than a yard or so from him as they circled. From time to time one would peel out of formation and move a bit closer, but then it would shake its head as if it had spotted a hook in the bait and shy away. He got it. It was the paint the witch-chief had smeared him with. Brujo had mixed some sort of fish repellent into the pigment. Good old Brujo. It was so simple it was dumb, when you thought about it. But her primitive followers didn't think all that much. As he surfaced, took a deep breath, and simply swam ashore, the tribe seemed terribly impressed. As he rejoined Brujo on the bank he asked, "How did you know there'd be piranha there this morning, doll?" She said, simply, "I had some ground meat thrown in the water. How do you like my witchcraft. Deek?"

"It's almost as good as your other talents. Does it work in the dark?"

"Of course. The main medicine is cayman bile. Everything that swims thinks you are a cayman when they smell you, and caymans eat everything, so . . ."

"Back up, what if I meet another cayman?"

"They don't like the smell, either. Only a badly injured cayman spills it's juices in the water and an injured cayman is very surly."

"I heard they cannibalize each other, too."

"They do. But they only attack others smaller than themselves. You are very big, Deek. No cayman less than two meters long would attack you with my medicine paint on you."

"Okay, what if I met one *three* meters long?"

"Try never to do that, Deek."

"That's what I thought. But it does cut down the odds a lot and I see another way to use this stuff."

She shrugged and said, "You have passed the test. Why don't you wash it off and let us see how it is together in a hammock, eh?"

"I know how it is in a hammock. I'll show you later. Right now I want some more of this fish repellent and I want to be painted solid black, too."

"You want to dive back in the river again, Deek?"

"Yeah, but not here. Let's go. I'll explain along the way."

Later, about high noon, Gaston sat fully dressed on a log near the tripod of the machinegun the Indian girls had happily portaged through the selva for them. The other men and Los Mujeros had taken cover up and down the shoreline of the backwater, screened by the wall of greenery and the dark shadows behind them cast by the overhead sun. Out on the water the gunboat of Commodore Barboza seemed to shimmer in the humid heat and nobody was on deck. They'd chosen the siesta hour with that in mind.

Near Gaston, the tall Brujo smiled and said, "He comes. The river spirits smile on my medicine." As Captain Gringo rose from the dark water, painted black as the ace of spades, and waded ashore in an inlet screened from view from the gunboat. He was trailing a length of what looked like thick fishing line. He uncoiled more as he moved over to Gaston and the machinegun. He said, "Jesus, that oxbow's lousy with piranha. They've been throwing garbage over the side and there's no current in this backwater."

"Meet any caymans?" Gaston asked, dryly. The tall American reached over to take the smoke from Gaston's lips as he growled, "None as big as me." He took a puff, then applied the cigar end to the end of the waterproof fuze he was holding. As it began to sputter he dropped it and said, "We'd better get set. I placed the dynamite amidships, under their boiler room. Brujo, do your girls understand that there's going to be a big boom?"

The witch-chief nodded and said, "Yes, Deek. We are not ignorant people. We sometimes get shotguns from the traders, but we don't like them much. They never go poof when they are supposed to, and they sometimes blow up in one's face."

"Yeah, rust would be a problem in this steam bath. Okay, tell them to get set. Gaston, move your ass and let me get behind that Maxim. That's quick-fuse I just lit."

As they changed places on the log Gaston saw the fuse had burned to the water's edge and that bubbles of smoke were rising off shore. Captain Gringo checked the chamber and straightened the hanging belt of ammo as Thomé moved closer to say, "The men are all posted, my Captain. Oswaldo asked what about prisoners?"

"Oswaldo's talking pretty silly. We haven't any place to put a prisoner, and we don't owe the bastards any favors. Pass the word that if anybody's squeamish he should just stand aside and let the Indians do it."

"Thomé moved off, silently. Gaston put a foot on the log and said, "I have been looking at those uncut diamonds you stole from Maureen, Dick."

"Later. The fuse should be about gone."

"Mais non, I have been watching the bubbles. Fortunately they are not too noticeable. Barboza's friends double-

194

crossed her, too. They must not have expected her to get through, knowing she'd be with us."

"Shit, you mean I swiped a cuntful of fakes?"

"Oh, they are diamonds. A few of the smaller ones are gem quality. But it's mostly *bort*. Industrial diamonds. I think we can unload them for a couple of thousand or so, if we ever *get* anywhere with them, alive. But, alas, we've just about made expenses on this trip."

Captain Gringo shrugged his bare, black shoulders and said, "I didn't really want that yacht and Lillian Russell anyway. We'll talk about it later. Hang on to your hat."

Out on the water, the mid-section of the gunboat was hidden by a geyser of water as the dynamite Captain Gringo had placed under her hull broke her back with a muffled roar.

As the spray settled, the gunboat looked much as she had before, save for all the white clad figures rushing out on deck. A circle of stunned fish rose like silver leaves around the gunboat as Gaston dropped to his knees to feed ammo and Captain Gringo opened up with the machinegun, hosing back and forth along the iron clad's deck to spang screaming lead off the hard steel and tear big, red gobs out of soft flesh. Rifles squibbed all along the bank as his comrades opened up, picking targets with more care. Captain Gringo saw a couple of men running for the forward gun turret. But as he traversed left they both went down with rifle rounds in them. Gaston said, "Regardez, the boat is starting to settle!" as the American chased the last moving figure back inside with a stream of fire. The gunboat started to sink on even keel, then changed her mind and began to roll on her starboard side. He swore softly as he saw the hull rising to screen the superstructure from his fire. But then, as the men aboard saw they were turning turtle they threw caution to the wind and started diving overboard. It turned out to be a lousy move. The underwater blast had stunned the fish near the hull, but others were moving in to feed on them, and anything else in the water. He spotted Commodore Barboza clinging to a floating hatch cover. As he swung the machinegun muzzle to do something about that, a thing that looked like a giant goldfish rose to swallow the treacherous navy man in one gulp. It didn't seem fair, considering how many of the others were being eaten a small bite at a time by piranha.

The rounded hull of the gunboat vanished under the surface with a long sad hiss of escaping air. For a long time after the surface was white with foam and stuff kept bobbing to the surface. Then things settled down and in a short while the black water lay smoothly shimmering in the sun. Brujo said, "The river spirits must be very pleased."

Captain Gringo grimaced and said, "Yeah, let's get the hell out of here."

The witch-chief frowned down at him and asked, "For why must we run, Deek? Anyone can see there were no survivors to worry about."

"I'm not worried about survivors. Those Venezuelan border guards will have heard the noise and they ought to be sending a patrol this way about now. I don't want them to find anything here. We'll police up our brass and haul our ass. That channel looks deep enough to keep its secret and if they don't find anything on shore they'll eventually put it down as a thunder storm or something."

As he and Gaston began to pick up spent shells and toss them in the water Brujo said, "Pooh, my Mujeros and I are not afraid of any silly soldados from the other side of the border."

He said, "I know. That's one advantage of growing up without a library in town. But if it's all the same to you, Brujo, let's keep them on their own side of the border. I've only got one belt of ammo left and *they* have machineguns, too."

They never found out how the Venezuelan border guards reported the mysterious fire fight in the distance. They went to considerable trouble to avoid meeting them.

After casting the launches adrift on the main channel to add further mystery downstream, Captain Gringo and his remaining men got Los Mujeros to lead them across dry land, avoiding a wide-water detour as well as the Venezuelan Army. They made camp on a tributary of the Orinoco and Captain Gringo made love to Brujo while his men built a big balsa with a thatched cabin, amid ships and long sweeps at each end to keep her straight as she rode the current. It took them a couple of days, and his own chores damned near broke his back. Even the athletic Brujo was beginning to run out of ideas for new positions by the second night. So, while she said she'd never forget him and that she sincerely hoped she was pregnant, she only cried a little and didn't throw her spear at him when he said it was time to say adios.

He wasn't too thrilled with the idea of leaving a half-breed bastard somewhere in the headwater country, but he supposed kids you didn't know about one way or the other didn't count. By now, Gaston was cheerfully certain he'd fathered a full battalion in his wanderings. But as they floated down the Orinoco they decided it was better not to think about such matters. Ladies who didn't know how or didn't want to take care of themselves had no business putting out, and, what the hell, they hadn't raped Los Mujeres. Los Mujeres had raped *them!*

Just where, in this uncharted wilderness, Brazil became Venezuela was up for grabs, which was probably why Brazil and Venezuela spent so much time grabbing. The Orinoco looked just like the Negro, save for running the wrong way. It seemed odd to be drifting north instead of bucking the current for the first day or so, but they got used to it, and now it felt like the Negro was running the wrong way.

The balsa carried them slowly, and life on the river was lazy with no danger ahead. No known danger, anyway. Gaston, as usual, stewed about all sorts of things they might run into. But Captain Gringo told him they'd worry about it when they came to it.

They came to it about a week later.

As on the Negro, there was river traffic on the Orinoco. They tightened up a bit the first few times they passed other craft on the river, but when people only waved, they took to waving back and not taking it too seriously.

So one afternoon when they spotted a paddlewheeler

coming downstream to overtake them, moving full steam, they simply used their sweeps to swing over toward the nearest bank, out of the bigger vessel's way.

As it passed, a man up on the Texas shouted down to them. "Save yourselves, Señores! It is El Tigre!"

Captain Gringo looked upstream the way the guy was pointing as he tried to figure out what the hell a jaguar would be doing on the Orinoco. He knew the big cats could swim pretty good, but it still sounded pretty dumb.

Their balsa bobbed in the paddlewheeler's wake and then as it vanished around the bend downstream, a smaller steam launch tore around the bend above them with a bone in its teeth and black smoke shooting high above it. The second craft had a flag or a jaguar hide streaming from its jack staff and the men aboard looked like comic opera pirates. As they tore past Captain Gringo's party without slowing down, one of them fired a shot, apparently just for practice, and Thomé spun around and went over the side, hit bad!

"Oswaldo, swing that sweep and get us broadside!" Captain Gringo shouted as he stared down at the coffee-colored surface to see where Thomé might come up. Thomé didn't. Even had they been able to stop, he could see it was no use. The brainless bastard in that launch had popped Thomé off like a wicked boy shooting at songbirds, and the bastards were already around the bend. He couldn't even shake his fist at them!

He moved over by the thatched cabin and removed the matting from the mounted Maxim as Gaston observed, "They are gone, Dick, what is your point? We cannot catch them without the power, hein?"

"This fucking river ends *somewhere*, and they just killed one of our guys!"

He armed the machinegun and squatted behind it, chewing furiously on his unlit cigar as they drifted on around the bend. As they got a better view downstream they could see the paddlewheeler was still in sight. It was on a sand bar, churning coffee-colored foam in a vain effort to claw free as the river pirates in the smaller launch circled it, smoking up the gingerbread trim as well as anything that moved on the

198

igher decks above them. Captain Gringo grinned wolfishly as he said, "Everybody aft. Oswaldo, man that sweep and keep us aimed at them."

One of the river rats on El Tigre's launch spotted them coming, of course. A low-slung helpless-looking raft offered sport and a chance to show the people on the steamboat the advantages of surrendering. So the outlaws broke off their attack on the paddlewheeler to steam upstream, spouting smoke, curses, course laughter, and bullets.

Captain Gringo let them come until the water spouts around him showed him they were within range. Then he gritted his teeth, sighted along the water jacket, and emptied the whole belt into them, raking the launch from stem to stern. Those river pirates who weren't blasted into bloody hash, if any, went under as the riddled craft's boiler blew up, cracking the boat's keel, and dragging it under in a swirling steam cloud. One head bobbed to the surface downstream. A dapperly dressed man aboard the steamboat took careful aim with his pocket pistol, and that was that.

With nobody manning the forward sweep the balsa started to yaw starboard despite Oswaldo's efforts. As they crabbed sideways over the boil of the sandbar the steamer was on, a deck hand threw them a line. Campos caught it without asking why. Captain Gringo knew it would seem suspicious if he ordered Campos to toss it back, so there they were, being hauled in like a fish as he started making up a fast cover story.

The skipper of the streamboat and the dapper man who shot well were on the lower deck as the balsa bumped against the low hull of the bigger vessel. The skipper was holding out his hand. So Captain Gringo stepped aboard and shook with him, saying, "Buenas tardes. I am called Captain Ricardo and we've been up the river prospecting. Without much luck, I'm sorry to say."

The skipper laughed and said, "Forget the gold few find in any case. Your timely arrival was good luck indeed to all of us. Don't you realize you just killed El Tigre? There were ten thousand Bolivars on that river pirate's head, and I, for one, intend to see that you and your men get it!"

"I shall also be your witness, Señores." The fancy dresser smiled at the skipper's side, then added, "Allow me to present myself. I am called Luis Vicente de Miranda, Governor of Amacuro y Delta Province. Thanks to you I shall return safely to my home in Tucupita and, naturally, mi casa es su casa, should you ever visit there. May one ask where you and your brave men were headed, Captain Ricardo?"

"Uh, as a matter of fact we were thinking of leaving the country. Heard about a gold strike over in Panama, and, even if it doesn't pan out we might get a job with the new canal company they're starting."

De Miranda shook his head and said, "Forget Panama. The pay is terrible and the vomito negro fever is worse. You shall come with me to Tucupita as my guests while we consider your future. If you still wish to leave Venezuela after a month or so of my humble hospitality, I shall see you have no passport problems and make sure you board a decent ship. Some of the tramps putting into the delta are not fit for gentlemen." He didn't wait for an argument as he turned to the skipper and asked, "How long will it take you to get off this sand bar, Lopez?"

The skipper smiled and said, "Only a few minutes, with nobody shooting at us, Don Luis." So the governor turned back to Captain Gringo with a smile and said, "Bueno. Forgive me, but you are not properly dressed to ride First Class, Captain Ricardo."

"I, ah, didn't know I was going anywhere first class."

"But of course you are. Aside from being the governor of Amacuro y Delta, I own this steamship line. Your cabin presents no problem and, by good fortune, we are almost the same size. I am sure my clothes will fit you, and I always travel with plenty to spare. Have your odd-looking, little assistant and the others load your things on the cargo deck and I am sure Lopez, here, will make them comfortable. You come with me and we shall see about making you presentable." He put a finger to his nose and winked as he added, "There are many grateful Senoritas aboard who may wish to thank you for saving them from a fate worse than death."

Captain Gringo gave Gaston the high sign and the

Frenchman nodded. As he followed the governor he said, dryly, "I didn't know there was a fate worse than death."

De Miranda chuckled and said, "I agree, but women are odd that way. Many seem to feel that the only proper reward for a man who saves their fair white body is, of course, their fair white body. Do me one favor, however. The one in the lavender lace with the ugly dueña is the one I am after, if only I could get her away from that old dragon she travels with."

At the head of the stairs other passengers crowded around to press his hand and admire him. He was suddenly very aware of his ragged clothing and unshaven appearance. He spotted the pretty girl in the lavender dress among a bevy of perfumed bright young things. Some looked so good to Captain Gringo, but the moustached dueña hovering over Miss Lavender must have presented a challenge to Don Luis. As they entered his stateroom he told the governor, "My sidekick, Gaston, might be able to help you out with that older woman, Don Louis. He's an older guy."

The Venezuelan opened a closet full of suits and said, "Help yourself when you finish washing and shaving. The bath is ajoining. What do you mean your friend can help me? That old woman is so ugly she has to be a virgin."

"Gaston is French. He eats snails, too. Seriously, the old dame has a sort of interesting shape inside that rusty black dress. My sidekick likes his women like his cheese and wine, a little on the exprienced side."

De Miranda laughed incredulously and said, "My valet may have some clothes that will fit your little friend, and there are several spare cabins up here, now that I reconsider his station in life. But I still think the crone is a dried-up old maid."

Captain Gringo let him think about it as he showered and shaved next door. When he came out, the stateroom was empty. He picked out the shirt with the fewest ruffles and put on a vanilla linen suit, filling the pockets with his belongings and of course strapping his side arm under the frock coat. It was a snug fit, but as he looked at himself in the pier glass he decided he was *almost* as pretty as Don Luis.

The latter came in, smiling, to say, "It is settled. Your little friend is with my valet. He agrees with you that the dueña offers sport of a sort for an experienced huntsman. Let me show you to your own stateroom. We shall, how you say, play it cool and invite the ladies to dine with us later this evening! This will give you time to look the others over and decide which one you wish to invite to the captain's table, eh?"

It sounded fine with Captain Gringo. A short while later they were off the sandbar and on their way again when he left his new stateroom, alone, and entered the grand salon. It was going to take him a while to get used to these new surroundings after weeks on the river the hard way.

The ornately decorated salon smelled of perfume, powder, and good cigars. The passengers had settled down after all the exitement and while he drew smiles and nods as he passed, the men and women lounging about on the overstuffed furnishings remained sedately seated and it was pleasant to sit alone at a table in the corner, listening to the low hum of refined conversation and the tinkle of ice in tall glasses. A waiter in a spotless white jacket came over to ask if he wanted anything. Captain Gringo said he wanted it tall, cool, and wet. As the waiter moved off he leaned back and lit a claro. This was the way a guy with couth ought to travel. He wondered why he spent so much time doing it the other way.

As he waited for his drink he spotted Gaston through the window, walking the promenade deck with Miss Lavender's formidable dueña. You couldn't say the older woman looked so formidable, right now. Gaston looked sort of silly in that oversized dinner jacket as he strolled arm in arm with the taller woman, talking a blue streak. She was giggling like a school girl. Governor De Miranda would be pleased, and they still had to smuggle themselves and a cuntful of diamonds, bort or not, out of the damned country. Luck like this wasn't supposed to happen. But, what the hell, it was about *time!*

The waiter brought his drink and said it was on the governor. It was real Jamaica rum, too. He asked if they sold cigars and the waiter said he could have all the Havana Perfectos he wanted, on the house.

Captain Gringo knew he still had to get his own broad. So he started looking over the other passengers as he luxuriated in the corner. There were a couple of really nice looking dames across the way, if you didn't mind them sort of snooty and overdressed.

A small-boned, bubbly little thing with light brown hair came in off the promenade, furling her parasol. She wore a cream lace mantilla over the high shell comb in her hair and her pale rounded breasts were trying to escape over the top of her low cut bodice. She flounced sort of bubbly, too, as she crossed the red plush carpet in her ruffled skirts. He decided she was it. The contrast between her little rounded curves and the muscular Amazon he'd had last made his groin tingle just to think about. He wondered how he'd work it.

He didn't have to. The girl saw him, came over, and said, "Oh, there you are." She sat down next to him.

He smiled and said, "Here I am indeed, Señorita... ah?"

"You can call me Maria, Captain Gringo. It's not my real name, but, then, you're not Captain Ricardo, either, eh?"

He took a thoughtful drag on his cigar before he asked, "What gave you that idea, uh, Maria?"

"Silly, we've been expecting you. It was the other side who placed that bomb in your hotel room across the border. They knew you'd eventually wind up here near the Caribbean again and they hoped the Brazilians you were involved with would get blamed."

He nodded and said, "I've been wondering about that loose end. Who were they, Maria? More important, who the hell are you?"

She looked around and said, "It's rather public, here. Maybe we'd better go to my stateroom to talk it over." She was all dimples as she added, "We've several hours before supper time, so we won't be disturbed."

He rose with her and she took his elbow to lead him out on the promenade. As they strolled off, he said, "I was thinking about asking you to join me at the captain's table for supper, Maria. How do you feel about breakfast?"

"I'd love to have breakfast with you."

"Good. Do I call for you or nudge you in the morning?"

She laughed, but before she could answer they encountered Gaston going the other way with his over-the-hill but hour-glassed companion. Gaston nodded and said, in English, "Very nice. All's well that ends well, non?"

Captain Gringo shrugged and said, "I'll let you know, later. I'm not quite sure what's going on, but here we go again."

HE'S UNSHAKABLE, UNSTOPPABLE, UNKILLABLE...
CAPTAIN GRINGO

RENEGADE #1
by Ramsay Thorne   (C90-976, $1.95)

He's a man on the run—Captain Gringo. By wit, by guile, by masterful skill with guns and women, he'll burn his way across the Border—wiping out a troop of Rurales and the sadistic pervert who commands them, leading a guerilla band on daredevil raids, hijacking, fighting, killing, winning.

RENEGADE #2: BLOOD RUNNER
by Ramsay Thorne   (C90-977, $1.95)

They're waiting for a man like Captain Gringo in Panama! Every adventurer with a scheme, every rebel with a cause wants a man like Captain Gringo—running guns, unloosing a rain of death from his Maxim, fighting Yellow Jack, Indians, army ants, even the Devil himself if he stands in the way!

RENEGADE #3: FEAR MERCHANT
by Ramsay Thorne   (C90-761, $1.95)

In this revolution-wracked land, no one can be trusted. With his eyes wide open and his Maxim at the ready, the Captain is primed for action: in the bed of a Chinese girl, at the challenge of a one-eyed general, at the command to murder a high-born lady, at the demand for love in the savage stare of an Indian girl.

RENEGADE #4: DEATH HUNTER
by Ramsay Thorne   (C90-902, $1.95)

In these cool and quiet nights Captain Gringo trails the highlands with his profile low and his Maxim ready. It's been a year of hell fighting his way through three revolutions and a U.S. courtmartial. But before Captain Gringo's vacation ends, he will have a job—masterminding an attack on three of the world's major powers.

HE'S UNSHAKABLE, UNSTOPPABLE, UNKILLABLE, CAPTAIN GRINGO

RENEGADE #5: MACUMBA KILLER
by Ramsay Thorne (C90-234, $1.95)

On this sweltering, voo-doo crazed island, the British Empire is breathing its last, subject to the forays of a marauding army of runaways and doped-up derelicts who have unleashed a reign of terror, death, and destruction. The British need a man to take charge, shoot straight, and spit in the enemy's eye—Captain Gringo is that man.

RENEGADE #6: PANAMA GUNNER
by Ramsay Thorne (C90-235, $1.95)

Captain Gringo's trapped aboard a crippled gunboat in shark-infested waters. Sudden mutiny on the part of Gringo's crew just adds to his inconvenience, but what's really playing havoc with the Captain's mind is the inexplicable interest he's feeling in a young, red-haired kid named Mac.

RENEGADE #7: DEATH IN HIGH PLACES
by Ramsay Thorne (C90-548, $1.95)

Captain Gringo is leading a brigade through a maze of volcanoes whose molten lava fills the trail, while the burning sting of the common fly sets the pace. Colombia is a political powder keg, and he's bound for Bogota to light the fuse that will ignite an explosion of chaos, destroying the country's corrupt and depraved regime.

RENEGADE #8: OVER THE ANDES TO HELL
by Ramsay Thorne (C90-549, $1.95)

There's no rest for Gringo in Bogota. Between seduction in the eyes of the senoritas and murder in the minds of the Kaiser's spies, a man has to keep moving to stay alive. From the hot Amazon jungle thick with headhunters to the chilling Andes rife with rebels, the Captain is on a trek to trouble.

"THE KING OF THE WESTERN NOVEL" IS MAX BRAND

THE BIG TRAIL	(C94-333, $1.75)
BROTHERS ON THE TRAIL	(C90-302, $1.95)
DRIFTER'S VENGEANCE	(C84-783, $1.75)
FIRE BRAIN	(C88-629, $1.50)
FLAMING IRONS	(C98-019, $1.50)
FRONTIER FEUD	(C98-002, $1.50)
GALLOPING BRONCOS	(C94-265, $1.75)
THE GAMBLER	(C94-328, $1.75)
GARDEN OF EDEN	(C94-290, $1.75)
THE GENTLE GUNMAN	(C94-291, $1.75)
GUNMAN'S GOLD	(C90-619, $1.95)
GUNS OF DORKING HOLLOW	(C94-204, $1.75)
HAPPY JACK	(C90-303, $1.95)
HAPPY VALLEY	(C90-304, $1.95)
THE INVISIBLE OUTLAW	(C94-343, $1.75)
THE KING BIRD RIDES	(C90-305, $1.95)
THE LONG CHASE	(C94-266, $1.75)
LUCKY LARRIBEE	(C94-456, $1.75)
THE MAN FROM SAVAGE CREEK	(C90-815, $1.95)
MARBLEFACE	(C90-307, $1.95)

"THE KING OF THE WESTERN NOVEL"
is MAX BRAND

_____ **DRIFTER'S VENGEANCE** (84-783, $1.75)
_____ **GUNMAN'S GOLD** (90-619, $1.95)
_____ **FIRE BRAIN** (88-629, $1.50)
_____ **TRAILIN'** (88-717, $1.50)
_____ **MARBLEFACE** (90-307, $1.95)
_____ **WAR PARTY** (88-933, $1.50)
_____ **SILVERTIP** (88-685, $1.50)
_____ **TROUBLE TRAIL** (90-314, $1.95)
_____ **FRONTIER FEUD** (98-002, $1.50)
_____ **RIDER OF THE HIGH HILL** (88-884, $1.50)
_____ **FLAMING IRONS** (98-019, $1.50)
_____ **SILVERTIP'S CHASE** (98-048, $1.50)
_____ **SILVERTIP'S STRIKE** (98-096, $1.50)
_____ **HAPPY VALLEY** (90-304, $1.95)
_____ **MISTRAL** (90-316, $1.95)
_____ **THE KING BIRD RIDES** (90-305, $1.95)
_____ **BROTHERS ON THE TRAIL** (90-302, $1.95)
_____ **HAPPY JACK** (90-303, $1.95)